"When it comes to women, I take what I'm given and give what I can,"

Mac said tightly. "The lovers I choose don't expect me to stay, they don't whine about me spending the night."

Shadow would need so much more than that, he thought. She would *take* so much more, whether it was given willingly or not.

"Where do you go?" she whispered.

"Home."

"Where's that?"

"Wherever I want it to be at the time."

"Always?"

"Do I always wander, or do I always go home afterward?"

"Go." She already knew about the wandering. *A man with no home.* And she remembered his eyes at the waterfall. A man that haunted would keep on the move, running from something within. There would be no haven for him.

"Yeah," he said quietly.

"That's lonely."

"That's sane."

Dear Reader,

We're back with another fabulous month's worth of books, starting with the second of our Intimate Moments Extra titles. *Night of the Jaguar* by Merline Lovelace is the first of a new miniseries, Code Name: Danger. It's also a fabulously sexy, romantic and suspenseful tale of two people who never should have met but are clearly made for each other. And keep your eyes on two of the secondary characters, Maggie and Adam, because you're going to be seeing a lot more of them as this series continues.

Award-winner Justine Davis presents one of her irresistible tormented-but-oh-so-sexy heroes in *Out of the Dark*, another of her page-turning titles. And two miniseries continue: Kathleen Creighton's Into the Heartland, with *One Good Man*, and Beverly Bird's Wounded Warriors, with *A Man Without a Haven*. Welcome bestseller Linda Randall Wisdom back to Silhouette with her Intimate Moments debut, *No More Secrets*. And try out new-to-contemporaries author Elane Osborn, who offers *Shelter in His Arms*.

As promised, it's a great month—don't miss a single book.

Enjoy!

Leslie Wainger
Senior Editor and Editorial Coordinator

Please address questions and book requests to:
Silhouette Reader Service
U.S.: 3010 Walden Ave., P.O. Box 1325, Buffalo, NY 14269
Canadian: P.O. Box 609, Fort Erie, Ont. L2A 5X3

A MAN WITHOUT A HAVEN

BEVERLY BIRD

Silhouette®
INTIMATE™ MOMENTS®

Published by Silhouette Books

America's Publisher of Contemporary Romance

SILHOUETTE BOOKS

ISBN 0-373-07641-X

A MAN WITHOUT A HAVEN

Copyright © 1995 by Beverly Bird

Printed in U.S.A.

BEVERLY BIRD

has lived in several places in the United States, but she is currently back where her roots began—on an island in New Jersey. Her time is devoted to her family and her writing. She is the author of numerous romance novels, both contemporary and historical.

Chapter 1

It was the kind of day her Navajo ancestors had died trying to keep for their own. Shadow Bedonie tilted her head back to breathe in the sun, understanding why.

The sky was an unbroken bowl of varying shades of blue. It was silver gold near the horizon where the desert wind teased up distant clouds of dust. Overhead, where it met the blazing orb of the sun, it was nearly white. And in between there were a thousand shades of azure and robin's egg, without a single cloud to mar them.

Shadow guided her horse along the top of an arroyo, looking down at a narrow stream that trickled through there. Within another few weeks it would be gone along with the last of the rainy season—if these summer months in New Mexico's high country could be called rainy. The parched land drank water thirstily, leaving scarce evidence of the rare storms. The air was dry and very hot, thin and hard to breathe.

It was hard country, rugged and stark and unforgiving. Shadow loved it with all of her soul.

She nudged the horse homeward with her heels, thinking about the time after college when she had left this reservation. She had ached for it, had felt so lost and misplaced without it that she had left the man who had taken her from it and had come back home. She had realized this morning that that had been seven years ago. She wondered if Kevin was still alone and doubted it.

She shook her head, unconsciously tensing. Her horse felt it and picked up into a rough, weary trot. Shadow let her go, as though they could somehow outrun the truth. But time was like that on this Navajo Res, wandering by almost unnoticed, until one day you sighed and realized the seasons had changed, until you looked in the mirror and saw little sun lines at the corners of your eyes and realized you were thirty years old.

That had happened today. It was her birthday.

Thirty. Shadow didn't want to think about it. It made her feel strangely wild inside, as though she wanted to protest, to fight back, but had no idea what to swing her fist at.

She rode up onto another rise of land and saw her hogan in the distance, sitting back a little way from a rutted dirt road. Her sheep grazed not far behind it and the rickety old gate of the corral swung back and forth, clattering in the breeze. She decided she would fix it this afternoon. The chore was long overdue and she had nothing better to do, birthday or not.

Only one thing about the place was not as she had left it—an old Land Rover was parked beside her four-wheel-drive truck. The Rover belonged to her brother, and Jericho had not been venturing very far from his house up on the mountain these past couple of weeks. His wife, Catherine, was very, very pregnant.

So what was he doing here? Had the baby come or was something wrong?

Shadow forced her horse into a tired, ground-eating lope and swung breathlessly to the ground when she reached the Rover. Jericho pushed open the door to meet her.

"Hey," he greeted her.

She looked at him closely. His face was a bit haggard but he didn't seem particularly distraught. "Everything okay?"

"Right as rain," he answered, "unless you consider that Paddy and Uncle Ernie have moved in."

Shadow's jaw dropped. Paddy was Catherine's father, a blustering Irishman who never meddled—he simply barged in. Uncle Ernie was their Towering Rock Clan grandfather, a shaman so old no one truly knew how many years he had seen. Uncle Ernie didn't meddle either. He just slid in like smoke.

"*Both* of them?" she asked, startled.

"They're waiting for Catherine to do something."

"I don't think it's up to her," she answered dryly.

"Guess not. The baby was supposed to have been here two weeks ago."

Shadow waved him inside the hogan and put a coffeepot on the wood-burning stove that sat in the center of the single room. It was easily a hundred degrees outside, but the interior of the dwelling was cool enough. A breeze puffed sporadically through the open doorway and the heat from the stove rose straight up through a smoke hole in the ceiling. In the winter she could close the hole a little more to contain the heat and warm the place. The hogan was small, but it had everything she needed.

Everything but someone to tell her happy birthday, to explain to her how *seven years* had somehow passed without her being aware of it, with absolutely nothing changing in her life.

Thirty. She shook her head, still amazed by it.

"Catherine's mother died having her kid sister," Jericho was explaining. "Paddy won't go home to Boston until he's sure both she and the baby are fine. And you know how Uncle Ernie gets when he likes somebody. He's taken a shine to Cat, I guess.'' He rubbed a tired hand over his eyes. ''Anyway, one's following her around nagging and the other one's following her around chanting medicine songs, and I needed a break.''

Shadow looked at him curiously. ''How's Catherine taking it?'' His wife was Anglo, a resident with the Indian Health Service. She had adapted to reservation life well enough; in fact she seemed to thrive on it. But Shadow had to wonder how she was handling Uncle Ernie on a live-in basis. Even those who loved him considered him to be mildly eccentric.

Jericho shrugged, reading her mind. ''Cat was acting a few cards short of a deck even before Ernie came.''

''Hormones.''

''Yeah?'' He took the coffee she offered. ''Nasty little buggers.''

''I wouldn't know.''

Her voice was too tight. Shadow flinched. Suddenly she wondered how many times in the past seven years she had even worn a dress. How many times had a man looked at her with anything other than brotherly camaraderie, or, in rare cases like Diamond Eddie, with lascivious greed? Given that it took a man's help to make a baby, it was doubtful if she would ever know about hormones, Shadow realized. She was surprised to feel her throat close painfully.

''You okay?'' Jericho asked, giving her a hard look.

''Fine. What are the nasty little buggers doing to her?''

''I brought her flowers last week and she cried for four days.''

''That would do it.'' Shadow sipped her own coffee, watching him. ''But you wouldn't come down here to tell me Catherine's gone loopy with estrogen, not even if Uncle Ernie and Paddy were camped right in your bedroom.''

He grinned. ''Yeah, I might. If I had an excuse.''

"Such as?"

"Heard something I thought you might like to know. 'Course, I heard it from Lance, so its validity is open to some discussion." Lance was a clan relative who had taken to drinking when his children had moved off the Res. Anything he repeated had to be taken with a grain of salt because he was drunk more often than not.

"I think somebody's digging up the ruins over in Kokopelli's Canyon," Jericho went on. "Lance went hunting out that way last week, up in the Chuska Mountains. Said he saw the *chindi* ghost of old Kokopelli himself. Probably what he actually saw was a pot hunter."

"Oh, hell," Shadow muttered.

It had been only a matter of time before someone dared the canyon again, she thought, but she'd put money on the intruder being anything but Navajo. The People had a healthy fear of *chindis*—Navajo ghosts—and the dead. The canyon was about as haunted and filled with bones as a hole in the ground could get. But *chindis* wouldn't stop a determined pot hunter from digging illegally on the Res, not when mere fragments of Anasazi pottery sold for thousands of dollars. The pieces were almost older than time itself. Centuries before the Navajo had come to this red-rock desert, the Anasazi people had dwelled here—and, then, inexplicably, they had disappeared again. The Navajo had arrived to find only traces of the Anasazi's brief sojourn and they had named them for the Navajo word meaning "old ones," their predecessors, the ones who came before.

Most of the Old Ones' ruins were too remote to be found easily, but there were at least four relatively accessible and renowned sites in the canyon that was named after the Anasazi's roaming fertility god.

The only thing that kept most of the hordes of archaeologists and thieves away from the place was the legend of the canyon itself. Those who went in were said never to return. Not all of the bones hidden in the ancient, crumbling ruins were hundreds of years old. Or so they said, Shadow thought dryly. She had been in and out of there once as an anthropology student, and she was still warm to the touch.

"I'll drive out there and see what's going on," she decided.

Jericho's face took on a wary cast. "When?"

Shadow looked at her watch. "Today. It's still early enough that I can get in and out before dark." She didn't actually believe in the legends—much—but she wasn't keen on being trapped in the canyon when the moon rose. Still, it was something to do. It was better than mending corral gates.

Jericho was still scowling. "Don't you have to work?"

"Diamond Eddie isn't expecting me until tomorrow." She was assistant curator for the Navajo Nation Museum in Shiprock. The place was only open four days a week.

But her brother knew that. She narrowed her eyes at him. "You don't even like Eddie."

"I don't trust any man who wears three diamond earrings."

"So now you're worried about him firing me? You've told me a hundred times that I should find another job instead of putting up with him."

Jericho didn't answer. Shadow waited. Conversational silences weren't uncomfortable for anyone raised Navajo—even if they had spent a chunk of their lives in the cities, as she and Jericho had done. Their parents had insisted they go to school in Gallup rather than on the Res.

"There's too much death in the canyon," he muttered finally.

"So you can do a sing for me when I get back." Jericho was a shaman himself, and the Navajo had rites to combat exposure to *chindi* ghosts.

"Hell, it's not your responsibility," Jericho argued. "Notify the tribal police. Let *them* flush him out."

"When? On Navajo time? If you didn't want me to go out there, Jericho, then you shouldn't have told me."

"If I didn't tell you and you found out that I knew about it, I'd never hear the end of it," he snapped.

Shadow gave a brief nod. She would have grinned if she hadn't been so preoccupied. She began moving around the hogan, collecting what she would need for the long drive— most notably water. She had broken down once in the desert in the summer months and she wouldn't be unprepared again. She filled a canteen and looked at Jericho.

"Besides, you know how it goes with the authorities here," she went on. "One day of real time equals five days of Res time. The pot hunter will be gone with his loot before an officer can be convinced to brave the *chindis* and the legend and go in there after him."

"So you're going to go after him yourself like some kind of fearless pit bull?"

Shadow shrugged. "Why not? Somebody has to." On impulse she added a flashlight to her duffel bag, although she really intended to be out of there by dark.

"And one of these days you're going to get yourself in trouble," Jericho said tightly. "Those guys can be dangerous."

She held up a small revolver for his inspection, then she belted it neatly around her waist. "Jericho, it doesn't matter if it's my responsibility. It doesn't matter if I get paid for it or even thanked for it. It's the principle of the thing. It's illegal to dig on the Res. It's immoral and wrong to disturb the Old Ones' bones. It's some kind of heinous thievery to take their pots from their graves and sell them to the highest bidder." *And I can't stay here today.* But she kept that last excuse to herself, not sure if she could explain it even if she wanted to.

"You and your damned causes," he complained.

"They're all I have."

"What about Catherine?" he demanded.

Ah, Shadow thought, therein lies the rub. "She's going to have a baby," she answered quietly. "Women have been doing it for centuries."

"What if we can't get into Albuquerque or Gallup in time?"

"Then you and Cat will deliver your baby yourselves."

Jericho blanched.

"She's a doctor!"

"Things go wrong."

She shook her head. "You don't need me this time. What could I possibly do? Offer moral support?"

"Well, at least you've delivered babies before. You could help in an emergency."

"So could Catherine."

Suddenly, for one brief, uncharacteristic moment, she wished fervently for a different kind of life, one where nobody needed her ever. Jericho always said she had an unnatural penchant for saving what he called broken doves—the weak, the wounded, the needy. Maybe she did. From her earliest childhood she had been prone to bring home lame, abandoned ponies and Anglo friends whose parents didn't share the People's devout love of children. She had established a precedent early on, she realized grimly.

By now—by *thirty*—it seemed everyone came to her for every favor they needed. She was always burying pieces of herself to take care of someone else. And somehow, in the meantime, too much of her own life slid right by without notice.

Thirty years old?

She realized she was almost desperate to get in her truck and drive away from it all. She slung her duffel bag over her shoulder and started for the door.

After a moment, Jericho followed her outside. "Be careful."

"I always am. These pot hunters are sneak thieves, Jericho. At the first sign they've been caught, they turn tail and run."

"Then they come back at night."

"Not always, and I'll be gone by then anyway."

She climbed into the cab of her truck. By the time she had backed it up to the horse trailer beneath the brush arbor, Jericho had given up the fight and his Rover was headed back down the road.

Shadow leaned her head against the steering wheel for one rare, vulnerable moment. The fact of the matter was, a "Happy Birthday" would have been nice.

She straightened and rubbed a hand over her eyes. Her brother wasn't cold. He cared deeply about those closest to him. Any day now Catherine would have their baby and his head would clear. He would realize that he had forgotten, and he would be appalled.

In the meantime, there was the shameful truth that she really didn't want to be anywhere around when his baby was born. The biggest part of her would gaze down upon the child, hold it close to her breast, and her heart would swell for this new life born into their family. But another small, nasty part would whisper, *thirty years old.*

Almost too old to be having babies of her own—especially since the next seven years showed every indication of passing the way the previous seven had done.

She was definitely having an age crisis, she decided. She got out of the truck again to hook up the trailer, unsaddling her horse and shoving the tack into the storage compartment. She brushed down the mare quickly and loaded her on, glancing at her watch only when she was finished.

It was nine o'clock. Later than she would have liked, but she could still make it. It was about three hours to the Chuska Mountains, then two hours up to Kokopelli's Canyon, hidden in their peaks. The mare would make the last leg of the trip less arduous, she thought. Even if there were complications, she should be there absolutely no later than three o'clock if she rode. That would still leave her a couple hours of daylight to get back down to her truck again.

No problem. She climbed up into the cab, slamming the door hard.

Mac Tshongely bit back a curse as he carefully maneuvered a potsherd out from beneath several still-connected pieces of vertebrae. The Old Ones tended to bury their dead in their trash middens. They had also been fond of disposing their pottery right along with their corpses. Both habits made digging for shards a messy, spooky business, especially if a man happened to be possessed of any superstitious Navajo blood.

But his Navajo blood was something Mac rarely chose to think about. As far as he was concerned, bones were just bones. And at the moment they were in the way of the pot he wanted.

He finally got the shard free and reached a hand behind him without looking, skimming the rocky sand for the brush he had laid there. But he already knew that the piece wasn't one of the ones he was looking for. For one thing, it was the wrong color and it bore several wavering lines. As his fingers closed around the brush handle, a drop of perspiration freed itself from his brow and landed wetly on the shard.

His hands moved fast now, drying it, dusting it, before the salt could do any damage. Then he swore again. He doubted if there was a hotter place on earth than this Navajo reservation. Unless it was hell. But it seemed to Mac that the ancient Greeks had attested to a river around that place—presumably a man could dive in and cool off once in a while.

Not so in Kokopelli's Canyon.

He laid the shard carefully on a pallet—he would take it anyway and hand it over to men who dealt with that sort of thing. Finally he straightened, stretching. His thighs felt cramped and achy from squatting so long. Another day gone and he still hadn't found what he knew was here...somewhere.

He looked down the canyon from where he stood at its easternmost edge. The walls were bloodred in the dying light, sweeping starkly upward, pockmarked with crevices and treacherous caves. Stunted junipers grew out from the rock, twisting up toward the sun, defying logic. The floor was a maze, angling first north, then south, then turning back on itself entirely. And in places where the cliff walls faced the winter sun, where mountain water had carved chasms in its downward path, were all that remained here of the vanished, ancient Anasazi.

As always, he wondered where they had gone and why. It was a mystery that had haunted him for as long as he could remember.

The particular pots he sought might tell him, but they would probably be in the last of the four ruins he searched—that was the way his luck usually went, but Mac had no complaints. He wasn't a man to protest long, tedious weeks in hot, dusty isolation. In fact, it soothed his soul.

The sun was sinking inexorably to the west, throwing light up from behind those peaks. He wouldn't be doing any more digging tonight, he realized.

He pulled a sweat-soaked bandanna from his back pocket to wipe the clinging red dust from the face of his watch. Almost five-thirty. Up on the desert floor the land would still be awash in sunlight, but down here, in the mountain's bowels, shadows were gathering with steady enthusiasm. Darkness moved in the caves and the crevices like a live, threatening thing. He thought of the legends he didn't believe in and went back to his campsite for some water.

Mac had learned a bit from the Anasazi over the years. He had chosen a place that remained in the shade except for the hour or so when the sun was at its highest. He had backed his tent up against the canyon wall so that anything coming at him would have to do it from the front. And less than a hundred feet away was a trickling stream offering fresh mountain runoff.

He grabbed his canteen and went to fill it. The first time he upended it over the general direction of his mouth, letting it spill over onto his neck and his chest as he swallowed. Then he refilled it and put it aside, wading into the calf-deep water to wash the dust and the grime off his skin.

That was when he heard a horse whinny.

At first it seemed almost a ghostly sound and the meager bit of Navajo in him stiffened. He came slowly out of the stream again, looking around, and saw nothing. With slow, silent steps he went back to his campsite, thinking about what he had heard. He finally identified the sound, although he had limited experience with horses. It would have been relatively difficult to drag one around with him considering the life-style he had chosen.

Still, he knew what one sounded like when it was frightened and angry. He slipped into his tent for his gun, then came out to scan the cliffs again. Still nothing, but someone was definitely out there. He could feel the intrusion into his privacy like some kind of living thing poking a cold, nasty finger into his ribs.

He remained standing to the side of his tent, using the site as he had intended, keeping his back to the rock. He held the gun with deceptive nonchalance at his side.

Then he saw her.

For one wild, mind-boggling moment, he thought it was She Who Waits, the woman of obscure legend, the one he was here seeking proof of. But before his mouth could go dry, his mind cleared. He understood why he might have thought such a thing even as his jaw hardened.

She stood on the southern rim directly across from him and she was significantly without a horse. The sunlight up there seemed to illuminate her. Very long, very black hair streamed to her waist, looking disheveled. Though the air on the canyon floor was deathly still there was a breeze up on the rim. It was just enough to tease errant strands. It lifted them here and there as though by a phantom hand.

It fluttered the loose white blouse she wore as well, or at least one sleeve of it. Mac realized that the sleeve was torn and that was why it moved the way it did, like the ghostly raiment of a woman long dead.

That was where all supernatural illusions ended. She had on tight black jeans. The sun glinted off silver near her neck—some sort of looped earrings, he thought. She was one hell of a good-looking woman, even from this distance, the kind who didn't need makeup or elaborate hair to make men pause and look twice. That irritated him as much as the fact that she would disrupt his solitude here, would surely chatter her way through the night when he preferred to be alone.

What the hell was she doing here at this time of day? It was too late to get back down the mountain tonight, at least by way of the eastern slopes, and she had no camping gear that he could see. So whoever she was, he was stuck with her until tomorrow.

Maybe longer.

Mac's jaw dropped as the woman took a single step to move toward him. Then she plummeted, bouncing and rolling, down the canyon wall when her feet found only air.

Chapter 2

Shadow shook the dazed feeling out of her head and looked up into the coldest, most prohibitive blue eyes she had ever seen.

No, not blue, she realized. *Gray* blue, the dark, threatening color of a storm sky. Even more than the gun in the man's hand, they made her feel cautious on some primal level. The fall had left her reeling, but she pushed quickly to her feet to face him anyway.

"Who the hell are you?" he demanded harshly.

Shadow pulled her hair back reflexively, knotting it quickly into a loop at her neck so it wouldn't be in the way if she had to run or—God forbid—fight him. The ponytail she always wore had come loose when her horse had thrown her. When she had tried to refasten it the band had snapped.

That was just about the time when everything had started going wrong. She'd had to urge the mare up the rest of the trail, a time-consuming and frustrating progress, and now she was hours off schedule.

"Actually, I came to ask you that," she answered, planting her hands on her hips, struggling to appear calm.

His face took on a look of cold surprise. "So you thought you'd just drop in—" he waved the gun up and down to show he meant it literally "—and find out?"

Shadow looked away, embarrassed. "That's right."

"Why?"

"Why what?"

"Why'd you do that? Why'd you step over, knowing there was nothing there but air?" He wondered for the first time if she was crazy, if she had escaped from some kind of protective incarceration. Then he looked at her eyes.

No. They were black, clear, sharp, even as she tried to avoid looking at him.

Shadow felt her heart give a hard, uncharacteristic thump of uncertainty. She didn't know *why* she had taken that step. One minute she had been looking down at him, at his stark, utilitarian camp. And in the next heartbeat she had found herself moving toward him as though he had called her name, beckoning her down with soft, unspoken promises that things would be better between these canyon walls, that everything she sought was right here, had always been right here inside.

Her throat closed in panic and she looked around the canyon a little wildly. Yes, oh, yes, she could understand how it had come by its reputation.

She forced a shrug. "I didn't know I was so close to the edge."

His eyes hardened dangerously. Somehow he doubted that. Somehow he got the impression that she knew where her feet were at all times—firmly planted.

"On what authority?" he growled. "What gives you the right to come poking into my business here?"

Shadow kept her eyes on the canyon. He had her with that question.

"I'm waiting."

She finally looked back at him. His face was just as forbidding as his eyes, she realized, although it possessed a certain rugged attractiveness. He had a strong if not large nose, and a hard, chiseled jaw—clenched at the moment. His hair was dark, but exposure to the sun had elicited hints of gold from it. It was a little long, pulled straight back from his forehead and gathered together by a rubber band at his nape. He clearly spent a great deal of time outdoors and that made her frown. Just as her brother had said, most pot hunters preferred to work under the cover of darkness, sneaking in and out of the ruins fast.

He was very tanned, Shadow thought. She could tell even in this light because he wore only boots and a pair of khaki shorts, and the shorts were lighter than his skin tone. That was a rich, burnished color. He really was handsome in a very male, very unpretentious sort of way. He was a big man, strongly muscled, and she felt dwarfed beside him.

Her heart started moving oddly again and suddenly her skin felt warm. Maybe it was just the matter of the gun in his hand.

"You won't need that," she said shortly, motioning at it.

He looked at the weapon, then back at her. "I'll be the judge. Keep talking."

"About what?"

"Who you are, what you're doing here, and when you'll be going home." He paused. "Are you hurt?" he finally asked, but she didn't think it was because he was concerned. More than likely, he knew it would complicate things if she was injured.

Shadow scowled, rubbing a sore elbow. "Not really."

"You should be. You could have killed yourself."

"Well, I didn't," she snapped. "I've been riding a horse since I was two and I was born and raised in this country. I know how to fall."

He nodded as though this satisfied him. "Okay. So where's your horse?"

She was surprised. "How'd you know I had one?"

"I heard it."

So he had good ears. She imagined that all of his senses were probably as sharp as a cat's. He had that way about him.

"Not very far," she answered finally. "I hobbled her in a glade. She balked, refused to come any further." Actually, the mare had balked so hard and so suddenly, she had pulled Shadow right off her feet. It had spooked her enough that her stomach still felt queasy. Animals knew . . . things. And that particular animal definitely had not been willing to come any closer to this canyon.

She shook her head. This was all wrong. She was supposed to be the one asking questions.

There wasn't time. He shot more of his own at her, keeping her off balance.

"Where's your camp stuff?"

"I'm not staying."

He snorted, giving that pipe dream about as much respect as it deserved. The western mountain slopes would still be bright, but the eastern ones leading back down to her truck would be as dark and treacherous as this canyon was becoming.

"I don't want to stay," she amended.

"That makes two of us. I don't want you to, either," he said shortly. "Okay. One more time. Who sent you?"

Her eyes narrowed. So they were back to that again. "No one. This is my country. I want to know what you're doing taking pieces of it."

She started off toward the place where he was digging. After a moment, she heard his slow, almost predatory footsteps come after her.

She wouldn't admit to fear; it wasn't in her nature. But she wished he would put that damned gun down. She wondered how quickly she could get her own free if she needed it.

Mac watched her, one brow lifting. Nice little sway to her hips, he thought. Her hair bounced and shone in the knot at her neck. But he wasn't interested in any of that under the current circumstances. He had no real aversion to rolling around in the dust with a good-looking woman, but there was no possibility he would peel those jeans off this particular woman tonight. There was no possibility she would be leaving before dawn. And since he sure as hell didn't plan to do so, that would be breaking one of his carved-in-granite rules—never, under any circumstances, would he spend the night with a woman.

Still, there was something about this one. It called to him, whispering in a very physical, very elemental sense. It made him follow her when he hadn't intended to. It made him want to delve into her deeper than this night would permit.

It was more than just her looks. She really did possess an air of efficiency. He thought she was used to being in charge of her own life and he liked that kind of strength in a woman. Clinging vines made him itch, made him start looking for the nearest door.

Of course, she was Navajo, and their women were always strong and pushy. Even if she hadn't more or less told him so, Mac would have recognized her heritage in her high cheekbones, in her wide, generous mouth and the midnight blackness of her eyes. And there was that business about her not wanting to spend the night, too. Only a Navajo would walk a hundred miles barefoot before lingering in a canyon where the ghosts whispered their secrets to each other.

He might not believe in them, but he knew she would. Yet she was trudging right up to the midden he'd been working on, self-assured, almost defiant. He raised a brow.

Maybe she didn't know there were bones in it. Very old, very dead bones.

She knew. Despite her bravado, she stopped judiciously several feet away.

"Do you have papers for this?" she called back.

Mac finished closing the distance between them. "Yes."

"Can I see them?"

"No."

Shadow felt as surprised as though he had slapped her. "Why?"

"Why should I show them to you?" he countered. "They're none of your business."

She bristled. She was getting tired of his cool hostility and the fact that she couldn't make him cooperate. It was frustrating, something she wasn't entirely used to.

"Maybe not," she snapped. "But if I don't see them, if you can't prove to me that you're on the level here, then I'm just going to notify the tribal police when I get back to Shiprock. Sooner or later you're going to have to show your papers to someone. I'd think you'd prefer to get it out of the way now."

"And why do you think that?"

"Because you want to be left alone."

Her words surprised her as much as him. He wondered if he was that readable—it had never been a shortcoming he'd had cause to apply to himself.

And that, of course, was why she'd said what she had.

Shadow realized it as soon as she thought about it. His eyes were like the rock at her feet, like the stone that swept up on all sides of her. Hard, keeping the world out and his feelings in. Assuming he had any feelings. It occurred to her that that might be a long shot.

"Good argument," he allowed finally. "Go ahead."

"Go ahead with what?"

"Send in your guns. When I see a badge, they'll see my papers."

Shadow's eyes sparked. "That's absolutely ridiculous! What are you hiding?"

The problem, she thought, was that he *didn't* seem to be hiding anything. She looked wildly down at the midden again. His work was meticulous and careful, while pot hunters tended to bring in backhoes with the teeth sawed down. They raped and pillaged Mother Earth, dragging everything to the surface, destroying her secrets. They callously tossed aside anything that wasn't worth big money. They worked fast, out of greed and fear of discovery. But this dig had been going on for a while.

The surface sand had been painstakingly brushed away, deeper and deeper, until he had come to the hidden past. The bones appeared untouched as much as possible. He obviously didn't want them, but neither had he disturbed them. In many places he had actually dug beneath them to extract the shards, and those shards were all placed neatly on a pallet. She could tell by their position that he had put them in order of discovery. There was a notebook nearby as well, undoubtedly detailing the exact positions in which he'd found them.

So he appeared legitimate. But then why wouldn't he show her his authorization? And why the gun? There was no doubt in her mind that he was hiding *something*.

"How did you know to start digging here," she demanded, "at this particular place?"

His eyes narrowed on her as though he was suspicious of the question. As well he should be, Shadow thought. She was trying to find out if he had any real schooling, any knowledge of the Anasazi. A genuine student or archaeologist would. But he appeared too old to be a student.

Finally he answered by pointing to the cliff above them. There were crumbling, connected squares in the rock there—the Old Ones' apartments.

"They rarely went far to dump their refuse," he explained, "or even their dead. They had enough traveling to do in pursuit of the merest essentials of living."

Okay, she thought. He was right about that. But then, suddenly, she forgot that she was grilling him. She studied the cliff houses, feeling the same eerie curiosity she had always felt in their presence.

"Why, do you suppose? Why did they come to such an inhospitable place as this, when they were obviously migrating and could have settled anywhere?"

Again he hesitated before answering. His blue gray eyes scanned her face. "Why did the Navajo do it?"

She looked back at him. "Our origin stories say we came up from another world beneath this one. This was where it happened, so this is where we've stayed."

"Anthropology says you're Athabascan, that your ancestors migrated down from the north."

Shadow shrugged, clearly unperturbed. "That's science. We know better. But the Anasazi clearly did come here from the south. Their flight has been tracked, more or less."

"They were running from something," he said.

"Or to something."

"No. They were hiding, afraid."

"But they dug in as though they were planning to stay for a long time. They wouldn't go to the trouble of plowing roads and carving out the cliff walls if they thought they were going to be flushed out soon by an enemy."

"Why did they plow roads when they had no wheels or horses?"

Shadow realized they were both watching each other intently as they debated. It made her feel uncomfortable and she looked away again.

"I have no idea," she mused. "I wish I did."

Why? He wanted to ask, but old, old instinct had him holding the word back. "You'd better go get your horse," he said instead, tightly. "I've heard bobcats these last few nights."

He actually saw her shudder. She closed her eyes as though to gather strength. Somehow he knew she would find it.

He was right. She squared her shoulders and went back to the place where she had fallen. Coincidentally, the best hand- and toeholds were there. Somewhere along the line, she had obviously noted that.

Shadow climbed up the slope, conscious of the feel of his eyes on her back. She knew that if she turned around to look at him they would close down again. A part of her wanted to do it just to try to establish some sort of one-upmanship over him. Another part knew—probably wisely—that it was best not to provoke him. She was going to have to spend the night here, after all.

Oh, how she dreaded it.

It wasn't just the *chindis,* although her skin already felt crawly at the thought of being trapped amid so much death. It was him. There was definitely something about him that didn't sit right with her, something that put her nerves on edge. Her instincts felt . . . endangered.

She reached her mare and guided her back to the canyon by hand, something she hadn't been willing to do earlier when she'd still harbored some misguided hopes of getting in and out before dark. She thought briefly of simply camping up here on the rim, then she discarded the idea. If the man said he had heard cats, then they were probably a more immediate threat than *chindis* and legends. She had only a .22-caliber handgun.

The horse fought her. She had to work slowly, coaxing her. "If I can do it, you can do it, old girl. We're in this thing together."

The mare gave her a reproachful look. Shadow supposed that if the mare could talk she would tell Shadow that coming here hadn't been her idea.

They finally reached the canyon and Shadow began circling it, looking for the best way to get the mare down.

Surreptitiously, she looked for the man as well. He was back at his tent now and it looked as though he had finally put the gun away. At least she didn't see it in the gathering darkness. If he was going to harm her, logic told her he would have done it already.

So why didn't that make her feel any better?

She found a wall in a switchback that was more sloped than the others. The mare was white eyed, sweating with nerves, but she allowed herself to be led down with reasonable obedience now and, Shadow thought, probably a good bit of resignation. They reached the canyon floor and came out of the switchback, and Shadow paused to try to place the ruins.

The one he was digging was to her left, and his campsite was between her and it. That was good. If memory served her correctly, there were three other ruins to her right. Two were distant, but one was sort of catercornered across from her. She wasn't sure how long it had been since anyone had tried to dig there, disturbing old spirits, but she wasn't inclined to take any chances.

Reluctantly she moved a little closer to the man's camp.

She felt his eyes on her again as he worked up a fire, but she ignored him. She tied hobbles around the mare's fetlocks to keep her from straying, then she untacked her, untying her duffel bag and dropping it on the ground. She rummaged through it for her water and chugged gratefully. Her thirst sated, she looked around, trying to figure out the quickest, easiest way to get through the night.

"I've got a little extra wood," he volunteered.

She saw some dry sage and a dead juniper halfway up the opposite slope. "No need."

She found her knife and climbed up to tackle the tree. The work took a while because she was hanging onto a precarious finger hold with one hand, chopping with the other. It would have been infinitely easier and probably more sensible to accept his wood, but for some reason she couldn't really define, she was loath to do it.

It was probably just as simple as the fact that he wouldn't cooperate with her. And it was obvious that he resented her presence here. But this was Navajo land and she had the blood right to wander wherever she chose upon it, undoubtedly more right than he had. So she would spend the night here whether he liked it or not, and she would do it on her own terms.

She was efficient, he thought. Desertwise and determined. He watched her bring the wood back and pile it. He wished she hadn't moved so close to him that he couldn't escape awareness of her presence, and wondered if he could have forgotten she was here even if she had stayed out of sight. Yes, she was very good-looking. There was something about the darkness of her hair and eyes that suggested a hot-blooded passion beneath her cool skin.

He found himself enjoying the diversion that watching her provided, even as it disgruntled him. "Matches?" he offered.

"I have them."

A moment later her sage sputtered and lit. A short time after that, the juniper blazed. The flames threw orange and black shadows up at her face. Mac jolted. In that moment, again, she reminded him of the vague image he held in his head of what She Who Waits would look like.

He wrenched his eyes away, irritated with himself.

He finally got his own fire going and went downstream, where he had left the last of the venison he had hunted up a few days earlier. The cold water and the aluminum foil he had brought with him were just enough to keep it from spoiling. He gave her campsite a wide berth both going and returning, and found himself relatively convinced that she would know of some way to eliminate the need for the aluminum foil—just one more thing he had to pack and carry to all his sites.

He settled at his fire and spitted the meat, and damned if he didn't hear himself calling out to her again.

"Hungry?"

"I brought food just in case."

Why wasn't he surprised?

It occurred to him then that while he had fully anticipated that she would chatter her way through the night, she hadn't spoken one single word to him that he hadn't provoked, at least not since she had come back with the horse. He shifted his position a little, to be able to watch her more easily. She seemed so at ease with her own company and silences.

He noted that she ate with quick intent, more for sustenance than enjoyment. But then, her meal consisted of a candy bar and a prepackaged sandwich, not exactly mouthwatering fare. She washed it all down with the water she had brought.

So what did she think she needed the fire for? Not for cooking and certainly not for warmth. The night air was warm and clinging. Then he figured it out. The *chindis*. He thought he remembered hearing somewhere that fire kept Navajo ghosts at bay.

So there *was* a soft, vulnerable spot inside her somewhere. He wasn't sure if he was pleased or not. He thought it probably had more to do with her being Navajo than with her being a woman.

She finished eating, neatly replacing the wrappers in her bag. Then she fussed around with her tack some, positioning the saddle just so, covering it with the saddle pad, keeping the side up that wasn't damp with horse sweat. When the moon started to rise, she dug out a little place in the ground for her hips and laid down. She seemed to do it carefully with her head against the makeshift pillow, her back to him. Almost as an afterthought, she reached behind her and pulled the knot in her hair out.

Her hair spilled to the ground, pooling there, long and silky. He had the stunning, almost overpowering urge to go over there and run his fingers through it, through something so sleek and alive with its own light.

How long had it been since he had touched anything that was *alive?*

He clenched his hands into fists, then she called out to him for the first time.

"What's your name, by the way?"

"What?" he asked hoarsely.

"Your name."

"Mac Tshongely." Too late, he realized that she probably had some sort of ulterior motive for asking. She clearly wasn't prone to casual conversation—unless she was discussing the ancient Anasazi.

"Hopi?" she guessed.

"That's right. Half of me is, anyway."

"What's the other half?"

I don't have another half. It left when I was ten. He was stunned to hear himself answer anyway, talking to her back.

"Some Navajo but she was mostly white."

"I guess that explains your eyes."

After that she was so entirely still he had to wonder if she was already asleep. But when he spoke again, she answered.

"What do they call you?"

"Shadow."

Shadow. Shade. Ghost. Like the image of a long dead woman plunging down a canyon wall to land at his feet.

Mac got up abruptly and went into his tent. It was long past time he stopped talking to her.

Shadow couldn't sleep. It wasn't the fact that she was outdoors without a bed. She was accustomed to that—she almost always camped out whenever she went to one of Jericho's medicine sings. No, it was the idea of Mac

Tshongely that kept her awake, the maybe-archaeologist with hard eyes and a rough voice and a mongrel mix of Hopi-Navajo-Anglo blood which theoretically put him at rights to be here also.

It was the thought that he was undoubtedly sound asleep himself no more than ten yards away. Leaving her alone. Giving her a wide berth.

What was wrong with her?

Why didn't men ever react to her? Was it, as Catherine had once said, that there was something just so no-nonsense practical about her? Cat had meant it as a compliment, but did it make her seem sexless? She didn't actually want Mac to come sniffing around her campsite—something about him told her that touching him would be an unsettling, dangerous experience indeed. If she ever *did* get around to loving a man again, she would prefer him to be someone with some heat, and Mac Tshongely seemed to be all cold antagonism.

No, it wasn't that she wanted him; it was just that she was very tired of being unwanted herself. She twisted and turned, and then she found herself thinking about his hands again.

She had watched them only briefly in the flickering light of his own fire, but they wouldn't leave her mind. They were definitely archaeologist hands—or at least they belonged to someone who dug in the dirt often. His nails were blunt, his fingers deft and strong. His skin had looked tough, hard, callused. In spite of herself, she wondered what such a cool touch would feel like against smooth, tender skin that never saw the blistering sun.

She heard herself groan aloud and was appalled at herself.

It didn't matter anyway—he couldn't have heard her. Almost simultaneously, she heard movement from his tent and knew that he had come outside again. Her heart began thundering and her palms went damp. *Would* he approach her? They were, after all, a man and woman very much alone.

And what would she do if he did?

Then she heard his footsteps receding. She waited a safe time and rolled a bit to see where he was going. He walked to his dig site, his sleeping bag jumbled up and thrown over his shoulder. She watched disbelievingly as he dropped it near the refuse midden and hunkered down to straighten it out.

That was when she realized he slept naked.

The strong lines of his body showed in the moonlight, gold and silver and shadowed. There was no spare meat on him despite his size, just lean, hard muscle. His buttocks were tight, his thighs powerful, his shoulders broad. Shadow's heart slammed and her throat went dry, then it closed over unshed tears.

Did he think she was asleep? Did he not care one way or another? Was it simply a foregone conclusion that thirty-year-old practically-spinsters weren't supposed to get turned on by ruggedly handsome, naked men?

She was turned on. Oh, God, she was turned on. A sharp, stunning sense of need ripped through her.

He laid down, pulling the top of the sleeping bag up over his shoulders.

Apparently, ten yards had been too close.

Chapter 3

Shadow saddled her mare again before the first new light touched the canyon floor. She worked stiffly, without looking anywhere near the refuse midden.

The small of her back ached and there was a sharp pain in her neck from holding herself rigidly on her back all night. If she'd rolled left, she would have been confronted by the sight of Mac Tshongely, naked inside his sleeping bag. To her right were the ruins and she'd been afraid to look that way, too—she had worried that she would see something ghostly moving there. Now she was tired and she hurt and she was irritable.

When her campsite showed not a single sign of human trespass except the vague indentation where she had lain, she finally glanced over at Mac's dig. He was gone. She breathed a little more easily, then her breath hitched. She didn't entirely like not knowing where he was, either. It left her with a vulnerable, exposed feeling.

Well, she could put an end to that by simply leaving. She had a lot to take care of today—first and foremost a sweatbath to rid herself of the threat of ghost sickness from spending the night here. Then she would go to the tribal-police subagency in Shiprock and report Mac Tshongely. She should probably check in at the museum, too, to see if Diamond Eddie had any work for her. After that, she would drive up the mountain to check on Cat and her brother.

She closed her eyes briefly. She wondered if Jericho knew any chants to erase the image of a naked Mac Tshongely from her mind. Somehow she doubted it.

Where was he?

She briefly considered looking for him, but it seemed absurd to search him out just to say goodbye. He hadn't wanted her here and she hadn't wanted to be here, so she would just go.

She gathered up her mare's reins and led her back up the sloped switchback wall to the rim.

She was halfway up when a flash of something caught her eye near the side of the trail. She paused, scowling. She *hated* litter. It was an affront to the earth, to the raw beauty the Holy Ones had given to the People. It was bad enough that Mac Tshongely was digging up the soil—as an anthropology student, she had long ago accepted the necessity of that. But to spoil the land with his trash, his refuse . . . that was something again.

She bent and snatched up the sparkly thing angrily, then she winced. It cut into her hand.

She uncurled her fingers slowly, looking down at the object. It was a very small, very sharp piece of Anasazi pottery.

Mac watched her from the top of the wall.

The carcass of another small buck lay at his feet and he rested one boot against its ribs. Conveniently, the animals gathered at a watering hole farther up the mountain at dawn. It had been all the excuse he'd needed to get up before the sun and get the hell out of that canyon.

He scrubbed a hand over his jaw. He needed a shave and decided he'd put it off until tomorrow. Today he was bone-deep exhausted.

He was getting too old to be laying awake all night like a teenager, hard and wanting something he couldn't have. No, that wasn't quite accurate. Couldn't was too prohibitive a word. Shouldn't was more apt. It would have been insanity to have answered her silent call.

He hadn't wanted any woman so much in as long as he could remember. The mere fact that she was spending the night had put her off-limits. But out of sight hadn't equaled out of mind.

Moving out of the tent hadn't helped. In the tent, he had sworn to God he could hear her slow, even breathing, so nearby. But at the dig, he had sworn he could *smell* her on the air, some soft, feminine scent, warm and musky and inviting. He hadn't known then and he didn't know now what made him so damnably aware of her. He had made the move to the midden instinctively, feeling like a hunted animal, needing to get away and put distance between them. He hadn't even realized until he got there that he had forgotten to dress again.

Not that it mattered. Something told him that naked men wouldn't skew her orderly world. She had probably been asleep, but on the off chance that she wasn't, he was pretty sure she had taken it right in stride without any blushing or gasping.

And now she was finally leaving. Now he didn't have to worry about it at all. He simply had to step back into the brush as she passed here and she would go on her way never knowing he was nearby.

But she didn't pass. She paused and stooped to pick up something from the dirt.

He laid his bow against a rock in the tangle of growth, then he bent and hefted the deer, slinging it over his shoulder. Despite his determination to keep hidden, he moved out into her path.

Shadow gasped, jerking to her feet, clearly startled. Her hand closed protectively over whatever she had found, then something in her eyes flared. The look caught him by the throat, strangling him, making him want her with an ungodly, mind-boggling rush that came out of nowhere. At first it was only suspicion and wariness in her gaze, but then her eyes widened ever so slight and her breath seemed to catch.

He knew instantly that she *had* been awake last night. Maybe she hadn't blushed or gasped, but there sure as hell was something probing and curious about her gaze now, something that made him want to satisfy her curiosity very much.

"Leaving so soon?" he snarled.

"It was the company."

She was quick, he'd give her that. He finally stepped back.

"Then don't let me keep you."

"I hadn't intended to."

She started moving again, leading the horse. *Let her go.* "Are you going to come back with the cops?"

She looked around at him, vaguely startled. "Why should I?"

"So you can see for yourself that I'm legitimate."

"If you're so concerned with my opinion, then why don't you just show me your papers now?"

His eyes narrowed. "Maybe I want to see if you'll give up without a fight."

"No," she said simply. "I never do that when something's important."

He had known that, and it was precisely why he didn't want to give them to her. He guessed that she would pretty much organize the people in her life the way she attacked an unplanned night in the outdoors. Something perverse in him refused to give her that power, that satisfaction, even if it meant he had to deal with the tribal police later.

He turned away abruptly. "Have it your way." His best hope was that the legends and the *chindis* would keep the cops at bay for at least another day.

His consolation was that they would undoubtedly be easier to deal with than a lithe, capable female with a great backside and hot black eyes.

Shadow headed east on Navajo Route 504 as fast as she dared with the mare trailing behind her. She reached Shiprock by lunchtime and slowed to a crawl where the narrow road intersected with the four-lane stretch of U.S. Route 666 that would take her home again. Then she made a decision and stomped on the accelerator. There was no sense in going home for a sweatbath, then driving all the way back up here to town. She'd hit the subagency and the museum first—the subagency being her top priority.

But when she pulled into the subagency parking lot, maneuvering carefully with the horse trailer, she hesitated again. She put the truck in neutral and jiggled her toe against the gas pedal, thinking.

Mac Tshongely was probably on the level. And what a shame it would be to send some poor Navajo cop into that horrible canyon for nothing. But what if he wasn't legitimate? *Something* wasn't right about him. Five hours of riding and driving hadn't changed her impression of that. She looked down pensively at the small piece of ice blue pottery that she had laid on the seat beside her. If she had found it on the canyon floor, it wouldn't have disturbed her particularly. But on the trail leading *out* of the canyon? Someone had to have dropped it there. Someone taking pottery away from Kokopelli's Canyon.

Mac Tshongely? Legitimate archaeologists packed their finds much more carefully than that—too carefully to be losing bits and pieces of it.

Abruptly she put the truck in reverse. No one would be in the subagency now but the dispatcher anyway. Everyone in town would be either at the Burger King or the coffee shop eating lunch. She would go to the museum first. It would give her time to do a little investigating, to think this through more clearly.

Diamond Eddie was in his office. He heard her footsteps in the museum lobby and came out, fairly buzzing with the kind of nervous energy that apparently didn't need food for sustenance. Shadow had worked here for seven years and she couldn't ever remember seeing him eat.

"*Yutaheh,*" he said in traditional Navajo greeting.

"*Yu te,*" she muttered back. "I need to use the computer."

"That's your job, *señorita.*"

"Knock it off, Eddie. You're not Mexican, and I'm not working today."

He shrugged, following her into her office. He was barely taller than she was. The three diamonds at his left ear twinkled in the fluorescent overhead light when she hit the wall switch. As usual, he moved closer to her than he had to.

"But Spanish is such a romantic language, no?"

"No." She turned her back to him, leaning over the computer, turning it on. When he pressed himself into her back, she paused to elbow him hard.

"Go away," she snapped without looking at him. "I'm tired and I'm cranky and I'm in no mood for your antics today."

"Ah, but you're still beautiful."

Well, at least *somebody* thought so. Apparently the man in Kokopelli's Canyon hadn't been very impressed. The thought jolted her and Shadow turned back to face her boss.

"There's something I need to do here, Eddie. Can I have some privacy?"

"You're beautiful even with dirt smudged on your cheek," he went on, licking his finger, making a move to wipe it off. Shadow reared back.

"Please."

He held up his hands in surrender. "Okay, okay. Maybe someday you'll change your mind."

"Maybe." Who knew how desperate she'd feel when thirty-five came sneaking up out of nowhere and nailed her? She looked at the little Navajo closer. No. No way. She wasn't even desperate now, just...itchy. And befuddled. Wondering how her life had come to be the way it was.

Diamond Eddie left, and she followed him as far as the door to close it behind him. Then she went back and sat down at the computer. If Mac Tshongely was indeed authorized, where was that authorization most likely to come from? The Smithsonian was always a logical place to start. They gave grants to three area universities that she knew of—New Mexico, Arizona State and the University of Arizona. Then there was the Chaco Culture National Historical Park just east of the Res. They always had somebody working out of there, too.

She used the modem to access Chaco first. They were a rough-hewn bunch over there. Tshongely seemed to fit their mold.

Nothing. Okay, back to the schools.

She tried New Mexico and came up with zilch again. By the time she drew a blank with ASU as well, she was thinking that there was nothing legitimate about him at all unless some Utah college worked in the field and had sent him. University of Arizona proved equally fruitless.

She sat back, rubbing her temples. Was it possible he worked directly for the big guys themselves? She made a phone call and found out how to access the Smithsonian personnel and grant files—illegally, but who was going to split hairs when she was trying to do them a favor? She tapped in, but then she found herself strangely reluctant to type out his name on the keys.

She hardened her jaw and did it. FILE NOT FOUND.

"Damn it." She was more distressed at his perfidy than she knew she ought to be. But he had *said* he was authorized. If he was legal in any way, shape or form, then the tribal council would have to know of him. But she couldn't access their brains by modem—checking with them would necessitate a trip over to their headquarters. And for some reason she couldn't understand, she didn't want anyone to know she was doing this.

Maybe it was just the little added bonus that a computer file would probably cough up all kinds of personal info about him.

She sat back in her chair, sighing. What kind of a man strolled naked from his tent in the moonlight when there was a stranger sleeping ten yards away? What kind of man made it clear that she was intruding, then offered to help her get settled—in a manner of speaking?

And why in the hell had he stopped her this morning? Why hadn't he just let her go?

She typed again, grasping at straws, trying Hopi phonetics to spell his name this time. Finally his file leapt onto the screen. Shadow sat back. *A Smithsonian file.* So he did work for the head honchos. She gave a shaky little breath and leaned forward again to read.

"Tshongely, Mackenzie." Now there was a mouthful. No wonder he had shortened it. "Birthdate 29 May," and he was thirty-seven years old. Her brows went up. "No permanent address. No telephone. Mail received General Delivery, Winslow, Arizona."

A man without a home?

"Will not work with team." That was even odder, unless he really was a pot hunter. Then he would want all the privacy he could get.

Shadow scrolled down. He had two degrees, a bachelor of science and a master's, both from Arizona State. She would have found some trace of him there after all if she had used the right spelling. He didn't appear to have a wife, but there was a father who lived on the Hopi Mesas and a brother who seemed to spend an inordinate amount of time in the Arizona prison system. He had been published many times, and his current grant had something to do with Kokopelli himself. He wouldn't be the first archaeologist who had tried to prove that the legend had actually lived and breathed, but Shadow was disappointed. It was such a mundane goal. He'd seemed too hard to be sucked into that fanciful game. He had struck her as the type who would try to unearth proof of something that really mattered—like where the Anasazi had gone and why.

She rubbed the back of her sore neck and left the file, turning the computer off. So that was that. Mac Tshongely had papers directly from the Smithsonian. She could go home now, take a sweatbath, and nap in her own bed. She could forget this business. The Kokopelli *chindis* could have him.

Except something still didn't feel right about the whole thing. Why wouldn't he work with a team? Maybe she should go back, she thought, just to watch him for a little while, just to... make sure.

She was out of her mind.

One night in that place had practically undone her. Was she actually considering spending *several* nights there? She was due for a vacation, but there was absolutely nothing wrong with Phoenix or Tucson or Palm Springs. Maybe *that* was actually what she needed—to get off the Res for a little while, to go somewhere where nobody knew her name. She had some money saved; it didn't take much of her salary to live out here. She picked up the phone to dial an airline, then put it down again slowly.

That wouldn't fix whatever was wrong in Kokopelli's Canyon. And something was. She couldn't put her finger on it, but she felt it on a subconscious level, a vague sense of misgiving right in the pit of her stomach. There was no rational explanation for that potsherd on the trail, but that didn't mean she wasn't using it as an excuse to stay away while Cat and Jericho had their baby.

Worse still, it didn't mean that something about Mac Tshongely, something about him personally, wasn't calling her back.

She groaned, closing her eyes. Was she that desperate? On some hidden level, did she think that if she hung out there long enough he might finally touch her with those rough, cool hands? That was *pathetic!* But... there was some lure of delicious danger about him, some squirming curiosity that couldn't be sated by the computer. She remembered the naked moonlit image of him at the refuse midden and something in the vicinity of her middle tightened again with a painful ache. She groaned and jumped to her feet to pace.

A man without a home. Why?

In the end none of it mattered. Mac didn't want her and Jericho didn't need her this time, whether he knew it or not. So she would follow her instincts purely for their own sake. She leaned down and pulled open her bottom desk drawer. There was a pile of steno books in there—her job demanded a lot of meticulous note taking. She found one with a relative abundance of blank pages and left her office.

Diamond Eddie was in the display area, talking to a family of tourists. Summer on the Res was tapering off, but there were still stragglers who wanted to see scalps and peace pipes. Unfortunately for them, the Navajo had never believed in scalping and all the pipes they had ever smoked with the white man had long since been destroyed in anger.

She waited until the family had moved on and approached Eddie. "I'm taking a week off."

He looked startled for a moment, then he shook his head. "Shadow, Shadow, when will you learn to ask a man for what you want, instead of telling him? When you smile, a man would give you any wish."

She forced a meaningless grin. "I wish to take a week off, and I have some time coming to me." She turned to leave.

"Where will you go?" he called after her. "Acapulco? California? You should have company."

"Kokopelli's Canyon, and I'll have company." *Whether Mac likes it or not.* "Some guy's digging up there," she explained from the door. "He's got credentials, but it wouldn't be the first time somebody used their papers to slip a few things away on the side. I found a piece of pottery on the trail leading out of there, so that's a pretty clear indication that somebody is taking stuff out of there. I'm going to write down everything he pulls out of the ground. Then I'll compare it with the Smithsonian list of what they collect from him and make sure he's not keeping anything for himself."

Diamond Eddie scowled. "There are four ruins up there. He could be working for a long time. What good is a week going to do?"

"Well, it's a place to start."

"He's not going to sell anything he takes while you're there. He'll wait and take those pieces after you're gone."

"If he's smart." But he was. At least he seemed to be, and all those degrees and published works had to mean something. "If he thinks I'm smart," she added, and that remained to be seen.

She went outside, then stuck her head back in. "My brother will probably come around looking for me. Tell him I'm fine and not to worry."

She'd worry enough for both of them. She was clearly out of her mind.

* * *

It was midnight before she got back to the rim. She hesitated there, remembering the gun he had.

His fire was mere embers. She didn't see him, even though the moon was getting full and there was a lot of milky light. He was probably fast asleep inside his tent. If he had been any other man, she would have been reasonably sure she could get down to the canyon floor without waking him. Uncle Ernie himself had tutored her in the art and value of silence.

But this wasn't any man. And her flashlight batteries were going out again—she had already changed them once in her careful, painstaking climb up the mountain. She had left the mare at home this time.

She took a tight breath and called out. If she tried to sneak in without waking him, he would probably shoot her.

"*Yutaheh!*" What were the odds of him speaking Navajo?

"*Yu te.*"

Shadow screamed and spun. He was right behind her.

One look at his face had her instinctively retreating. If he had resented her intrusion before, now he was menacingly angry. She put a hand out instinctively as though to ward off a blow, and felt her heel slide on the edge of the rim where the rocky surface began to crumble.

"Oh, hell, not again," he groaned.

She felt her balance sway and knew it was going to be a bad fall this time. She had a pack on her back and it was heavy; it wouldn't let her roll. The earth gave way beneath her and she pinwheeled her arms, struggling desperately to right herself. But it was too late and the pack gave the upper half of her body too much weight.

He came with her.

One moment there was only air, and then his body slammed into hers, so much bigger and stronger, absorbing the first bone-jarring bump. His hard arms came around her, then somehow he was at her back, her pack between them, his legs tangled with hers as they fell. They rolled, then came to an abrupt stop that had her jaws snapping together. Shadow bit her tongue hard and felt blood pooling in her mouth.

She had landed face down and she spat it out. Her cheek was pressed flat and hard against a rocky ledge, and his full weight was on top of her. Between that and the pack, she could barely breathe. She craned her neck, gasping for air, and saw that he had managed to grab hold of one of the juniper branches with his left hand. That and the ledge had broken their fall.

Then she saw that his right arm was close against her right shoulder and that at the end of it, in that hand, was the gun.

"Don't move," he snarled.

Chapter 4

Shadow couldn't have moved if she had wanted to.

Her heart was still galloping from the surprise he had given her, and from the sickening, plummeting sensation of the fall. Numbing fear filled her at the tone of his voice and the curl of his finger so near the trigger guard. And finally, awareness of him came sliding through her, fluid and hot and breath robbing. There was every indication that she was going to get hurt here, yet suddenly the thing uppermost in her mind was the *feel* of him.

His left leg was lodged between her and the canyon wall. But his right one was *between* hers, his hard thigh pressed intimately against her. She felt heat pooling deep inside her in response. She had worn shorts instead of jeans, because she wasn't riding this time, and his skin felt as cool and rough against her inner thighs as she had thought it would. The weight of him was solid and powerful.

"I'm alone," she gasped. "I didn't bring the cops."

"Why?" he growled. "Why'd you come back here? What the hell do you want from me?"

Her head swam with too many answers to that one, answers she wasn't sure she fully understood herself. "Can we talk about this in an upright position?" she groaned.

"I'd prefer it."

Shadow flinched. She was painfully aware of him, and he wanted nothing more than to get away from her.

"So move," she snapped hoarsely.

"Believe me, I'm working on it."

Then she realized the problem. There was really no way for him to do it without both of them plunging all the way to the bottom this time. The ledge was too tiny. Unless . . .

"Put your hands on either side of my head and get to your knees," she suggested. It was a few moments before he responded, but then he did it fast and almost violently, tossing the gun over the edge to get it safely out of the way. It went off as it hit the floor, an explosion that made her flinch, and she held her breath as she waited for the bullet to ricochet off all that rock. But there was only one distant ping, then silence except for the echoing reverberations.

"Can you see a handhold?" she asked.

"Yeah."

"Take it."

"I already have," he said tightly.

She felt him moving upright, smoothly for a man of his size. "Where are your feet?" she asked.

"Between your calves."

"Step between me and the wall."

Shadow felt him move and she rolled half onto her back so that she faced the outside of the ledge. They had fallen about halfway down. Moving as little as possible, she struggled out of her pack.

"I'm going over," she said.

He looked down at her incredulously.

"I managed it the first time without getting hurt," she pointed out. "I should be able to do it again, especially since I'm dropping deliberately this time. You go up."

"Yes, ma'am. You're damned good at giving orders."

"Then save your own stupid hide," she hissed. "I really don't care how you do it. I was just trying to help."

There was a short silence. "Fair enough," he conceded finally. "You got us into this, so you can get us out."

"*I* did? You sneaked up behind me like some kind of commando guerrilla."

"I was trying to find out who was coming up the mountain, trying to be quiet and doing a bad job of it."

Shadow flushed. It was true that she had stumbled into the brush once or twice the first time her flashlight had gone out, but she wasn't going to dignify his observation with an answer. She swung her legs over the edge, belly down, then she inched out farther until she was barely holding on with her arms.

She let go, her legs slamming painfully against the wall, but there was little she could do about that. She felt skin tear from her knee and she winced. But just as she had told him, she knew how to fall. She made her body go limp and loose and when she landed she protected her head, rolling onto the canyon floor.

She let out a harsh burst of breath, gingerly checking for injuries. The knee was the worst of it. She sat up and looked to see how he was faring.

He was several yards farther along the wall, coming down where the Anasazi had left the toeholds. He had her backpack. She stood, hurting.

He reached her and thrust the pack at her. "Let's get one thing straight, Sergeant. From the looks of this bag, you're planning on staying a while. I don't know why, and I don't care. But this ruin is mine. This area of the canyon is mine. It's a big place. You want to commune with nature and *chindis,* go do it in some other part."

Sergeant? She watched mutely as he stalked back to his tent.

"Why?" she demanded. "What are you doing here that you don't want me to see?"

He turned back on her so hard and fast she cringed. "I like my privacy."

"Then why didn't you just let me fall on my own? That would have sent me limping home in a hurry."

"*After* I carried you eight damned miles down to my truck and drove you to the nearest hospital. Either that, or buried you so you wouldn't stink when the sun found you. It's late. I'm tired. I didn't feeling like doing either one."

He snatched back the door flap of his tent and ducked in. A lantern went on inside. She watched his silhouette as he ripped off his shorts and dropped down onto his sleeping bag. Her mouth went dry. The lantern went out.

She tried to shout after him and had to clear her throat to do it. Finally she found her voice. "I'm going to camp tonight right where I camped last night. It's too dark and I don't know the canyon well enough to look for a new site now." Not to mention the fact that she was damned if she was going to fumble around the ruins in the moonlight.

She flinched as his voice drifted out to her again. It was muffled, but she understood enough to know that he swore darkly.

Shadow went back to the place where she had slept the previous night. She dropped her pack with a ragged sigh, then she kicked it angrily. She was too exhausted to set up her tent tonight. Oh, God, what was she doing here?

Finally she wrenched her sleeping bag free of the pack and laid down, wadding a sweater beneath her head for a pillow and thumping it hard with her fist. Maybe there were *chindis,* she thought, maybe he was dangerous and up to no good, but right now she was too tired to care. He could parade naked right under her nose and she wouldn't care. Much.

It was her last thought before Shadow closed her eyes and dropped immediately into a dreamless sleep.

* * *

She woke hard and fast when sunlight angled down over the southeastern rim, spearing into her eyes. She sat up, rubbing them, and looked over at Mac's campsite.

He was already at his fire, making breakfast. The smell of reconstituted eggs didn't do much for her, but oh, the coffee! She craved a cup so badly she could almost taste it. Well, she could have some of her own—it would just take her half an hour or so to make it.

She kicked her sleeping bag off and stood, stretching. Then she rolled it back up neatly and fastened it onto her pack again. If she was going to look for wood for a fire, she might as well find a new campsite at the same time, she thought. She actually didn't want to keep sleeping any closer to him than she had to. She didn't want a repeat of what had happened two nights ago. It made her feel too... achy and empty. She couldn't handle wanting someone that much and for no explicable reason—someone she didn't particularly like, someone who definitely didn't like her.

She didn't bother to fix the pack onto her back this time. She simply dragged it along with her, scanning the canyon walls as she went. She took several steps before his voice stopped her.

"Where are you going?"

She turned back to face him, surprised. "To find a place of my own. I think we'll both be a lot happier."

She thought she saw his jaw harden. "So you're planning to stay," he said finally.

She lifted her pack as proof. "You figured that out last night."

"Want a kick start?"

He held up his coffeepot. Shadow felt her heart thump oddly. What was his story?

He clearly wanted her out of the way, so why was he—again—trying to help her with a few creature comforts in the meantime? Whatever the reason, there was a time and a place for pride and principle, and she decided this wasn't it. "All right," she said cautiously.

Mac watched her drop the pack and dig through it for a metal cup. It took no more than a blink of an eye for her to find it. He knew nothing in there would be jumbled, the way his own packs usually were. Hell, he wouldn't even be surprised if everything was imprinted with her name and Social Security number.

Why was he doing this? She marched around like a damned drill sergeant, tossing out orders and expecting everyone and everything to jump to attention. She had shattered his solitude for reasons known only to her and he was angry about it. She was as tenacious as a bulldog... and, he thought, she stretched like a cat.

Deep inside, he was just a man after all, and she had some strange effect on his libido. He was a man with rules, he reminded himself, but as long as he kept the big ones intact, bending the small ones a little shouldn't matter. He watched expressionlessly as she approached him, then he gave her the coffeepot.

"Thanks," she said stiffly, pouring.

He made a sound that was half growl, half acknowledgment. She had great legs, especially when they weren't hidden in jeans, but the shredded skin on her right knee looked nasty.

"Do you have anything in your pack to take care of that?" He motioned at it.

Shadow sipped and nodded. The coffee was strong and black—perfect.

"I'd be really stupid to come out here without a first-aid kit. I was just too tired to do anything about it last night."

His voice got suddenly tight again. "And you wouldn't do anything stupid, would you?"

She lifted one shoulder. "I'm here. The wisdom of that could be debated."

"Why?" he asked again. "Why did you come back?"

"I don't trust you."

She was honest. He could deal with that. "Then why not just send the cops in?"

Because I read your dossier. "Because for the most part you seem on the level. I have nothing to go on but instinct and that wouldn't be enough to get them to risk coming into this place."

"And you trust your instincts?"

"Always."

That surprised him. Navajo or not, she just didn't seem the type to rely upon anything so tenuous.

He ran his eyes down her small, trim body. "Just out of curiosity, how do you intend to stop me if I *am* doing something illegal?"

His perusal unnerved her. It made her feel naked. She swallowed carefully and fought the urge to fidget.

"I have a gun, too."

"Should I shake in my boots?"

"Something tells me you don't do that often."

For a wild moment, she actually thought he might smile. But it was true—he was so hard and strong, so capable. She got the distinct impression that absolutely nothing could hurt him. He wouldn't allow it to.

Her gaze coasted past him, to the refuse midden. "Why this canyon?" she asked suddenly. "You said you were part Navajo. It couldn't be high on your list of places to visit."

"My mother was barely Navajo," he said flatly. "She never taught me about Navajo spirituality." And even if she had, Mac thought, he wouldn't have embraced it. He would have treated it like everything else that reminded him of the woman—he would have cast it off and shut it out.

"I was raised in Salt Lake City my first ten years," he volunteered finally. "The Hopi Mesas after that."

"So you don't believe in *chindis?*"

"I believe the past lives on in more concrete form."

"In pots and antiquities and bones."

"Exactly."

She shivered. It was the concrete stuff that bothered her the most. A *chindi*'s belongings, most notably its name and bones, were the things surest to call it back from the dead.

It was going to be a long week.

Mac drained the last of his own coffee and stood. Finally his gaze followed hers to the midden.

"This site is next in a long, curving line I've followed up from the Yucatán," he explained almost absently. "What I'm looking for should either be here, or it's within a thirty-mile radius."

With his disturbing eyes safely elsewhere, Shadow looked at him more closely. He wore shorts and boots again, nothing else. His thighs were as muscled as she remembered, covered with curly, almost blond hair. His broad shoulders tapered down to narrow hips. His shorts rode low there; he hadn't bothered with a belt. Despite his size, he reminded her of one of the scrappy Navajo sheep-camp dogs that could react like lightning when provoked. She remembered how hard and solid he had felt against her the previous night, the way his strong body had so easily absorbed the blows of their fall.

That strange, treacherous ache was starting deep inside her again. She looked away.

"What...what are you looking for?" she asked hoarsely.

"A particular style of pot. Ice blue glazing. Painted with figures instead of lines or geometric patterns." Why was he telling her this? he wondered. He rarely shared information. For all he knew she was a professional, trying to scoop him on this thing. He still wasn't entirely satisfied with her explanation for coming back.

Maybe it was as simple as the fact that it had been a fairly long time since he had talked to another living soul, and something within him needed the contact whether he liked it or not.

Shadow jolted. Ice blue glazing? She remembered the potsherd she had found on the trail. There had been no figures on it, but it had definitely been blue. He'd implied that he hadn't found what he was looking for yet—but *someone* had dropped that shard and it certainly hadn't been the Anasazi.

Mac went into his tent to gather his tools. When he came out, she was still standing there.

"These pots—you've found examples of them all the way up from the Yucatán?" she asked.

"Yeah."

"But not here."

"Not yet." He frowned at her. If he was lying, she thought, then he was master of the art.

"So you're tracking one individual potter?"

"Seems that way," he answered. "The style is distinctive, unique."

"And you think it was Kokopelli himself?"

His eyes narrowed on her face. "Why would you guess that?"

Shadow flushed. Too late she realized the only basis she had for such an assumption was his grant information. She made a halfhearted gesture at the walls. "Kokopelli's Canyon."

He seemed to consider this, then he shook his head. "There's an obscure story that says he traveled with a woman. I'm thinking it was her."

Shadow frowned. "I don't know that story."

"It's got Hopi origins."

"Still . . . I was an anthro student at New Mexico State."

That jolted him. *Was* she here for some professional reason? Then why not tell him that?

"What do you do now?" he demanded harshly.

"I'm assistant curator at the Navajo Nation Museum in Shiprock. Why?"

"Just wondered if your interest in this is more than meets the eye."

So there was distrust on both sides, she thought. Well, her being here was an admittedly odd development. She forced herself to meet his hard, gray blue gaze.

"It fascinates me," she admitted.

He held her eyes for a long while—too long, she thought, feeling somehow...invaded. It was as if he could see a lot more of her than he was revealing about himself.

"Like I said, the legend's obscure," he went on finally. "They say she was his mate. She Who Waits."

Shadow's brows shot up. "*Mate?* Sort of an open relationship, wasn't it? He traveled from pueblo to pueblo impregnating the women."

"Ergo her name."

"She was waiting for him to finish sowing his wild oats and settle down?"

"So to speak. Actually, Kokopelli was a trader. If women lined up for his services at each pueblo he visited, you can hardly blame him for taking advantage of it."

There was something hawkish about his gaze again, as though he was watching for her reaction. Shadow looked away.

"I guess not. It wouldn't exactly be human nature to turn away from that kind of bounty."

"No. Not average human nature, at any rate. But some of us have different rules, different motivations."

What did that mean? She frowned over it for a minute, then pushed past it. "Why do you think this pottery was hers?" she asked.

"Because of the trail. She seemed to make some and trade it at every pueblo she visited. Women didn't usually wander. They stayed at home and tended the hearths. And there's something distinctly feminine about the artwork on these pieces."

Shadow was beginning to comprehend the full implications of his search. "When you come to the end of her trail, you're likely to find her."

He nodded.

"She'd be buried with a lot of her own work."

"Theoretically."

"Or maybe her trail doesn't end. Maybe she went wherever the Anasazi vanished to."

"That's what I'm thinking."

"Wow."

This time one corner of his mouth did kick up. "Yeah. Wow."

He took his tools and started off toward the dig site. To Shadow's knowledge, no archaeologist yet had undertaken such a staggering find. So far no one had been able to figure out a way to do it, had been able to unearth enough information to go on. But then, she had sensed from the first that he wouldn't be content with the mundane.

She watched him leave, then she remembered what she was supposed to be doing here. She couldn't believe he would sell the potsherds of She Who Waits. But maybe the ice blue piece she had found wasn't one of She Who Waits. Maybe the piece was similar, but not the real McCoy. But he was bound to have to dig through a lot of clouds before he found a silver lining.

"What are you going to do with those other pieces you found?" she asked. "The stuff that's not hers?"

He gave her a dark look over his shoulder. Any light that had come into his rugged features as he had talked about his work was gone now. His eyes became hooded.

"Didn't you say you were going to find your own place to camp?" he said. "Goodbye."

Chapter 5

Mac's mind wasn't on his work. For the first time in what could possibly be years—in fact, he couldn't remember the last time it had happened—he tore a fragile scrap of sandal as he tried to remove it to get to a shard.

He straightened away from the dig, looking down at his hands as though they had somehow betrayed him. He supposed they had every right. They hadn't touched anything warm and responsive in far too long now. He thought of her hair again. He swore and raked his hands through the top of his own.

Where the hell was she?

He went back to his campsite for his canteen, looking around the canyon as he went. The place she had used the past couple of nights was pristine now, returned to its natural condition. He looked down past the other ruins and saw no sign of her.

So she had taken him at his word and had gotten lost. It had been nearly an hour now since she had left to find her own site. But it didn't seem characteristic of her not to have come back. He would have put money on her spending the day right here at the dig, watching every tiny piece he pulled out of the ground.

Was she hurt? Had she fallen again? God knew she had a propensity for it.

It wasn't his problem. Then again, there was something exceptionally cold about going back to his work when she could be lying injured somewhere, without water, in this broiling sun.

"Damn it," he snarled. This was exactly why he hated to work with anyone. It was why he hated company when he was digging. No matter what that person's intentions might be, they were *there* and that was distracting.

Well, she was here. He couldn't do anything about that. So he would find her and when he saw for himself what she was up to, then he could come back and get some work done without images of her lying broken and bent cluttering up his mind.

He drank deeply from the canteen, capped it again, then set off down the canyon floor. He found her as soon as he turned the bend into the switchback. She hadn't gone far.

A small waterfall splashed down from the higher elevations at the very back of it. The water crashed into the stream, then wandered across the canyon floor to disappear into a cave on the far side. He had been bathing on the cave side although he knew that the fresh runoff would be hard to contaminate—the water moved through the canyon too quickly. But Shadow with her ghostly name had apparently found the cold tumbling water on this side too much to resist.

She stood under the waterfall, naked, her head tilted back in pure, sensuous pleasure. The water cascaded through her hair. She faced his way, and the sight of her drove a hard, burning fist right into his gut. It brought an airless sensation to his chest, close to pain.

His gaze moved over her, even though he had meant to turn right around and go back to his dig. She was lithe and supple, delicate yet strong. Her back was arched so that her breasts were thrust toward him, small and high, her dark nipples tightening as the cold water splashed over them. His gaze moved down from there, past a narrow waist and the flare of her hips, past the little tangle of black hair at the juncture of her thighs. He already knew how athletic those legs were, had watched her climb up and down the cliff wall as nimbly as a cat. But seeing all of their smooth, clean lines was something else entirely.

He had to get out of here. He stood riveted.

Shadow was in heaven. There was a ravine near her hogan that rarely went dry and afforded her fresh water to wash in, but an actual waterfall in this desert country was an oasis, as rare as a diamond in a drugstore. She hadn't even noticed it the first couple of times she had been through here because it was in the back, cloaked in shadows. But that was exactly the sort of spot she'd wanted to camp in—a protected alcove—and when she had walked deeper into the switchback to investigate, she had found it.

She had immediately dumped her backpack and stripped off her clothes, wading in. Everything else could wait, and Mac was safely off working.

Still, she did have a purpose for this excursion, she thought now. No matter how delightful the water was, she really ought to go see what he was doing. Who knew how many pieces he could slide to the side while she was here soaking up pleasure like a satisfied cat?

She groaned reluctantly and finally stepped out of the cascade. She gathered up her hair, wringing it out, then she saw him.

Her heart slammed up into her throat. Never, ever, had a man looked at her like that, with such heat and raw hunger, with such *wanting*. She was so stunned she couldn't even react. She simply stood there, her arms over her head, her hands frozen in her hair and her eyes huge.

He turned abruptly and left the switchback.

Shadow's heart plummeted back where it belonged, so hard and fast it made her feel dizzy. She lowered her arms slowly, her hands trembling, and hugged herself. What had that been about? Why had he come in here?

More importantly, why had he left that way, without a word?

She could no longer tell herself that it was because he didn't want her. She wasn't blind and she wasn't stupid. She knew what she had seen in his eyes in that moment before he had turned away, and even now it made her knees feel weak. She couldn't shake the memory of it, of all the unbearable emotion that had stormed there—wanting all tangled up with torment and denial.

That torment and denial changed everything. Somewhere inside he was broken.

Every protective, nurturing instinct she possessed swept through her suddenly, making her ache for him. Crazy. The last thing in the world a man like him would want was her care and concern. Slowly, frowning, she left the stream, moving to warm herself in a patch of sunlight.

She should go home, she thought suddenly, should just forget about whatever he was doing over there in the refuse midden. Instead, she found herself hunkering down to pull her pack free from its aluminum frame.

She found a clean pair of shorts and some underwear, and finally slid a comfortable tank top over her head. Her hands continued to shake as she combed out her hair and fastened it, still wet, into a ponytail. Finally she looked down again at the backpack frame. She was procrastinating and knew she really had to. She had to gain some control over herself before she went to find him.

She took a few minutes to unfold the frame, opening it up into tent poles. She emptied the pack. The durable nylon weave spread out into a cover. When it was finished, it formed a small, lightweight tent, just big enough for one person.

She put her gear neatly inside, then she straightened and took a deep breath. There was nothing else to do here. She grabbed the notebook and a pen and left the switchback.

He was working.

His broad back was to her, his skin golden-red in the sun. The heat in the canyon seemed to make his image shimmer. Shadow approached silently, slipping around him to sit on a nearby boulder.

She flipped through the pages for a blank one before he finally looked up. She met his gaze, swallowing carefully, but his eyes were neutral, closed as only they could be. He looked down at his work again without speaking to her.

There was nothing new on the pallet except a swatch of what looked to have once been leather. She jotted it down, with meticulous detail as to its size and shape. That finally got a reaction out of him.

"Get out of here," he snarled, his eyes fast on a piece of bone.

Shadow's chin came up. "Not a chance."

He finally looked at her again. "What the hell do you think you're trying to accomplish here?"

She opened her jaw and shut it again. She was no longer entirely sure.

"If I show you my papers, will you go?"

She thought about it. "No. I already checked your credentials on the museum computer."

His eyes narrowed at that, then he looked incredulous. "So what are you doing here, if you know I'm legitimate?"

"Instincts," she said again, softly. "Just...instincts." And a small, inexplicable piece of pottery that she had found lying on the trail.

"So take your instincts and go home."

He went back to his work, pulling a shard out too roughly. He paused, flexing his hands with deliberate patience, then he reached behind him for a small chisel to work some more dirt away from the piece. It was lodged between crumbled rock and stone and what appeared to be a piece of skull. Shadow didn't want to look at the human remains, but Mac's hands gave her no choice. She watched them, rapt.

His strong fingers worked with exquisite care, gentle but firm. He touched the piece as if it were a woman he was trying to coax a response from, working it this way, then that, pulling when it gave, smoothing more dirt away when it resisted. Her heart started to pound.

He finally got it free and stood to brush it off. He put it on the pallet and her gaze followed him.

"I don't get it," she said hoarsely.

He answered with hard reluctance. "What?"

"How can you be so incredibly sensitive with things that are dead, while your eyes shut out life?"

He turned around very slowly. She saw that a muscle moved at his jaw. Then he bent again to work the piece of skull free of the sand. He straightened and brought it to her.

Shadow recoiled.

"Go ahead," he said too quietly. "Touch it."

"I . . . can't."

"If you're going to play around graveyards, then be a big girl and do it. Stop hiding in safe, distant shadows."

She did because it was a dare. Because something within her wouldn't let him back her down.

She ran her fingertips over the closest curve of it, shuddering and closing her eyes. It was smooth and eerily warm from the sun, as though life still pulsed within it. She fought the urge to snatch back her hand. Beneath her fingertips, she felt cracks and fissures left by immeasurable years, the grit of the dirt that still clung to it.

"Okay," she said finally, pulling her hand away, looking at him. "There. Satisfied?"

"What did you feel?"

He didn't mean the question literally. She looked into his storm-colored eyes.

"Time," she answered simply.

He nodded almost imperceptibly. "That's why."

Finally he moved away from her. He laid the skull piece carefully on the pallet as well.

"I date this site to sometime around the mid to late 1200's," he went on shortly. "Bones, pottery, history—they endure. Life doesn't, and people sure as hell don't."

"So you shut people out?" she asked breathlessly.

"You said that. I didn't." He began collecting his tools and the pieces that he had already excavated. Only then did she realize that a rare cloud had moved over the sun. It was probably going to rain. The heat had acquired an oppressive, damp feeling.

"You work alone," she persisted. "Most archaeologists work in teams."

"I've earned the right. I produce results. I do it best when I'm not stepping over people, trying to cooperate with their half-baked methods when mine are better."

She slid off the boulder as he started back toward his campsite. He had clearly ended the conversation. She followed him slowly, thoughtfully, then went on to her own tent. After the rain passed, she would go back to see if he had resumed digging.

Everything he had told her about his work and his methods seemed perfectly reasonable. Maybe she should just give it another day and go home.

That would probably be safest—but for which of them, she was no longer sure.

The wind started tunneling into the canyon like an angry spirit. Mac struggled against it, securing his tent firmly.

He finished just as the downpour began—big, heavy drops that seemed to mock him, as though telling him that more were coming and there was absolutely nothing a mere mortal could do about it.

He had no doubt that Shadow would try anyway.

Damn her.

He paused, scrubbing his unshaven jaw, looking down the canyon. She had lived her whole life in this land. She had to know what mountain squalls could be like, how fierce they could be when a man—or woman—found himself trapped right in the middle of the cloud that was crashing in torment. She'd be fine.

He went inside and lit the lantern, settling down with his notes of the dig. There was precious little to report regarding this morning's work. He wrote what he could, then his mind wandered to the naked woman in the waterfall. He cursed her again, aloud this time, and threw the notebook aside.

Did she actually think he would try to sell anything he found here? If she had read his dossier, then she should know better. He was too acclaimed in his field—there was no way in hell he could keep such a transaction anonymous. Not when he was considered something of an oddity to begin with, a loner and wanderer to whom money meant very little. He had no mortgage. He camped out at his digs more often than not, and his biggest monthly expense was his truck payment—a whopper, but one he fully considered worth it. The vehicle was a big, comfortable Explorer, and he had slept in it more times than he cared to remember.

Sergeant Shadow just had a bee in her bonnet, he thought, and she wasn't going to be satisfied until she satisfied herself. There was nothing he could say, nothing he could do about it but hope that she reached some kind of conclusion soon.

Then the canyon would be empty again. Silent, except for the moaning wind, the way he preferred it. He wondered why that thought suddenly made him feel itchy.

It was the storm, of course, getting under his skin. The gales buffeted his tent, gusting stronger, and rain drummed against the taut canvas. He wondered again if she was okay down there. What was she using for shelter?

"Oh, hell. No way." He thought about it, then he closed his eyes in disbelief and resignation.

That backpack had to be one of those contraptions that opened up into a tent. A very small tent, very lightweight, great for flat, dry desert surfaces. He didn't care how strong or pragmatic she was, she wouldn't be able to carry anything up this mountain that was heavy enough to survive a canyon storm at five thousand feet. So she was moderately fallible after all.

He swore again, getting up to duck out into the storm. He fought the wind even as thunder began to roll. There was a faint sulfer scent to the air through the rain. Lightning had found one of the trees up on the slopes.

He turned into the switchback. If she had ever had a tent, it was gone now. The wind had taken it off to parts unknown. She sat huddled, her sleeping bag pulled over her head for cover. Her belongings were scattered all over the cranny, strewn by the fury of the storm.

He reached her and caught her arm, hauling her to her feet.

"Only a woman would be stupid enough not to ask for help when she needs it," he snapped. "Let's go, Sergeant. You're coming with me."

She didn't argue exactly, although he half expected it. "Wait!" she cried. Then she turned back and he saw that she had been sitting on her notebook, trying to keep it dry. She snatched it up and let him drag her back into the main canyon, but when they were halfway to his tent, she shook his grip off.

"I'm not going to blow away," she snapped.

They reached the tent and he let her duck in first. He came in after her, pulling the rubber band out of his hair, combing his fingers through it so it could dry. Shadow turned to face him and her breath stalled.

The tent was certainly bigger than hers had been, but he filled it so...so *inexorably*. Suddenly all her senses felt filled with him. He was too close—and too far away. His broad shoulders were inches from her nose. She caught the damp male scent of him, unique to him and as rugged as everything else about him. The look he had given her at the waterfall flashed through her mind again and she felt weak, too warm.

She wanted to back up and protect herself against the feeling, but there was nowhere to go. She wanted to lean forward and touch her tongue to the raindrops beaded on his chest, and the thought flabbergasted her. She wondered where her mind had gone these past several days.

She clenched her jaw and got a grip on herself. She might have seen desire in his eyes, but he obviously had no respect for her as an individual. And she wasn't desperate enough to settle for that any more than she would have settled for Diamond Eddie. Neither man could fill the hole in her life.

She swallowed carefully. "You don't have a very high opinion of women."

"They're not in my rules."

She blinked at him. "Never?"

He let out a rough burst of laughter. "I'm not gay. I just know how to pick and choose."

And she, he thought, would be a very, very bad choice.

He supposed he had known that from the start. It hadn't been just the fact that she would be staying in the canyon that first night that had had him roaming for a place to sleep, like a wild animal. She just wasn't the sort of woman he tangled with. Oh, he sensed a simmering, bottled heat behind her cool, practical exterior, and that appealed to him readily enough. But there was also an inherent fear beneath her stubborn courage, a certain sensitivity that had allowed her to feel time in a bone, her simple joy at splashing naked in a waterfall. And those were the sorts of things he had learned to distrust most of all.

"What rules?" she asked. Her voice had a vaguely husky quality and they both noticed it. She thought she saw something flash in his eyes, but then they narrowed and it was gone.

"My turn to ask questions," he said shortly. "What's so all-fired important about that notebook that it was the single thing you saved from the storm? What have you written down in there?"

Shadow stiffened. *Had* he set some piece aside that he thought she had noticed?

"It's not what I've written," she answered levelly. "It's what my boss has written. There are notes on museum pieces in here that I haven't put in the computer yet."

"Yeah? Let's see."

It was another dare of sorts. Her chin came up and she handed over the notebook.

He rifled through its pages, then looked up at her, his blue gray eyes incredulous. "You weren't kidding."

"Of course not."

"The storm blew your tent away—probably with you sitting right beneath it—and you maintained the presence of mind to grab *this?*"

She shrugged. "You've got to know Diamond Eddie. I don't dare give him anything to hold over me."

He thought about it. His eyes were watchful. "Bet you hate that."

"Bet you're right."

"So quit."

"I can't. I want his job. When and if he finally goes, I'm the logical choice to replace him."

He finally settled down on the sleeping bag, his back against a duffel bag, stretching out his long legs. She felt her heartbeat hitch. Why was she so aware of him? He was just a man, and not even a very pleasant one... although he did possess a rough, reluctant edge of chivalry that hinted of something warm and generous inside.

She wrenched her eyes away from his legs only to fall into his own eyes again. They were steady now but they still looked like storm clouds and there was a certain wary curiosity there, too. For some reason, that shook her even more.

She looked around awkwardly for a place to sit.

"Over there." He pointed to a small chest.

She settled upon it carefully, drawing her feet up to brace her heels on its edge and hug her knees to her chest.

"So tell me, Sergeant. What else do you want?"

Her heart moved hard and uncomfortably. "What do you mean?"

"Out of life. You want this Diamond Eddie's job and what else? Come on. We've got time to kill. Let's hear it."

"Okay." Shadow ran her tongue nervously over her lower lip and thought about it. Two days ago she had been sure that she had it all figured out.

"My own life," she said finally, putting it into words.

"What's holding you back?"

"The land I love, the people I love... and... and me." She was shocked as she heard herself say it, but as soon as she did she knew it was true, knew it deep inside herself in that spot where no lies could live.

He was both startled and unnerved by her honesty. Apparently it extended to her own self-evaluations, as well.

"How so?" he asked after a moment.

"I don't like saying no." She reached up and wrenched her own hair free, fanning it out so it could dry. "People ask me for help, ask me to do this or that, and I'm always jumping to it as though no one else could handle the favor just as well. Then someone else gets all the happiness and the satisfaction. I get . . . nothing. They're gone, Mac. All those *years* are gone. The other day something happened to snap me awake and I realized I've accomplished absolutely nothing for myself. I'm living the same exact way I did seven years ago. Not one single detail of my world has changed.''

So that was why she was here, he realized. He had suspected from the first that his pots were just an excuse. In some measure she was hiding from herself—or maybe she was trying to reclaim some small piece of her.

He watched her jump up to pace, even though the tent would scarcely allow it. Energy seemed to crackle around her, frustrated, hungry for something more. It tightened something inside him again. That, and all that hair, sleek and damp, flowing around her shoulders, bouncing each time she made a sharp turn. He had another flash of how it had looked all slicked back beneath the waterfall.

"Sit down," he said too sharply.

She stopped to look at him warily.

"In another minute you're going to have *this* tent loose and flying down the mountain."

"Oh." She sat again stiffly.

"I guess you don't think of everything, huh?"

Her gaze turned defiant. She wasn't sure if he was talking about the tent or her life. "I never said I did."

"You never had to." He looked away toward the door as though wishing desperately the storm would end soon. Shadow followed his gaze, suddenly wishing the same thing herself.

When he spoke again, his voice was too quiet, almost musing. "In those seven years, did you ever let a man take care of you? Just pour himself over you without taking anything back for himself? Did you ever stop being the one in control?"

Shadow's mouth went dry. For one breath-robbing moment she could only think of his hands moving over her skin the way they had worked that shard. The ache came back inside her, and with it an undeniable heat, sliding through her, staining her skin, stealing her breath.

He glanced back at her idly, then his face changed, hardening fast.

That hunger inside her was alive now. It was in her deep black eyes, questing, searching for something as she watched him. It flared there, that inner heat, ready and wanting...knowing on some level what it was that she needed, and he could have sworn in that moment that that something was him.

This time he pushed abruptly to his feet before she could actually ask for something he couldn't give. He wondered if she would be as blunt and honest about her physical needs as she was about everything else.

"Sorry, Sergeant," he said hoarsely. "I'm not the man for the job."

He heard her sharp, indrawn breath but didn't see the color drain from her face. He yanked back the door flap and squatted down on his haunches to look out at the storm.

"When it comes to women, I take what I'm given and give what I can," he went on tightly. "The lovers I choose know that. They don't expect me to stay, they don't whine about me spending the night. They're tougher than that, stronger. I share touches with them, then I go."

She would need so much more than that, he thought. She would *take* so much more than that, whether it was given willingly or not. And that was his biggest, most ironclad rule.

How had this gotten so personal? Shadow wondered wildly. But then she realized that on some level it had been from the first. She, at least, had reacted to him even before she had watched him stroll about naked. He, on the other hand, seemed determined not to react to her at all.

"Where?" she whispered. "Where do you go?"

"Home."

"Where's that?"

"Wherever I want it to be at the time."

"Always?"

He finally looked over his shoulder at her. "Do I always wander or do I always go home afterward?"

"Go." She already knew about the wandering. *A man with no home.* And she remembered his eyes at the waterfall. A man that haunted would keep on the move, running from something within. There would be no haven for him.

"Yeah," he said quietly.

"That's lonely."

"That's sane."

"Why?"

She had been honest. He could be the same. He met those dark, searching eyes of hers, feeling an unaccustomed pain, one he had not allowed himself to feel in a very long time now.

"Because you can't lose something you never claimed for your own." He stood again. "The storm's breaking, Sergeant. Take my sleeping bag for the night. Yours'll be soaked."

He bent and gathered it up for her, telling her in no uncertain terms that it was time for her to go.

Chapter 6

The heat rose steadily as the sun climbed. By the time it blazed directly over Kokopelli's Canyon, strands of Shadow's ponytail clung to the back of her sweaty neck. Little runnels of perspiration slid down between her breasts, and she had to be careful not to touch the boulder she was sitting on with her bare skin.

She wanted to go back to the waterfall so badly that her mind kept returning to the possibility again and again. But she doggedly kept on with her notes, watching Mac work. If the heat bothered him, it didn't show.

He worked late into the night before he stopped. At sunset, he rigged up a pair of battery-powered spotlights over the dig, illuminating a small section of it almost as bright as day. Still, Shadow was painfully aware of the dark ruins behind her, of the eerie abandoned dwellings over her head. She fidgeted uncomfortably on the very hard boulder as she made notations on the last piece he had taken out of the midden.

"Call it a night and go back to your camp," he suggested dryly, without looking up. "You won't offend me."

"I'm fine."

"Then how about some more water?"

"In a second." She finished what she was writing and put the notebook down, then she stood. Mac sensed rather than saw what she did next—he wasn't stupid enough to look. But he knew that she slowly rolled one shoulder then the other to get the kinks out, arching her back so that her tank top clearly outlined her breasts. He knew that she bent over to touch her toes and stretch out the muscles along the backs of her legs, presenting him with a tantalizing view from behind.

His jaw hardened and a dull heat started throbbing low inside him again, getting stronger the more he tried to ignore it. He willed her silently to cut it out and go get the water.

But when she finally did, he glanced over his shoulder to watch her leave. His eyes narrowed at the easy yet somehow purposeful way she moved. There were no wasteful gestures about her motion; each one flowed into the next with unconscious grace. He wondered if loving her would be like that, flowing, smooth, yet subtly driven.

A headache started behind his eyes, one of frustration and restraint.

Both were why he was still working at ten o'clock at night. Restraint took his concentration away from the dig, and the night ahead would bring frustration he preferred to avoid as long as possible. She had returned his sleeping bag this morning. He had no doubt that her scent would linger on the cloth, in the down.

His fingers grew rigid. Very carefully, very slowly, he pulled his hands back from his work.

She had to know by now that she was wasting her time here, he thought. She wouldn't catch him doing anything illegal, and she wouldn't find the piece of herself she had somehow lost. He gave her another day or two at the outside and then she would probably go home. The realization eased the tension across his shoulders a little, but it also brought a hollow feeling to his gut. The plain, bald truth was that her company—in and of itself—hadn't been an entirely bad thing. If she hadn't looked as good as she did, he might actually have enjoyed it.

For the most part she had remained silent, but occasionally she had asked a well-placed question. And when the sun had begun fading in the canyon, she had simply retrieved the last of his venison, skewered it, roasted it, and brought it back to him without comment so that he could eat without breaking from his work. He had finished the meat and was absently wiping the juice from his mouth before he even realized what had just happened.

She brought the water to him now, setting his cup on a rock without comment.

"Did you say blue?" she asked suddenly. "That the pieces you're looking for have ice blue glazing?"

He went still in mid-swallow, watching her warily from over the rim. "Yeah. So?"

She pointed into the dig. "Is that a trick of the light?"

He followed the line of her outstretched finger and his heart gave an odd hitch. "I'll be damned," he said softly, tossing his cup back over his shoulder. "Oh, sweetheart, good eyes."

Shadow's own heart gave a kind of twisting squeeze that almost took her breath away. She knew the endearment had been casual, without meaning, probably even unconscious...and she knew that she didn't want endearments from this complicated, unhappy man. She didn't want anything from him except perhaps the whole truth about what he was doing here. Yet her blood surged as she watched him ease his way carefully down into the midden, several feet deep now.

He barely disturbed dust. It still amazed her how he could move like that when he was so strong, so large.

A fraction of pale blue stuck out from one of the side walls of the excavation—maybe half an inch of the piece. The glazing had taken on some odd quality in the artificial light—not quite shining, not quite glimmering, but almost luminescent. Shadow found herself biting her lip as he worked it free. It was only a shard. He cupped it gently in his palm and the way he touched it took her breath away.

"Is it one of her pieces?" she asked.

"Yeah. Oh, yeah."

"So she was here."

"Looks that way."

"How do you know she didn't trade the pots to other travelers, people who might have taken them to places she never visited?"

Mac finally looked up at her. It was a good question. "Because I've never found them anywhere else but in this Yucatán-Four Corners sector."

"And no one else has either?"

He shrugged. "There's no way to track what illegal pot hunters have done, but reasonable control is kept over these reservation sites. There are no pieces in any private collections that I know of. None have shown up for auction. There are none in museums. About all that proves is that no one else has stumbled upon the mother lode I'm looking for—the place where she's buried with most of her possessions. There'd be a bunch of pieces there, so some of them would almost have to have come to public light."

Shadow considered that. "Can I . . . can I see it?"

He looked at her for a long moment, then he finally shrugged. "You found it."

Shadow stepped carefully into the excavation and looked down at the small piece in his palm. Her heart slammed. It could be the artificial light, but it looked exactly like the piece she had found up on the trail. And if it was, if Mac was telling the truth about his work, then that meant that someone else was moving the pottery of She Who Waits out of here.

If Mac was telling the truth. Every instinct she possessed insisted that he was, but she'd be a fool to confide her find in him until she had more proof than that.

She stepped away from him carefully. "So will you move on now?" she asked. "Now that you know she's been here to this canyon?"

He made a motion over his shoulder at the other three ruins. "She could be buried down there somewhere. I'll dig a little more at this midden tomorrow, but I'm almost to the bottom now and she doesn't appear to be here. I'll move down there on Thursday and start working the next one."

"How long will it take you to go through all four of them—assuming you have to?"

He shrugged again. "Six more weeks at the outside. What I'm doing is a lot less time-consuming than a full dig where every single thing that comes out of the ground has to be labeled and sorted. I don't pull anything unless I have to. It's too much unnecessary work with pieces I'm not interested in."

He came out of the hole to stand close to her. Though he didn't touch her, she was suddenly aware of the *feel* of him again, powerful and implacable.

"What's the matter, Sergeant?" he asked. "You worried about running out of vacation time?"

Shadow brought up her chin. "The problem's occurred to me. When I have to leave, I figure I can just trace any new pieces that come up for sale. There's more than one way to skin a cat."

"Not without it screaming."

He turned away and flicked off the spotlights. They were plunged suddenly into darkness and Shadow gasped. She began to back up carefully, away from the ruins, then his voice came quietly out of the night.

"You don't believe I'm stealing pots any more than you believe the sun's going to fall out of the sky tomorrow."

She found that she couldn't respond to that one way or the other. And by the time she found her voice and her vision adjusted to the darkness, he was gone.

She washed at the waterfall. She stood under the spray, shivering with it now that the sun had gone. Goose bumps prickled over her skin and tightened her nipples. It was just the cold, she thought, such a shock after the heat of the day. It had nothing to do with her body clamoring to be touched again. It had nothing to do with the memories of the day that kept taunting her, flashing in and out of her mind . . . his hard-gentle hands working, his muscles moving under his skin as he stretched and lifted and moved.

She moved out of the waterfall and grabbed the towel she had left on the bank, wondering where he was.

Mac peeled out of his shorts and stepped into the comparatively tepid water at the cave side of the stream. Against all reason, he glanced back toward the switchback. The closest rock wall hid her camp from sight. He could barely hear the waterfall from here, only if he strained, only if he knew what he was listening for.

She was in it. He didn't have to see it, didn't need to hear it, to know that. The day had been so ungodly hot that he doubted if either of them had a stronger priority right now than getting into wet, clean water.

In spite of himself, another image flashed in his mind, of what she had looked like standing in that water yesterday. He got it into his head that she was standing just exactly that way now, sleek and bare, her back arched, her arms raised over her head.

He growled an inarticulate curse and grabbed his soap from the rocky bank, suddenly anxious to finish here and get into his sleeping bag whether it smelled of her or not.

Sleep was what he needed, something that would ease his mind. He needed an escape. She was haunting him.

He stepped out of the water, bending to swipe up his towel as he started back to his tent, drying himself as he walked. He ducked inside, compelled to pull on a pair of clean shorts to sleep in, as though that was somehow safer.

He finally laid down and closed his eyes. Then he knew he had been right about the sleeping bag.

Something of her lingered in it, a scent of smoke and woman. He thought of kicking it off, of hurling it to the other side of the tent, but in the end it wasn't worth the energy it would take.

It wouldn't get her out of his head.

She *was* wholly unlike most of the women he had known, and the one he desperately needed to forget. She was capable rather than mewling. Generous instead of clawing. Quiet most of the time, insightful at others. Tenacious, honest and strong. In short, he couldn't attribute any of the qualities he disliked about her gender to her. For all intents and purposes, she was the kind of woman he normally gravitated toward for a night, a weekend, a brief time in the sun.

And she wasn't anything like those indifferent, self-serving females at all because he knew instinctively that she wouldn't let him go afterward.

He could go down to that switchback, he thought, could slide into that bag with her and sink himself into her hidden fire, and he doubted if she would object. They were a man and a woman alone, and he could still remember her hungry gaze yesterday during the storm, wanting him, wanting any man who could give her back that piece of herself, whether she realized that or not. He could still remember that innocently speculative look in her eyes the morning she had left only to come back, a look he now doubted she had even been aware of giving.

It would be like Kokopelli and one of his maidens, he thought, fast, mutually satisfying, and theoretically at least, someday he could wander on. But he had the strong sense that if he sank into her, into this particular woman, even for one night, he wouldn't be able to leave again. She wouldn't hold him, but she would ensnare him.

It wasn't worth it. He wasn't Kokopelli. He was too old, too scarred, to change.

He groaned and rolled over in his sleeping bag, deliberately closing his eyes.

Shadow listened to the scurrying sounds of some nocturnal animal, then she shifted, rolling to her left, wondering why the ground seemed so much harder tonight. True, her sleeping bag was not as well stuffed and as heavy as Mac's had been. But she had slept the first two nights without his and the rocky ground hadn't bothered her then. Of course, you never missed something until you had it and it was taken away.

He had said something like that yesterday, in the storm. What was it? She scowled, trying to remember his exact words. *You can't lose something you never claimed for your own.*

She rolled to her right side and wondered what he had lost.

A wife, probably. That was usually the story, and the sort of thing that would make a man as bitter as Mac seemed to be. And yet she had the sense that it was something deeper than that, something that had scarred him while he was still too young, too vulnerable to deal with the blow.

Shadow grimaced in the darkness. Some small part of her yearned to fill the angry, hurting hole inside Mac Tshongely. She wanted to mend his wings, but in the end it would be the same as it always was. He would fly, whole and strong, and she would be left on the ground. She couldn't do that anymore. She felt strongly that she was running out of pieces of herself to give, and Mac Tshongely would take a lot from her. If she shared touches with him, even a few, then she knew somehow that she would never be able to forget him.

She thought of leaving the switchback anyway.

She thought of going down there, slipping inside his tent. She didn't think he would send her away. She could make the ache inside him go for a little while, could give him a brief respite, a temporary haven in her arms. She could assuage this new, clawing hunger inside herself. She could slide her hands over his cool, rough skin, could glory in the uncomplicated touch of his own hands. Like one of Kokopelli's maidens, she could meet him sweetly in darkness and say goodbye when the sun rose again.

She groaned.

More likely, she thought, she would play the role of She Who Waits, wanting, needing, always hoping until that last twilight came. She shivered in her sleeping bag, suddenly cold again. Mac Tshongely wasn't your average broken dove. He was surly... and instinctively kind. He was hard, yet he could coax life out of the sands of time. A loner who unconsciously shared. A man who didn't want her here yet had risked bodily injury to break her plunge to the canyon floor.

She groaned again and deliberately closed her eyes.

Impossibly, Mac felt himself harden. *Don't think about her.* He reached out and turned on his lantern, as though it could clear his mind along with the darkness. It didn't.

Clean lines, smooth skin, vibrant, alive, heated by the sun and cooled by the moon. A different voice began whispering in his head, this one cruel and cunning.

Go ahead. Do it anyway. Don't think about tomorrow... until tomorrow.

* * *

Shadow thought of the way he had filled the tent yesterday, so male, the raindrops beading on his golden skin, his hair shaggy and wet, his strong, deft fingers working the rubber band out of it. The ache came back to her, settling at all the central points of her, between her legs, in the pit of her stomach, in her throat. A sly, sibilant voice came to her head, one she barely recognized as part of her.

Go ahead. For once, just take something for yourself.

She considered that she wouldn't actually be left with nothing this time. She would have searing memories. She moaned, sitting up, hugging herself.

Could she do this? Did she dare? She kicked her sleeping bag back, scrambling to her knees, her heart pounding. She moved swiftly and silently down the switchback, out into the canyon, and collided with him solidly.

She started to gasp, but there was no time. His mouth finally came down on hers, even as his strong hands caught her shoulders to steady her. His kiss was bruising, angry, frustrated . . . and she had known it would be. She had wanted just this, exactly this, had wanted a touch every bit as hungry as what had come to live inside her lately, as what had shown in his eyes at the waterfall.

His tongue dove past her teeth, skimming them before finding hers. He moved his hands to tangle them in her hair, pulling her head back almost painfully, making her open to him even more. He looked fast into her eyes and groaned, then his mouth closed over hers again.

She had to touch him, had to feel his skin, this time beneath her palms. She flattened them against his chest, feeling hard, ungiving muscle and the brush of that near-golden hair. She clenched her fingers, digging them in as sensation stormed through her, frightening but right, somehow so right. . . .

He slanted his head, covering her mouth fully, breathing against her lips. "Let's just get this over with."

"Then we can forget about it," she agreed on a gasp.

"Put it behind us so I can think straight again."

"I can stop wondering what it would be like. . . ."

"Here, right here."

"Now. Please."

She slid her hands down his ribs, to his waist, to his hips. He had shorts on this time. She pulled at them, feeling frantic now that she had made the decision, now that she had finally let herself go.

His hands moved down her back. She wore a T-shirt, big and roomy. He swore impatiently at the obstacle it presented, and pulled it up so he could find skin, warm, smooth skin still pulsing with life. She wore panties. He cursed at that, too, sliding his hands beneath them, cupping her bottom, pulling her hard against him before exquisite pain exploded from behind him, from his thigh.

He gripped her tighter, confused for a moment, feeling like a wounded, savage animal. Then his brain cleared and he understood that something was very, very wrong. Shadow looked up into his face, dazed, then past his shoulder. She screamed.

It was a blood-curdling sound that ripped through him. Mac let her go to spin around, hunkering down slightly in an instinctive fighter's stance, pushing her behind him. Ready. . . but there was no enemy to fight, only a hail of arrows, one after another coming down from the eastern rim. They spat and hissed through the air, digging into the sand with little *cht-cht* sounds, smacking against the rocks, almost faster than a man could shoot them.

Almost, but not quite.

"What the hell?" Mac snarled. He started into their fire. Then something froze him, a thin, mewling sound.

He turned around and looked back at her. She sank slowly to her haunches, quivering in pure terror, her eyes huge and white and stricken. Something happened to his heart. He closed the distance between them again in two long strides, pulling her to her feet.

"*Ch...chi...chi...*" she began.

"*Chindis,*" he said for her. "No." He wondered if he was going to have to hit her to snap her out of it, and prayed to God that he wouldn't.

On some distant level, he realized that the arrows had stopped. He shook her instead.

"Stop it. Listen to me. It's over."

Her eyes darted frenziedly, looking. Arrows littered the ground all around the place where they were standing, but no more flew.

"The legend," she breathed. "Oh, God, it's the legend." She was still shaking badly. She groped for his arms, digging her fingers in to hold on.

"Or someone who wants us to think about the legend," he corrected. He had guessed that immediately, but he couldn't for the life of him figure out why. In any event, he'd never convince her of it, at least not now.

"Come on," he said.

He pulled at her. Her legs were rooted where she stood. He finally scooped her up and carried her back to his tent, putting her on her feet again at the last moment, pushing her a little to make her go inside. "Hey, Sergeant, you're fine. It's okay now."

"Okay," she repeated hollowly. "Fine."

She slipped inside, then stood, looking about vacantly as though wondering where she was. He followed her and something tightened inside him again in the area of his heart.

It was something dangerously different from what he had felt when he had finally gone to her, both at odds with that and yet totally a part of it. Real fear slammed into him this time. The little drill sergeant was no longer in control. She had been, very much so, when they had been groping at each other. Later he would have to examine how they had both come to be in that place at the same time, both with the same thoughts, and that would scare him too. But now she was not strong, was not giving anybody orders or pushing them around. Now she was terrified on a primal, inherent level that had nothing to do with practicality and common sense, everything to do with her Navajo upbringing and faith. Right now she was vulnerable and she needed him, and that shook him more deeply than anything that had happened tonight so far. Because he wanted to wrap himself around her as he had when they had gone over the cliff, protecting her from whatever it was she thought she should fear.

He put an awkward hand to the back of her neck, kneading away the knotted tension there. For the first time in his life, he realized that he really didn't know how to be kind, how to give care. He had never needed to learn.

"Sit down, sweetheart. There, right there. That's it."

She did it hard, dropping onto the chest, her teeth clacking together. She followed his movements with wide, stricken eyes.

"What are you doing?" she whispered.

Good, he thought, she was aware of her surroundings now.

"Following an age-old remedy for shock," he answered. "I don't know if your medicine men teach it, but it's always worked where I come from." He found a small flask of brandy he kept in his duffel bag and went back to hold it to her mouth.

Shadow chugged it gratefully, then she sputtered. He wanted to laugh, but there was a tender spot at the base of his throat that wouldn't let him. He started to hunker down in front of her, then fresh, blazing pain caught him up short.

He reached around behind him. He remembered being hit now. His hand closed over an arrow protruding from the back of his thigh.

"Damn it."

"What?" she breathed. Her eyes were clearing.

"You're going to have to snap out of it now, sweetheart. I need you to do something for me." That, he realized, was probably the best way to bring her back—giving her something to do, putting her back in charge. For the moment he would allow it because they both needed it.

He stood and turned around, looking back over his shoulder to watch her. Her face blanched, but then a grim set came to her mouth. More color came back to her face.

"Oh, my God. One got you," she muttered. And he had *carried* her here. But she would think about that later. She pushed the flask back up at him. "I guess you're going to need this worse than I do."

Mac took it and swallowed. "All right. Go ahead. Pull."

"I can't."

He looked around at her again. "Are you going to wimp out on me, Sergeant?"

Something flashed in her eyes. "I never wimp out."

"Then pull the damned thing."

"Do you want to lose half of your leg in the bargain?" she snapped. "It's in deep. I'm going to have to push it through. But it's got barbed feathers on the nock end. I need a knife."

He moved to get one, then winced as she began cutting the feathers away, pain searing through his leg with even the scant pressure she applied.

"I'm sorry," she said tightly. "It's the only way."

He realized that he was suddenly, profoundly grateful she wasn't the type to faint or weep. He took another strong swig.

"All right. I'm ready. Go for it."

He waited for the pain, but there wasn't any. "Oh, my God," she breathed instead.

"Now what?"

"Wait."

Suddenly she was up, dashing through the door. When she came back with a handful of the arrows her face was white again, her eyes glassy. She looked down at the little pile of feathers she had cut away from the arrow in his leg and examined the chipped metal points of the ones she held. Mac noticed that they were slightly misshapen. The feathers were black and red.

"I'm not in the mood for guessing games right now, Sergeant. What in the hell are you doing?"

"These arrows..." she breathed. "The lead. I've seen some like this before."

"So?"

"In museums. In private collections. They're...Mac, they've got to be over a hundred years old."

Chapter 7

"Let me see that."

Mac grabbed one of the arrows out of her hand and carried it closer to the lantern. After a moment, Shadow got a grip on herself and followed him.

"Look," she said hoarsely. "Here." She pointed to the tip. "And here." She drew a finger down the shaft.

"Okay. So?"

"Imperfect."

"It's an imperfect world, Sergeant."

"It was even more so a hundred and forty years ago," she snapped. Then she took a deep breath. "Come on, Mac. You're an archaeologist. You know what I'm talking about."

He did; he just didn't know what to make of it. The shape of the points was irregular, not stamped out by a machine. Navajo warriors had once had to melt lead down and pour it into their molds by hand, so each one they made had been marginally different. Like these. And the lines and the feathers on them were clearly handpainted.

He touched a very gentle finger to one of the feathers. It was incredibly fragile.

"Someone shot *artifacts* at us?" he said disbelievingly.

She had to think about it more, but on a gut level Shadow couldn't accept that that was what they were. "So to speak," she whispered, sitting on the chest again carefully.

Mac made a rude, snorting sound. "Forget your legends, sweetheart. These things are real, not ghostly." But he closed his hand around the one he held as though to make sure.

Shadow laid hers neatly on the floor. "Whatever," she said quietly. "I'll get that one out of your leg now."

She didn't believe him, Mac realized. He could tell by the easy way she spoke, accepting too readily that their problem was real, not supernatural. She never accepted anything that easily. When she got a bee in her bonnet, she didn't give it up without a good fight.

Well, they could argue about it later. He realized with an odd sensation—half sinking, half a lurch of his gut—that he couldn't let her go back to the switchback now. It had little to do with what had happened between them, everything to do with what had happened *to* them. He wasn't sure if someone had meant to kill them and was just a very bad shot, or if someone had only been trying to scare them. But either way, he wasn't comfortable having her out of sight, beyond shouting distance.

Tomorrow she was going to have to go home.

He turned around in front of her again, tensing his jaw hard as she worked the arrow through the fleshy part of his thigh. He took another deep chug of brandy and almost laughed in spite of the pain. This time he was thinking about her deliberately to get his mind off what she was doing to his leg.

Pound your head with a hammer, and your smashed thumb doesn't hurt anymore.

He raked a hand through his hair, wondering at the insanity that had led him down to the switchback earlier. God, what hormones could do to a man's brain! Maybe that old adage was right—maybe all his thought processes were centered right down there between his legs.

Well, he was thinking with his brain now. He was thinking how incredibly grateful he ought to be for that idiot's perfectly timed assault. It had saved him from himself.

"It's through," she said softly and he flinched at the sound of her voice—steady in spite of everything, though with a certain reedy thinness that made her still seem vulnerable, which she probably was. It threatened to undo all the nice, practical thinking he had just done.

"Do you feel all right?" she asked.

"It hurts," he answered tightly. "About what you'd expect."

"No light-headedness, any odd stinging sensation at the point of entry, nausea—that sort of thing?"

"None of the above." He scowled. "You're thinking something was on the arrow tips? Some poison?"

She murmured a sound of agreement. "Lay down, give me the rest of that brandy, and grit your teeth," she ordered.

"Yes, sir, Sergeant."

When he was down on his sleeping bag she splashed more of it in than she had to. He ground his teeth at the extent of the sting.

"Roll over," she snapped.

"I'll do the other side myself, thanks."

"Fine. Then you can bandage it yourself, too, while you're at it. I'm going back to my camp."

"Not by yourself, you're not."

"Watch me."

She ran. The little minx ran, knowing he wasn't up to speed. Anger pounded at his temples and Mac launched himself to his feet to go after her, cursing at the pain. He caught her at the point of the switchback and swung her around.

"We can do this my way, or we can do it your way. It's your choice, Sergeant."

"What's your way?" she asked too compliantly.

"I'll throw you over my shoulder and carry you. Or you can pack up your stuff as neatly and precisely as you do everything else and bring it back to where you spent the first couple of nights."

"Chivalry ends at your tent door, huh?"

He felt something squirm in his gut. "That's right."

"You think the bogeyman's going to get me, but you don't care enough to let me in? That's a pretty deep paranoia you've got going there, friend."

His jaw turned to granite. "I don't spend the night with women. I told you that. It's one of my rules."

Why was she pushing it? Shadow thought wildly. It didn't matter.

But it did.

"Nothing happened between us, Mac," she said more softly. "Not really. A night between us would be totally nonsexual."

"The hell it would. I wasn't kissing myself out in that canyon. You're staying in your own sleeping bag, Sergeant."

She took a step backward, feeling her skin color, feeling as if he had struck her. "I don't remember being the one to suggest otherwise," she said tightly. "I'll sleep in my own bag in my own camp."

"On second thought, I don't give a tinker's damn what you do," he snarled. "It's your skin."

He turned on his heel and returned to his tent. After a long time Shadow went on to her own camp. She crawled, shivering, back into her sleeping bag.

It was a long time before she remembered her gun and got up to make sure it was within reach.

* * *

Mac was a bear in the morning.

Shadow woke from a drowsy half sleep when his broad shoulders blocked out the first sun of the day. She sat up and looked at him groggily.

He was standing over her, holding the arrows. "We have to decide what to do with these," he said tightly.

Her brain felt sluggish. She hadn't slept well. There was that bizarre assault, of course, but more than anything she had thought about those few moments when they had touched, of the wild heat that had flared, of the shattering potential that had been promised . . . potential unlike anything she had known before.

Granted, she had limited experience. Maybe that was why she had gone running to him like some kind of sex-starved fool.

Oh, God.

She scrubbed her face with her hands. "I need a tooth-brush. Coffee. Then we'll talk."

He went on as though she hadn't spoken. "I think you should drop them off at the nearest tribal-police sub-agency when you leave here. I think there's one right down the western slope in Chinle."

"I'm not leaving," she murmured, standing.

His gaze moved down her legs. He thought of pushing that T-shirt up the previous night, of the warm skin he had found underneath, of sliding his hands beneath her panties. . . .

Impossibly, he felt himself begin to harden again, like a teenager, like a fool, like a man who couldn't keep his mind on what was important and off what was not.

"Yes, you are," he growled huskily.

"No. I'm not."

She was about to bend over to find her toothbrush. He caught her arm to stop her. He couldn't take anymore.

His grip almost hurt. Shadow felt her heart squirm. "You have no right to tell me where to go and what to do," she managed. "This is a free canyon. I'm camping here whether you like it or not, so leave me alone."

"We have a problem," he retorted.

"We have a lot of problems," she said softly. He dropped his hand as though she had burned him.

"I have coffee on," he said rigidly. "Go brush your teeth, do whatever you have to do, then come and have some. We'll discuss this like two civilized adults." *When you're dressed.*

"There's a start."

He watched her for a moment, then turned and stalked out of the switchback. Shadow let out a deep, ragged sigh and found her toothbrush.

She took her time dressing. When she went back around into the main canyon, he was sitting at his fire, looking both hard and torn. Something painful moved in the region of her heart. She closed her eyes.

She couldn't heal him, couldn't save this one. She would only end up hurting herself. She had known that with startling clarity the moment he had said she should camp where she had spent the first two nights...close, but not too close.

She swallowed carefully and closed the last distance between them. She took his coffeepot off the little metal stand that held it over the flames.

"I'm not taking hundred-and-forty-year-old arrows to the cops," she told him flatly. "If you want to try to convince them that there's some mortal cause for what happened, then *you* do it."

He wouldn't look at her, but he surprised her by nodding. "Yeah, there are some holes in that approach."

She sat down across from him. "Not the least of which is the fact that they'd chalk it all up to the legend. No one would come in here to investigate—not unless they've got a cop on the force who's converted to Christianity. Even so, the stories of this place wouldn't make it a high-priority case. You don't necessarily have to fear *chindis* to worry that no one who has ever come in here has left alive."

"You did," he said pointedly.

"More than once," she agreed. She nudged the arrows with her toe. "But there's the proof that it doesn't happen easily."

He finally looked at her. His eyes were more dark gray than blue now, as impenetrable as the stone at all sides of them. "So then what do you suggest we do?"

"Nothing."

His mouth twisted. "That's not your style, Sergeant."

She tried to shrug, but her heart wasn't in it. "The legend's been active for hundreds of years, since my ancestors' time. I can't totally disregard it."

"You think some *ghost* did this?"

"I think it's an unexplained phenomenon."

"Oh, for God's sake."

He was getting angry again. She could feel it. The problem was, so was she.

"To use your phrase, I don't give *a tinker's damn* what you think. I'm not going to try to leave and put it to the test."

"So you're going to stay here forever?" he demanded incredulously.

"I don't know what I'm going to do yet—except that I'm not going to fly out of here in a panic, only to discover that something won't let me."

He scrubbed a hand over his jaw. "I don't believe this," he muttered.

"Fine. *You* try leaving."

"I've got work to do."

"Coincidentally, so do I."

He looked at her narrowly. "You're wasting your time and you know it."

Shadow brought up her chin. "I was beginning to think so, but now I'm not so sure."

"Meaning?"

"Meaning maybe *you're* responsible for those arrows. Maybe you thought you could scare me into running for my life, get me out of the way so you can do whatever it is you really want to do here."

He leaned across the fire embers at her, deadly calm. Shadow fought the urge to cringe back.

"I was with you when those arrows started flying," he said quietly. "As much as I'd like to take back that fact, I can't."

It hurt worse than she thought it would. She *knew* he regretted what had happened—what had almost happened—between them. And she told herself that she did, too. Yet hearing him say it was like a knife inside, slashing and deep.

"You were with me," she agreed evenly, "but who's to say you're not working with someone?"

Mac very nearly choked. "You're unbelievable, do you know that? And how do you suppose I got word to this accomplice? How do you suppose I told him that I was going to meet you in the canyon near the switchback at that particular time of night? Smoke signals, maybe?"

Shadow flushed. Her theory did reach.

He stood and stalked into his tent for his tools. When he came out he started for his dig, then turned back to her abruptly.

"There's one other small detail you're neglecting here, Sergeant."

"Stop calling me that," she said stiffly.

He ignored her, going on implacably. "I didn't find you in the switchback."

No. No, he hadn't. She had been going to him, had met him halfway, driven by that strange, indefinable hunger that filled her even now as she watched him standing poised and ready for a fight, the sunlight teasing the gold in his dark hair. She closed her eyes because it was too easy to remember when she was looking at him, too easy to want again.

"You were headed for my tent, sweetheart," he continued, and now the endearment sounded more like a curse. "*You were coming to me.* And there was no way in hell I could have told anybody that that was going to happen because I didn't even expect it myself. There was no way I could have told anyone to lie in wait at that precise place instead of near your sleeping bag, where *I* was headed. And God help me, but at the time I really didn't want to be interrupted."

He went to the dig and she let him go. Her throat felt painfully tight with a million emotions. But finally the one that was first and foremost was fear.

She had been grasping at straws when she had tried to throw the blame at him. Because she really couldn't deal with the alternative . . . that she was trapped here by some malicious legend, by an ancient *chindi* spirit, and she was scared senseless to try to leave and prove it didn't exist.

Or worse still, maybe she just didn't *want* to leave. Maybe, in full denial of all her better judgment, she was trying to give time the opportunity to bring them together again.

Several hours passed, and she didn't appear at the dig. Mac was at the bottom of the midden, coming up with nothing but ageless rock and sand now. There was nowhere farther to go. Literally and figuratively, he thought, standing away from it and scowling.

He looked down toward the switchback. The next logical step would be to sort and label the few things he had taken out of here this morning and go on to the next ruins. It was distantly at an angle from the place where she had first been camping, hidden by the switchback outcropping from the place where she was now. Either way, he'd be working much closer to her.

Why the hell wouldn't she move? he wondered. Why was she being so stubborn? She had to know she was putting herself in danger. But she wouldn't leave and she wouldn't move and now, apparently, she wouldn't even visit his dig site.

He had hurt her.

He knew that and it made something writhe a little inside him. But he'd had no choice. He was the man he was, and he'd been honest about that long before he'd touched her. Honesty was the single unblemished thing he knew he was able to give anyone, and he had done it freely.

So now there was nowhere else to go. Nothing to do.

"Damn it." Damn her. Damn the canyon and the arrows and the fool who had shot them. She had him so tangled up inside he hadn't even given much thought to that yet; to who it had been and why anyone would want to do such a crazy thing. First things first. If she was going to get herself killed, then he had to make sure she didn't do it on *his* conscience.

He left the dig and went down to the switchback. She was sitting on her sleeping bag, writing furiously in her notebook. His steps seemed to slow of their own accord as they carried him toward her.

"Hide it in the rocks," he said. "Then when they find your body and scour the place for evidence, they'll know to come looking for me. Is that the idea?"

Shadow jumped nearly out of her skin. She gasped, then pressed a hand to her heart. "You scared me. I didn't hear you coming."

"Then you ought to be thanking your Holy People that it was me and not our prankster," he said tightly. "What are you writing that's more important than cataloging what I pull out of the ground?"

Shadow set the notebook aside. "I wanted to put down everything that happened last night while it was still fresh in my mind. When I finally get out of here, I might decide to take those arrows to the authorities after all."

Mac stuck his hands in his pockets. Suddenly he wasn't sure what else to do with them.

"Having second thoughts about leaving?" he asked finally.

"Not right now. But you were right. I can't stay here forever. And I did consider hiding the notebook in the rocks, in case I don't make it out alive." Her faced paled ever so slightly as she said it, but her jaw was grim, her expression pragmatic.

"Great minds think alike." He took his hands out of his pockets and crossed his arms over his chest instead.

Shadow hesitated. "I never really thought you were responsible." Not for the arrows, at any rate, she told herself doggedly. Then she sighed aloud. The hell of it was, it was becoming almost impossible to convince herself that he had anything to do with the shard on the trail, either.

He had the sense that this was all backward, that he was the one who ought to be apologizing to her. "I know," he said finally. "You're not stupid."

Her chin came up. Odd, but he took that as a sign that she had stopped being angry or hurt or whatever she was.

"Well, thanks for that, anyway," she muttered stiffly. She got up and brushed off the seat of her shorts, then she finally met his eyes. "What are you doing here? Don't you have work to do?"

"Yeah. I've finished the one dig. I'm about to move on to the next ruins."

"So do it."

"Move your campsite," he said finally.

"Why? Worried about your conscience?"

She saw him flinch and was immediately sorry. Of course he was. What else could it be?

"Please," he said, and she seriously thought the word would strangle him.

"I'm sorry," she said quietly. "I can't."

"Why?" he demanded.

Because you're starting to scare me worse than chindis.

"Because we were both moving down the canyon last night," she answered simply.

She saw his eyes flare again. This time they didn't close down quickly enough. She saw desire there, heat, wanting, awareness. Then he half turned away from her to run a hand through the top of his hair.

"All right," he said. "Okay. Fair enough. We're both a little vulnerable to—to each other. But that doesn't make it sane to let this guy catch either one of us alone."

"Something tells me you could handle him, alone or otherwise, *chindi* ghost or mortal." She knew it was true as soon as she said it. She remembered the way he had half crouched down the previous night, putting her behind him, protecting her. The memory came to her clearly now even through the haze her terror had thrown over it. She swallowed carefully. She had let him do it. She was a woman who fought her own battles, and those of quite a few others as well. But she had let him do it.

"*You* can't," he said finally. "I would just feel better if I knew where you were."

"You do."

"I want to be able to see you, hear you. Damn it!" he snapped, turning suddenly back to her. "Call it my conscience, call it anything you want. I don't want you to get hurt."

"Okay."

"Okay?"

"I'll move."

It was a mistake. She knew it. It was just as dangerous as *chindi* legends, and they both knew that, but she turned away from him to start gathering up her stuff.

"Look," he said roughly, "if you don't want it to happen again and I don't want it to happen again, then there's no reason why it should."

He wasn't talking about the arrows. "That's right," she agreed.

"I'm thirty-seven years old," he went on. "Not some kid with raging hormones."

"I'm thirty. Old enough to know better."

"Good. Then that's that." He moved to take some of her gear from her. "It was temporary insanity."

"Moonlight madness."

As they left the switchback, Shadow wondered who they were trying to convince.

Chapter 8

Mac helped her carry her stuff back to the old site, then he moved on to his new dig. After she was settled, Shadow took her notebook again and followed him.

She knew there would be nothing to write for a long time. It would probably take him days just to get through the top layers of sand and crumbled rock. And the apartments up on this cliff face were more extensive, wider. Mac made the same educated guess Shadow would have made as to where this midden was most likely to be, but there was always the possibility that he would dig for days and find nothing; that he would have to move a little farther along the canyon floor and start over.

Shadow watched him absently and found her mind wandering. Suddenly she straightened. "Mac."

"What?" He threw a guarded glance at her. She was sitting Indian style on the ground this time. He wondered why she always wore her hair pulled back like that and answered his own question immediately. It was more practical.

And safer. He had, after all, buried his hands in it the first chance he'd gotten.

"Correct me if I'm wrong," she continued, "but neither of us thought to look up on the rim where the arrows came from. Did we?"

"What?" he asked again, still thinking about her hair.

"The rim," she repeated. "Did you look up there?"

He stopped brushing sand away and settled back on his haunches. For a moment, he looked almost embarrassed.

"I didn't check it," he said finally.

"Me neither."

"Okay. Let's do it."

"I'll go. You have work to do." She had noticed that he was limping a little on his sore leg, but she didn't think male pride would allow him to take that for an excuse.

She pulled herself halfway up by the nearest handholds before she heard him behind her anyway. They reached the top and found exactly what she was afraid they would find.

Nothing.

She hugged herself against a chill, telling herself that the breeze made it just a little bit cooler up here than it was on the canyon floor.

"Maybe this wasn't the place," she mused.

Mac moved to peer over the rim. He studied the switchback and his tent.

"We were about right there," he said, pointing. "And the arrows came from this side. You go right, I'll take the left."

They met back at the place they had started five minutes later. "Anything?" he asked.

This time Shadow shivered outright. "No."

Mac shook his head and rubbed his jaw. "Not on my side either."

"Maybe..." Her throat went dry and she had to force the words through it. "Maybe they didn't come from up here at the top. Maybe they came from the cliff dwellings."

"More than likely he erased his tracks," Mac said flatly. "He wasn't stupid. In fact, my guess is that he never meant to hit us at all. If he had been trying to kill us, the arrows would have come more slowly, would have been better aimed. Hell, two good shots could have killed each of us, and that would have been that."

"We'll never know," she answered quietly. "If he used sagebrush or something to rub out his footprints, there's no sign of it now. There was wind last night."

"I know." He had laid awake too damned long listening to it. "Look, it can't possibly be an Anasazi ghost, because every time I've heard the legend that's about the way it went—some pissed-off Old One still protecting his home against outsiders."

Shadow nodded, wondering what he was getting at.

"Those relic arrows aren't seven hundred years old, Sergeant."

She hadn't thought of that. It made her feel somewhat better, more in control. "That's true."

"Can I get back to work now?"

"I didn't ask you to come up here in the first place."

She had a point there, but he was still strangely reluctant to let her out of his sight. The more he thought about it, the more convinced he was that the arrows—and the legend itself—were nothing more than pranks. A ghost story had gotten started somewhere along the line, and some fool had decided to breathe a little extra life into it, tormenting the few people who ventured into this place.

"The arrows probably aren't even a hundred years old," he said, going down. "They were probably handmade to look that way."

He got to the bottom and glanced up, shielding his eyes against the sun, making sure she climbed down this time rather than plummeted. He watched her legs stretch, her feet searching blindly for purchase in the rock. He looked away again quickly.

Too old for hormones.

She jumped down beside him. "If that's what you believe, then why do you care where I camp?"

His eyes narrowed on her. "If you're willing to accept that it's not an Anasazi *chindi,* then why don't you leave?" he countered.

"Maybe it's a Navajo *chindi.* Maybe the legend got twisted somewhere along the line out of sheer repetition. Maybe the ghost is a lot younger." And maybe I'm grasping at straws.

She sat down again to watch him work. There was yet another question, Mac thought, going back to the new dig, picking up his brush again. Why were they both so willing to do nothing about a prank that could have killed them? He found that he was no more eager to answer that one than he had been to go up to the rim and find that there was no real threat, no reason for her not to stay in the switchback, no real reason for her not to go home at all.

He worked late again without finding any trace of Anasazi habitation. It was half past nine before he finally straightened away from the dig, easing his sore leg carefully out of its bent position. Shadow was doodling in her notebook.

She hadn't brought him dinner this time. The last little buck he had killed was long gone. He had the absurd sense that he had failed at some primitive role—that of feeding her, providing for her. He looked around at the rugged, uncivilized canyon. Maybe there were no *chindis* here, but it sure could do some odd things to a man's mind.

He knew she had brought her own food. She didn't need him. No way in hell would Sergeant Shadow head off for a week in the wilderness without ample rations.

"I'm going to call it a night," he said finally.

She looked up. "Okay."

"Good night."

"Good night."

He switched off the floodlights and went to his tent. Shadow watched him disappear into the darkness, then she went to her sleeping bag. She had laid wood earlier. Now she lit it for her *chindi* fire, carefully sprinkling some sage around the outer perimeter of it. She had no doubt that it would keep ghosts away, but at least some small part of her wondered what affect it would have upon a more human intruder.

She fought the urge to dig the arrows out of her pile of supplies and look at them again. She found her little stash of chokecherries instead, and felt him watching her as she popped them one by one into her mouth, savoring them.

"What are you eating?" he called over.

"Berries."

"Where'd you get them?"

"There's a bunch of them growing in a ravine down past all the ruins."

"When'd you find time to pick them?"

She finally looked his way. "This morning while you were still at the first dig."

"And you're just going to eat them plain?"

"Well, gee, I guess I just forgot to bring whipped cream."

She couldn't actually see him scowl through the darkness, not even with his own fire beginning to sputter and light. But she felt it, even across the ten yards or so that separated them.

"Bring them over here," he said finally.

"Is that your way of asking me to share them?"

She thought she heard him curse. "It's my way of saying I can stretch them and make a real meal out of them."

Shadow was curious enough to take them over to him. She had collected them in one of her T-shirts and she handed the bundle over to him. But she found herself strangely reluctant—and afraid—to sit down and settle in at the fire with him.

Then again, this could take a while. She sat on the ground, keeping a careful distance between them.

Mac went into his tent and came out with some flour and a little metal tin. She pried the lid off it to peer inside and smelled animal tallow, probably left over from the deer.

"Go down to the stream and see if you can find some flat rocks," he said. "About this big." He demonstrated.

"Sure, Captain."

He raised a brow at her but made no response. Shadow went to the stream and found the rocks he had asked for. When she came back he had mashed the berries, mixing them with the flour and a little bit of water.

"Now what?" she asked.

"Smear the fat on the rocks."

She did.

"Lay them at the edges of the fire there so they get red-hot."

She did that, too. He spread some of the batter on each one.

The goo cooked in no time at all. He used a stick to slide the rocks away from the fire again, let the stuff cool, then peeled a piece off and handed it to her.

Shadow ate cautiously and her eyes widened. "It's delicious." It was paper-thin, sweet with the berries, rich with the tallow. It melted on her tongue. She hadn't expected anything so simple to be so good.

"It's an old Hopi recipe. It varies with whatever you happen to have on hand at the time, but the heating method is the same."

"A man who can cook," Shadow murmured. "I'll be darned." She tried to picture him as a boy, learning the art, and failed miserably.

His gaze skimmed over her expression. "What's the matter?"

"I can't see you at your mother's knee helping her to do something like this."

His face hardened so abruptly, so completely, her stomach rolled. "That's because it didn't happen that way," he said shortly. "My grandmother taught me."

She nodded and swallowed. "What happened to your mother?"

"How come you decided you don't want it to happen again?"

Shadow blinked at the way Mac steered the subject away so swiftly. It took her a moment to realize what he was talking about. Suddenly the cake seemed to stick to the roof of her mouth.

He needed to know. It had been bothering him all day. She had been willing enough last night before the arrows had come; had been hot and demanding in his arms. She had been as greedy as he had felt. Yet by midday she hadn't wanted to camp anywhere near him. The more he thought about it, the more he considered it an extreme reaction from her, too emotional even if he *had* somehow hurt her by not wanting her in his tent or—God forbid—his sleeping bag, even if he already sensed she was the type who would want so much more than a man like him could give.

He watched her face. A lot of emotions played there, but the one that finally came out on top was a sadness that tightened something inside him with surprising force.

"Because I can't save you without hurting myself," she said finally.

"*Save* me?" he repeated, dumbfounded. "From what?"

"Yourself."

"I don't need saving."

"You don't think you do, and that's my point."

"I'm not following you." And he found that he wanted to, very much. What crazy thing was going on in her mind now?

She put her cake down on her knee carefully. "I thought I could bring you some warmth for a while. But I was coming to you for myself, too. Because *I* needed something...something physical, something to make me feel like a woman again. I wanted to take something for *me*, finally." She shrugged, trying unsuccessfully to make light of the whole thing. "Hey, it's the nineties—I thought we could both get some satisfaction out of it and walk away feeling better."

His eyes narrowed. "No, you didn't. You're not a nineties kind of woman."

She wasn't sure if that was a compliment or an insult. "Maybe not," she allowed. "In the end I realized that I wouldn't feel better for it. I'd lose something of myself into your darkness, and I wouldn't be able to give you any light."

"My *darkness?*"

"You're complicated, Mac. You're an emotional mess."

His jaw dropped. He wasn't sure anyone had ever put it quite like that before. "How so?"

You're a man without a home, without a haven. "Every life needs an anchor. It's only human."

"I have an anchor." He realized his voice sounded defensive, and he didn't like it.

"What? Your work?"

"That's right."

"I rest my case. You give your best to dead pieces of the past that can't give you anything in return."

He frowned. "That's more or less what you said about yourself," he pointed out. "That you give all your best to other people and don't get anything back."

Shadow flinched. "But I have the good sense to realize it and try to figure out what to do about it."

She made a move as if to stand. "Wait," he said harshly. He wasn't done with this conversation yet. Something she had said earlier came sneaking back at him, demanding that he examine it. "You said you wanted to take something for yourself *finally.* Just how long has it been since you've done that? In a—uh, physical sense, I mean?"

He watched her chin come up. "Seven years."

"Seven *years?*" No, she definitely wasn't a nineties woman, and she sure as hell wasn't the kind of woman he needed. "What happened?" he demanded.

Shadow shrugged. "I left my husband in Santa Fe because I found I couldn't survive away from the Res, from my home. But the Navajo way is uniquely hard on relationships. Strangers from other clans are to be avoided. People from within your own clan are considered kin. To become involved with one of them would be the same as incest. So." She shrugged again deliberately. "It just happened. The years just passed."

"You haven't met anyone who struck your fancy?"

"I couldn't allow my fancy to be struck," she corrected. "And vice versa. Practically all the men I know are clan brothers." She thought of Diamond Eddie. "Or strangers I wouldn't give the time of day to, anyway."

So she had run. Something had happened and she had realized she was traveling a road going nowhere . . . and she had run in panic, straight into his canyon, straight into his arms.

She would probably have gone to any man she happened to find here on her headlong flight, Mac thought. He wasn't sure why that didn't make him feel any better. He only knew that it was a very, very good thing that nothing had happened last night after all. Because she needed so much more than she knew.

"How about you?" she asked. "Why do you need so badly to be alone?"

"I always have been," he answered, and that much was just about true. "It's a way of life that suits me."

"How long is always?"

He thought about it. "Since I was sixteen."

"You never married?"

"No."

Shadow scowled. That blew her wife theory right out of the water. Of course, even as she had hit upon it, it had felt...off. "So you've just been...wandering...for twenty-one years?"

Something about his shoulders was beginning to stiffen. He could ask hard, searching questions, she thought, but he didn't like them asked of himself.

"I stay in some places longer than others," he allowed finally.

"Like where?"

"I go back to the Yucatán whenever I get the chance."

"What's so great about the Yucatán?"

"A widow with fire in her eyes and plenty of tequila in her cupboard."

Shadow fought the urge to wince. She wasn't sure why that brought back the knife, slashing around inside her again. It was more or less what she had expected. "A widow who knows how to say goodbye," she clarified softly.

"Who *wants* to say goodbye. To my knowledge, Regina's been married six times. All of those husbands treated her badly. She's just as glad to close her door at the end of the night and sleep alone now."

"I see."

"No, you don't."

"I don't?"

"You're not a woman who needs to be left alone. Only someone who's been scarred can truly understand that need."

"How do you know I haven't been?" she asked, feeling almost defensive.

"Because you said you left your husband. Leaving doesn't take a bite out of you the same way being left does. I've been left and I know better than to let it happen again.

I'm not the man for you, Sergeant. You were right. I don't have anything you need, anything that'll make you feel good again.''

Who had left him? Shadow knew he wasn't going to tell her. That would definitely be letting her get too close, closer even than sharing a tent against the threat of bogeymen.

She finally stood. ''Thanks for the cake,'' she said quietly.

She was giving him what he wanted, what he had always wanted. She was leaving. So why didn't he feel better for it?

''No problem,'' he said tightly.

''Sweet dreams.''

She went back to her own campsite. His fire was dying. He threw sand over the last of the embers and went inside.

For a long time he only stood there in the darkness. He wondered if he would sleep better if he laid down outside tonight. Anyone could sneak up on him when he was inside the canvas. He wouldn't see them, wouldn't even know they were coming until they were on top of him.

But who was going to come? An ancient, pissed-off *chindi?* Some warped prankster?

A woman with fire in her eyes, who really didn't want to be left alone at the end of the night?

He pulled off his shorts and laid down on top of the sleeping bag, closing his eyes. It was good that they had talked, he decided. They understood each other now. There would be no more craziness about touching and loving. There would be no more groping each other in the darkness just because to do it and get it out of the way would mean neither of them would have to wonder about it anymore. It was the wrong thing to do, and they both accepted and agreed on that.

Now they could share her final days in the canyon as ... friends. He wondered if he had ever really had one before. The Yucatán widow was probably as close to one as he knew, unless he counted the blind bum beneath the highway overpass in Phoenix.

Mac wondered what had happened to that old man. He was probably dead by now. He hadn't thought about him in years.

The realization left him with an odd, sad feeling, almost a hollow sensation in the center of his gut. He pushed it away out of habit. For the next few days there would be Shadow, with her pertinent questions and her now-uncomplicated companionship.

They had disposed of the sex thing. Everything would be easy and fine from now on.

That was when he heard her scream.

Chapter 9

It was a curdling shriek, without end. It froze nearly every bodily function Mac had—his breath, his heart, even his saliva seemed to go dry for a moment. Then he was out of his tent and running.

There were no arrows. He looked around wildly, more than half expecting them. Shadow was sitting up in her sleeping bag with the same look that had been on her face last night, but this time she was pointing to the far canyon wall.

Mac looked that way and then he saw it. The moon was over the western rim. It was past full and shrinking again, but it still gave good light, enough light to cast shadows. And the shadow that was moving slowly across the eastern wall was that of . . . Kokopelli.

Mac's thought processes staggered. He knew it couldn't be, even as he knew what he was seeing. The figure was hunchbacked, stooped, grotesque, and it carried a flute at its mouth. From somewhere above the canyon rim came the reedy sound of its music.

Rage finally cleared his thinking. It was a hell of a good show, but *chindis* couldn't play the flute.

"Stay put," he growled at her. "Don't move."

There was only one way that anyone or anything could make a shadow at that particular spot—it would have to be standing between the moon and the eastern wall. Mac climbed up the western one, using the junipers, the craggy outcroppings, anything he could get his hands on to pull his way up. He felt the sting of blood on his palms and ignored it. From the top he could keep an eye on her, he thought, could make sure no one was sneaking back down there in her direction. And he could track the nut's footsteps, because there was no wind tonight and even if he was obliterating them as he retreated, there would be *some* sign.

But there wasn't. Mac reached the top and looked around, feeling dazed.

Slowly, shaken himself, he climbed back down to the canyon floor. He went to her sleeping bag, dropped down beside her and put a hand on her updrawn knee.

"It's all right. Easy now."

His assurances weren't working this time. She was shaking so badly. He caught her fingers as they plucked at the sleeping bag bunched at her knees. Her hands were ice cold.

"I w-want . . . I need . . ."

"What? Tell me, sweetheart. Come on, talk to me." She probably had some kind of Navajo medicine with her somewhere, he thought, something that would ward off the threat. If it made her feel better, he would find it. He would play the *chindi* game. He started to go to her small pile of possessions.

"No." She wouldn't let his hand go. "I need . . . you to hold me . . . please."

Mac went still. Of all the things she might have asked him for, he wondered if there was anything more difficult for him to give her than that.

Friends, he thought again. From somewhere far back in his mind, he remembered the blind bum beneath a highway overpass holding him as he cried.

"Sure. All right. Come here. Scoot over."

She came out of the sleeping bag, scrambling close to him. He closed his arms around her slowly, and then he closed his eyes.

He was so steady and solid and real, she thought, just what she needed right now. Instinctively, she spread her hands against his back, rubbing them over his skin. She wanted to feel strength. She wanted to feel warmth. What she found instead were muscles tensed with desperate restraint. She snatched her hands back.

"I'm...all right now." But she wasn't. Every one of her senses felt exquisitely raw. The feel of him lingered on her palms. The scent of him filled her head, something clean and earthy that reminded her of rainwater and rock. His breath sounded unnaturally loud to her, almost ragged. And then there was his face, rough and wary, and those gray blue eyes in the moonlight, as warm as they were cold.

She hugged herself this time. "What...what was it?"

"I don't know."

Her eyes widened. "You went up there."

"I didn't find anything."

"Nothing?"

His silence was so long it was an answer in itself. "I'll look again in the morning."

"That's a long time away," she whispered miserably.

In more ways than one, he thought.

He couldn't stand being this near to her, and found he couldn't bear to move away either. The sane thing to do would be to get up, tuck her in, go back and get his own sleeping bag and put it somewhere nearby...but not too nearby. Somewhere where she knew she'd be safe and he knew she'd be safe. Somewhere where he could watch that canyon rim while she slept.

That would be the sane thing, but he drew her head back down to his shoulder instead. For some reason, he needed the contact as much as she did.

"*If* we're talking about ghosts here, then it's two different ones—or something human and something not—or someone human who's pretty damned clever. Those arrows are no older than nineteenth century—if that—and Kokopelli, if he ever really lived, was dead by the fourteenth at the latest."

He felt her nod.

"So someone's playing games with us, sweetheart. I don't think ghosts are so inconsistent."

"Mmm."

He could have been telling her that the moon was made of cheese, he realized. She was aware of nothing but the comforting drone of his voice and his touch. He played with her hair and kept talking.

"Ghosts come from one time period—the one they died in. They don't play hopscotch over several eras." He was running out of things to say. He wasn't good at this. She shifted against him. His voice started to feel raw, scratchy.

"So Kokopelli didn't shoot the arrows and—"

"You're not dressed," she murmured, and in that instant everything changed.

It was too easy, he thought with the last part of himself that was capable of fighting it. Like some mystical hand *was* playing games with them, putting them in positions they couldn't easily extricate themselves from. Then she was pressing herself against him and his sanity was shattered.

She had changed into the big T-shirt again to sleep. He could feel her nipples harden against his bare chest even through the cotton. He dragged her closer, flattening them against him, and found her hair again. She had taken down the ponytail, too. He would just run his hands through it, he thought, just one more time. He gathered rich, glorious handfuls of it, then he groaned and covered her mouth with his.

Oh, how good he felt, she thought. His mouth worked on hers, brutal yet soft. His hands were so rough...and so gentle. His body was so ungiving...and his touch melted over her like hot wax, tangling in her hair, sliding down her back. It was like the night before, yet not like it at all. The night before they had both been frenzied, as if they were trying to grab something before sanity returned and brought them up short. This time there was a certain inevitability. She almost felt as if they were sinking into each other, slowly and sweetly, beyond care or control.

He still tried to push her away...although one hand remained at her neck, beneath her hair and his face stayed close to hers.

"Go do something," he said hoarsely. "Go on. Get out of here. Go wash your face in the stream. It'll make you feel better."

"Not me," she answered softly.

"You're going to regret this. I'm going to make you regret it, whether I mean to or not."

"I don't care."

"You will. Later."

"Not now. I need...too much."

He was damned. He found the hem of her T-shirt and dragged it up over her head, closing his mouth on hers again.

She was so hungry for touching. She couldn't fight this anymore, couldn't worry about what might happen later. He was here and she was here, and from the beginning he had made her ache with a desire that was almost unbearable. She had lived seven years without feeling any sense of hunger, had lived all her life without knowing hunger like this. She *needed* it, needed him, and she was neither capable nor willing to think beyond that.

Not now. Not while his mouth was warm and wet against her neck, not when he came back to ruthlessly reclaim her own. She drank in the taste on his lips.

He felt the need in her, in the way she quivered against him. Her mouth was too hungry, seeking his blindly. He had never wanted to hurt anyone less, and he had never needed another woman more.

"I want you," she said, sealing his fate. He felt as if he were going to explode.

"I want you, too, sweetheart." And then he took what she offered him.

He sought her tongue with his own, even as he found the elastic of her panties and tore them roughly down over her hips. She wriggled to help him, desperate, greedy. He tried to remember that she had no recent experience at this—for all he knew, she'd been with only the man she'd married. Common sense told him to go slowly, gently, not to scare her. And she wouldn't let him.

She came to her knees and his hard-gentle hands moved up her legs, kneading the back of her thighs, *touching* her. She moved closer and closer to him until he was forced to lay back, then she settled on top of him, molding her body to his. His hands moved higher on her legs and she moaned, shifting her weight, allowing him access. She craved his caress now as much as she'd ever needed air to breathe. But when his fingers slid between her legs, even as something bright and hot leapt through her, she still wanted, needed more.

She bit down on his lip, goading him, yes, knowing she was playing with fire and wanting to get burned. He made a harsh sound in his throat and twisted, pinning her beneath him. That was better, more... yet the ache wouldn't let her go. Frenziedly, she ran her hands across the back of his broad shoulders. She found his thighs, not cool anymore but warm, so warm... she slid her hands up. His buttocks were clenched. So were the muscles along his back and shoulders now. She realized he was struggling hard for control.

"Easy, sweetheart, take it easy," he groaned. "It's been a while for me, too."

She was both shocked and not surprised. But she couldn't heed his warning.

"Then let's not wait anymore."

She wrapped her legs around him hard. She gave him no place to go, no other move to make. She felt his unmistakable hardness press against her and she gave a little satisfied cry.

She was so ready for him, he thought, as if she had spent seven years simmering, waiting for him, waiting for this exact moment. He tried to go slowly, entering her with a steady, inexorable pressure, but he wanted her too badly and then she lifted her hips and caught him fully. He sank into her with a sensation that was almost pain. He felt her close around him tightly...welcoming him home.

She began trembling again.

"I know," he said. "I know."

She let him slow down then, the clench of her legs relaxing, because it was almost too much, too good. The way he filled her made her ache inside, but this time it was a good ache, warm and pervasive, like a glow. He rolled over again, taking her with him, holding her hips hard and tight against him as she straddled him. Then she was ready for more.

She fought against his grip until he finally began moving again in an opposing rhythm. An agony of wanting tangled inside her until she couldn't bear it any longer and she cried out again, louder this time.

He grabbed her hair, pulling her face down to his, smothering her voice with his mouth. She shuddered even more as the tension inside her built, then it exploded with an even more plummeting sensation than when she had plunged down the cliff. But he was with her this time too, absorbing her spasms, then his grip tightened on her hips again, pinning her against him as he thrust himself inside her. She felt his power over her, his strength, and it thrilled her even as it frightened her a little. He groaned and held her still a little longer, then she very slowly lowered her face to his neck.

She felt dazed, disassociated. His voice came to her as though from a long way away.

"Well, you didn't rust."

Shadow tried to laugh, but it was just a breathy little catch in her throat. She sat up, still straddling him.

Fascinated, Mac watched the play of moonlight on her breasts. Then she lifted her hair and let it fall again. It spilled down over her shoulders, covering her. He felt the absurd sense that it was somehow shutting him out, shutting her body and her heart away from him.

He wanted to tell her that it would be different next time, that he wouldn't let her take charge twice. This once she had overwhelmed him, had driven through his defenses before he could know or care. And maybe there really would be a next time—maybe there would even be a time after that. But sooner or later she would go home, and he would move on.

The thought blindsided him.

He stirred restlessly beneath her. He remembered the moment he had first entered her, feeling whole, complete, truly warm, for the first time in his life. A part of him wanted to keep that feeling, wanted to claim it for his own. And he knew such a thing was impossible. Even if he wanted to, even if he tried, he knew from firsthand experience that no man could claim anything forever.

"Where will you sleep?" she asked as if reading his mind. She didn't ask if he would go, or why he had to. She merely wanted to know how far away he would be.

Why was that so much worse?

"I'll stay close enough," he answered finally.

She eased her weight off him. Her expression was totally unreadable. "You don't have to worry about me. I'll be fine now."

She would, he thought. But would he?

Shadow woke before dawn. The canyon was cloaked in a filmy half light. She sat up slowly, feeling pains and twinges in parts of her body she'd forgotten she had. A fleeting grin touched her mouth, then faded abruptly.

What had she done?

But there was no going back, and even if she could she knew she wouldn't do things any differently. She wouldn't even grant herself the excuse of her terror. She had wanted him from the first night she'd spent here, and she'd taken what she'd wanted. She felt neither shame nor regret, only a shaky kind of doubt as she wondered what would happen now.

She could stretch her vacation four more days or so. Maybe she'd fill her senses with him until that time was over. Then she'd go back to her real life and Mac would dig on, here, then somewhere else. She knew beyond a doubt that she'd never see him again afterward. There would be nothing more than this one steamy, shining time in Kokopelli's Canyon, and her memory of it would inevitably fade as she grew older.

She could live with that. She *could*. The tapestry of her life was already far richer than it had been when she had arrived here.

She got up, found soap and shampoo, and started down to the switchback and the waterfall. Then she realized that he hadn't stayed in his tent last night after all.

Her steps faltered. He was in the middle of the canyon now, in his sleeping bag, sprawled on his back. His gun was near his right hand. She crept closer to him.

Something painfully tender closed around her heart. So he had come back to protect her. He had spent the night with her, whether he would admit it to himself or not.

In sleep, his face was neither hard nor closed. It was defenseless, open ... inherently kind. His demons were gone for a while.

She wondered what he dreamed about.

Shadow closed her eyes against a surge of emotion. She would fight those demons for him if he'd let her. He wouldn't, but given the chance she knew she'd battle them to the end of the earth. She had told herself that the previous night was just sex, that she was only a woman with needs somehow left too long unfulfilled. Now, as the first sun touched the rim of the canyon, she knew that it had never been that at all.

He was her most broken dove ever and she *had* lost something of herself to him. She had lost her very heart ... but she'd done it long before she'd touched him.

She hugged her bare shoulders and moved away from him again silently, heading into the switchback.

When she came back into the canyon, the sun was full and strong. The rocky floor was already beginning to shimmer in the heat and Mac was at his new dig.

She guessed that he had washed over at the cave side of the stream. His hair was still wet, long and free. It curled as the sun tried to dry it, tickling his shoulders at the back of his neck.

As though sensing her presence, he turned to look at her. For one awkward moment they only watched each other. Then he nodded curtly in the direction of his fire.

"The coffee should be ready by now."

"Thanks." So that was the way it was going to be, she thought. As if nothing had changed, but everything had.

She saw that he didn't have a cup yet, so she poured one for each of them. When she came to the dig, he saw that she didn't carry her notebook this time. So that was the way it was going to be, he thought. As if something had changed between them, but nothing had.

Her hair was still wet, long and sleek and free. His fingers itched for it. He wanted her as much as he had before he'd known what he was missing, and he knew it couldn't make a difference. An inexorable sadness filled him, the kind he hadn't let himself feel in a very long time.

"How much farther down are you going to go if you don't find anything here?" she asked. She sat on the ground, sipping, watching him.

It took him a moment to pull his thoughts back to his work. "Four feet. Maybe six. If I don't hit anything by then, the midden's probably somewhere else."

She nodded, hesitating. "Did you go up to the western rim yet by any chance?"

He lifted his coffee for her inspection. "I was waiting for this. I want my senses sharp and clear."

"Are they?"

"Close enough." He rested the cup in the sand. "You coming?"

She didn't want to and knew she had to see for herself. "Sure."

They climbed up the western wall, then stood looking around. The land here was much as the opposite wall had been after the arrow attack. There was nothing amiss. Nothing different leapt out at them, nothing that wasn't as it should have been.

"You're changing your mind, aren't you?" she asked finally. She saw it in his befuddled expression, as if he was struggling hard to accept something that had no place in his world. "You're starting to believe in the legend."

"Not yet," he said finally.

He began walking around, studying the ground. Every once in a while he would nudge something with the toe of his work boot, then he'd move on. But finally he stopped abruptly, staring hard at a boulder.

"What?" she demanded. "What is it?"

He motioned her over. She went to stand beside him and looked down.

"What do you see?" he asked.

"A very big rock."

He shot her a withering look out of the corner of his eye. She noticed for the first time that he had sun lines there of his own and she stared, fascinated.

"What about the ground?" he persisted.

"Uh . . . dirt," she said, dragging her eyes back to it. "Same as everywhere else—" Then she broke off and hunkered down.

"Uh-huh," he said from above her.

"It's . . ." She started to touch it, then pulled her hand back so as not to disturb anything. The dirt was absolutely flat here. It possessed none of the ridges that marked the rest of the land, no pebbles, no debris from the trees that began a little farther up the slope.

"What does it mean?" she asked.

"It means someone picked up that rock and moved it, from this spot to where it is now. No wonder I didn't see anything last night." He squatted, got a grip on the thing, and used his thighs to push up again, straightening. Shadow felt a little shiver at his strength, but then her eyes were fast on what they found beneath it.

"A *hole?*" She scowled. "I don't get it."

"Unless I miss my guess, that's about where Kokopelli was standing," Mac said, putting the rock down again.

"Kokopelli wasn't standing. He was moving," she pointed out.

"Only at first." He remembered that now. "Then he went still, probably while this idiot cleaned up his act and covered his tracks. Your *chindi* was some kind of life-size cutout figure, sweetheart, something braced upright by a stick."

"But why?" She was so confused she felt almost light-headed. She sat hard on the rock.

"I don't know," Mac answered. "But I'm going to find out."

"How?"

He looked at her oddly. Then, for the first time he truly smiled. It stole her breath away, made gooseflesh tickle over her skin. He shook his head at himself.

"Hell if I know. But I'll think of something."

He started back down the wall again. After a moment, Shadow got hold of herself and followed him. When they were back at the dig, she sipped thoughtfully at her cooling coffee.

"It has to be someone strong," she said. "You could barely lift that thing."

"The world is full of strong men. Which of them would want to try to scare the bejesus out of two unrelated people camping in a canyon? It's pure chance that we're both here at the same time. I still want to think it's just a prankster."

Shadow ran a hand through her loose hair. "It doesn't make any sense."

"Not if you try to make it sensible. Then even I'd have to say that I'm the only one who would have any motive."

He was working as he said it. Her heart hitched and she looked at him, but he was staring down into the dig and didn't meet her eyes.

She shook her head. He would hardly point out such a thing if it was true. Then she had a new thought. For the first time she wondered if their prankster, their tormentor, could be responsible for the shard she'd found up on the trail.

She glanced around the canyon and let her breath out slowly. No, that didn't seem likely, either. The only excavations in sight were Mac's. If their prankster had dropped the shard, then where had he unearthed it from in the first place? One of Mac's digs? There was no way he could manage that without Mac noticing. Maybe there were other digs farther down in the reaches of the canyon that she hadn't explored yet, but it just didn't make sense that whoever it was would carry their cache all the way back up here *then* ascend to the top.

No, she thought dismally, none of this made any sense whatsoever.

"So what do we do now?" she asked. "Even if we wanted to take it to the authorities, we don't even have the evidence of the cutout figure this time."

She said *we* so easily, he thought, feeling something sad move inside him again. It was a word he'd rarely used in his life. He finally looked at her.

"You're still not going to leave, are you? Even knowing it's something mortal?"

She thought about it. "No. That would be like letting him win." And, God help her, she just didn't want to go. Not yet. Not now. It was too soon. She wanted more memories to store.

He read all that in her face and frustration and fear and something else warred inside him, something far softer, far more yearning and far more dangerous.

"Then I guess we'd better figure out where we're both going to sleep tonight," he said tightly. "Because I don't think this nutcase is quite done with us yet."

Chapter 10

Shadow fully expected Mac to work late, to put off such a decision as long as possible, but he surprised her. Her watch read only a little past four when he threw his brush into the dig with a wordless sound of disgust.

"There's no midden here," he said finally. "They didn't follow the laws of reason this time."

"Where will you look next?"

"The second most logical place." He straightened and looked up. "Sometimes, if their apartments were big enough, they piled their dead and their refuse right up against the walls. These cliff dwellings are relatively large."

Shadow felt a very cold finger trace down her spine. "You're going to dig *in there?* You're going to go right up there into the dwellings themselves?" She could think of nothing worse than being trapped in an enclosed space with lingering *chindis.* At least out here in the canyon she had the sense that she could run, could somehow defend herself if they appeared.

PLACE FREE GIFT SEAL HERE

DETACH AND MAIL CARD TODAY!

THE SILHOUETTE READER SERVICE™: HERE'S HOW IT WORKS

Accepting free books places you under no obligation to buy anything. You may keep the books and gift and return the shipping statement marked "cancel". If you do not cancel, about a month later we will send you 6 additional novels, and bill you just $3.21 each plus 25¢ delivery and GST*. That's the complete price, and—compared to cover prices of $4.25 each—quite a bargain! You may cancel at any time, but if you choose to continue, every month we'll send you 6 more books, which you may either purchase at the discount price...or return at our expense and cancel your subscription.

*Terms and prices subject to change without notice. Canadian residents add applicable provincial taxes and GST.

If offer card is missing write to: Silhouette Reader Service, P.O. Box 609, Fort Erie, Ontario L2A 5X3

CDMA
Member

0195619199-L2A5X3-BR01

SILHOUETTE READER SERVICE
PO BOX 609
FORT ERIE, ONT.
L2A 9Z9

MAIL▷POSTE
Canada Post Corporation / Société canadienne des postes
Postage paid   Port payé
r mailed in Canada   si posté au Canada
Business   Réponse
Reply   d'affaires
0195619199   01

But Mac only shrugged. "I could save it until last, but I hate wasting time and that's probably where their trash is." Finally he noticed her stricken expression. "Hey, Sergeant, I've already told you that I'm not superstitious. I don't believe in Navajo *chindis.*"

"But you said you were part Navajo," she blurted, then she winced.

She had promised herself that she wouldn't ask him any more personal, intrusive questions. Something about having made love with him changed her right to do that. He had made it clear that any woman he touched was...well, for touching only. When she had crossed the line between acquaintance and lover, she had somehow given up all her chances to know him better. He would place her in some little niche now and keep her there, wouldn't risk letting her get any closer, wouldn't let her become an intimate part of both his body *and* his heart.

For Mac Tshongely, that was simply too much.

"Sorry," she muttered, getting to her feet. "None of my business."

He watched her go back to her sleeping bag. "Is that where you've decided to sleep tonight?" he demanded.

Decided? She looked back at him. "You haven't mentioned any other alternatives."

Mac shoved his hands into his pockets. After a moment, he followed her.

She sat on her sleeping bag and dug through her belongings for an envelope of reconstituted stew. She tore it open with her teeth and poured it into a lightweight tin pot. It had taken him two trips to get all his stuff up the mountain, he thought, and he still didn't have everything with him that would have made his stay comfortable. Sergeant Shadow, on the other hand, had brought one small backpack, and he had the feeling that if he asked her for a bathtub, she would have pulled that out from her little pile as well.

He chuckled aloud, a rough sound. She looked up, startled.

"What's so funny?"

"Nothing. If you share that tonight, I'll go out at dawn and see if I can find another deer."

"Sounds like bribery."

"It is."

She shrugged. "It'll work. I'm getting sick to death of this stuff."

She waited for him to point out again that she could always go home, but he didn't do it this time. Something moved in the pit of her stomach. She looked up at him cautiously.

"How about some more of those skinny little cakes?" she suggested. After all, he had already pretty much said that he would be eating with her. "I could go get some berries."

"That'll work, too."

She went down the canyon and he went to his tent for the flour and the stones. He hefted one in the palm of his hand and stared down at it pensively.

His rules were fraying badly around the edges, he thought, and he didn't even know which thread he should try to grab first to stop it all from unraveling. There was such a radiant warmth about her. He had the distinct impression that it was a solid warmth, something he could get his hands around and hold onto.

Fool. But as the day had passed he'd found himself wanting that more and more badly, wanting to be warm, to finally be warm inside again as he had been when he'd sank into her the night before. How had she put it? *I'd lose something of myself into your darkness, and I wouldn't be able to give you any light.* But she had. In a few impossibly short days, she had lit up his world.

It was the little things, he realized with a start. Cooking together, tracking their prankster together. It was the silly stuff that wasn't at all hard to do alone, but was so much better with company.

"Mac?"

He jolted, looking around at her. "Did you get the berries?" he asked. His voice sounded raw even to his own ears. He grimaced and cleared his throat.

"Not many. Most of them are sun-shriveled, almost rotten. I didn't notice that before." Small wonder, she thought, the way her head had been lately.

She had stopped at her own campsite and he went back there to join her. They worked in silence. A warm silence. He marveled again at the way she didn't feel the need to fill it up with inane talk.

He was the one to finally break the quiet and when he did his own words shocked him.

"My mother had the Navajo blood. She was a quarter Navajo. She didn't raise me."

Shadow nodded simply, pushing one of the finished cakes into her mouth, poking at her stew with her finger and a dissatisfied frown.

"She left when I was ten," he said.

She finally looked up at him. *I've been left and I know better than to let it happen again.* His mother, she thought. Of course it was his mother who had gone. She remembered now, the way he had steered the subject away when she had mentioned the woman before.

So why had he decided to tell her about it now? Suddenly she felt as if she was handling something very, very fragile, something her merest breath could break. She urged him on with another bare nod, just enough to let him know she was listening.

"In my earliest memories of her, she was happy. So...loving. So full of joy at the simplest things. I remember when I was five or six or so, she took me to Salt Lake. She was raised in Utah, not on your reservation. She just took me. It was our own special excursion. We left my father and brother behind. She...she thought of things like that. She was full of ways to make someone feel special." His face took on a pained, faraway cast. "She ran out into the water first that day. She had on a dress. The water...it buoyed her skirt up, billows of it, all gathered around her. She laughed. I can still remember her that way, her head thrown back, laughing, waving for me to come in...." It was, in fact, the only truly clear memory he had left of her.

He was quiet for a long time. Shadow finally cleared her throat carefully. "So what happened to her?"

"I'll be damned if I know. I just—I have an impression of the warmth, the life, going out of her over the years. At some point it just didn't seem like they loved each other anymore. And then she just...left." This time his laugh was ugly. "You've heard the stories. Papa went out for a pack of cigarettes and never came back. Only this time it was Mama, it was a loaf of goddamned bread and the station wagon, and that was that. She crumbled, fell apart...faded away. Whatever trials and tribulations there were in her life, I guess she just wasn't strong enough to meet them."

Shadow's heart squeezed for him. She doubted, somehow, that it had been trials and tribulations. Maybe it had been doing...always doing for others. It could be exhausting to think up ways to make people feel special. Maybe, she thought, Mac's mother had just gotten... tired.

She could almost understand it, then she looked at Mac. How could a woman get tired of a man she loved, of her *sons?* For one moment, for one horrible, fleeting moment, he was a little boy again, befuddled, lost and alone. Then the man was back, the man that little boy had become, and his face became stony, his eyes hard.

"Dad waited a while, and then he took us home to the Hopi Mesas. That was where he was from. But in the beginning, he would just go to the front door at odd times and stand there, staring down the street as though he still expected that damned station wagon to come cruising around the corner again at any time. I guess it took a while for him to accept that she wasn't coming back." Mac shook his head. "I never knew a man could hurt like that."

Now you do. But she didn't say it. Instead she asked, "Did the Mesas heal him?"

"I thought they would. But she destroyed him. When she gave up, when she ran, it ruined him. It was like the beauty had gone out of him. He was a jeweler by trade. He never bought his gems, his stones. He used what he found, whatever the land gave him. But after my mother left, he just stopped working and drew further and further into himself. It was almost as though he thought maybe the beauty just sank inside him somewhere, and if he went deep enough he could find it again."

What an eloquent way to put it. Shadow lost her breath to a sharp pain, both for Mac and for this man she would probably never know.

"Finally he started drinking," he went on. "Miller—my brother—was falling apart, too. And I guess Dad just wasn't strong enough to take that on top of everything else.

"Miller started stealing things, stupid things. God only knows what he thought that could give him. It went on until he was about twenty or so. I was sixteen. Then the Hopi elders called a meeting and decided he would have to go. What he was doing completely contradicted the Hopi way. He needed help, he needed their wisdom, but they sent him away. So I got mad and righteous the way only a kid can do, and I left with him."

"Where?"

"We wandered south and ended up in Phoenix. We lived on the street and Miller provided for us in his own warped way. But his stealing got bigger, worse. On the Mesas it was some old woman's blanket hanging from a laundry line. In Phoenix it was cars, cash registers. The cops finally caught up with him. It had to happen sooner or later. They packed him off to jail."

Shadow's throat felt so tight she could barely swallow. "So they all left you," she murmured, "all three of them."

He looked vaguely surprised, then his eyes hardened. "It wasn't their fault. My mother destroyed both of them. She set all of their failures into motion when she deserted us."

Shadow decided she would leave that one alone. She knew there would be no swaying him from the conviction. It was far too old. "It's a long jump from the streets to a master's degree," she said instead.

"How'd you know about my master's?" He looked at her hard, suspiciously. His eyes were on the verge of closing down again.

"The computer."

"Oh. That's right. You were playing supersleuth."

Shadow flushed, trying to hold his eyes. *Don't go. Don't stop talking to me now.*

Something from her heart must have reached him. After a moment, he went on.

"I was sleeping at nights under a highway overpass in the south part of the city. There was an old blind guy there too." She thought she almost saw him smile. "I was following Miller's way, doing anything to survive, when that old man realized what I was up to and smacked the hell out of me. I couldn't believe it. He couldn't even see, but no matter which way I tried to run from him, he'd find me with that damned cane and whale on my hide." *Until I sat down and cried.* He had never cried again, Mac realized, not once after that sultry, dark night. But for some reason, he felt like doing it now.

"A few whacks with a cane doesn't equal a college degree," Shadow responded carefully.

"Those few whacks went a long way. He said it was one thing for him to sleep under the overpass. He was old and he didn't have any good years left, anything to give. But I was only sixteen. I had a lifetime and a million potentials unless I squandered them all. I didn't pay him any mind at first, but eventually I came to realize that it was safe enough to rely on myself. I got a job and my G.E.D. and a scholarship. And that was that."

"Why archaeology?"

"The past endures."

And people sure as hell don't. She remembered the way he had said that and she understood now. "Some people do, too," she answered quietly.

He gave a deprecating snort, but she could think of a handful right off the top of her head. Her family, to begin with, and so many of the People on the Res. Jericho might have forgotten her birthday, but she had no doubt that by now he had grilled Diamond Eddie six ways to Sunday about where she'd gone.

Something trembled inside her as she realized how very, very different they were.

Mac's face was hardening again. "Don't try to tell me you're one of them," he said tightly. "I won't buy it. You're not that strong."

Her spine straightened defensively. "You don't have any way of knowing that."

"Sure I do. You've already left one man just because you wanted to go home."

That hurt. The truth of it was like a slap in the face, and she answered without thought. "I didn't love him."

She knew it as soon as she said it, though it had never consciously occurred to her before now. It shook her and she hugged herself, feeling like a hurt animal that needed to slink off to some dark corner to examine its wound. But Mac wouldn't allow her that. The moon was rising. It was a night for shared truths. She wondered where they would take them.

"You married a man you didn't love?" he drawled. "Now *there's* character."

Suddenly she was angry. "Do you think I knew it at the time and married him anyway?"

"Why, then?" He wanted her to feel hurt too, wanted to pay her back for making him dig up old memories, even though she hadn't actually asked him to. It was perverse, but he couldn't fight the urge. Emotion had been unleashed inside him and it was violent now; it had been chained up for too long.

"I was twenty-two!" she snapped. "He was the campus jock. Everything we did together was fun, a good time, lots of laughs. It wasn't until after we got married that I realized we really didn't have anything in common. I was sort of like his... his Indian princess, I guess, like an exotic toy to show off to people, something he had that none of his friends possessed. He wanted me to play the role in company, but he didn't want me to *be* it in private. He wanted me to bury my beliefs and embrace his because they were the only ones he could really accept. There wasn't anything there to sustain me after we got married. He didn't even want me to visit the Res anymore. There was nothing there to take the place of everything I did love, everything that I had lost because he wasn't able to share it."

"No sex like last night?" Mac queried cruelly.

Shadow flinched but then she met his eyes. "No. I've never known anything like last night."

"Well, I have. I've had it with the best of them and that wears thin, too, sweetheart. It's just not enough over the long haul."

He said it because he needed to believe it. As soon as he did, he felt lower than a worm for lying.

She went pale. She tried to scramble to her feet and couldn't quite manage it. She finally stood, swaying, then she looked at him through stricken eyes. Finally she stumbled around and headed for the far reaches of the canyon.

He had never hurt inside like he did at that moment.

In the days she had been here she had done nothing to threaten him, to bring him pain. She had not pressed too close; she had not wandered too far away. She had been true, solid, unflinching in the face of his temper. *Why?* And why did he need to hurt her for it?

Because no one else, no one other than a dead, blind bum had ever possessed that kind of guts where he was concerned, he realized. Because guts like that could last, could endure. And that scared the living hell out of him.

"Wait," he called out hoarsely. "Shadow!"

At the sound of his voice, she started running. He had to let her go, yet he couldn't let her flee down there into that pitch darkness alone. He couldn't let her leave him. Not yet. It was too soon.

He was on his feet and running after her before he knew he would do it. He caught her arm to stop her and she turned on him like a wild thing, clawing and hitting.

"I'm sorry," he apologized.

"Why do you have to... try to bring everything down... to your coarse, wretched level?" she gasped. One small fist connected hard with the side of his head before he managed to grasp both her wrists. "Can't you just let anything be *good?*"

"I don't know, Sergeant. I guess I just don't know how."

"Don't call me that!"

She managed to pull away from him. He tackled her because it was the only way he could stop her from running again. He caught her ankles and she spilled into the sand, then he scrambled quickly up over her, pinning her arms over her head.

"Shadow, stop it. God, stop it. I didn't mean it!"

But he did, she thought. In some scarred part of his soul he had meant every word, because he needed to believe them. She was out of her element here, couldn't save him, couldn't even *touch* that darkness inside him, because although he had opened the window to let her see it, he still kept bars in place to keep her out.

"Leave me alone," she moaned, "please."

"I can't."

She shuddered, then went very, very still. He moved his hands up her arms and felt the rigidity of her flesh. He forced himself to meet her gaze, though it was one of the hardest things he had ever done.

"Come on, sweetheart. Let me back in. It's cold out here."

She groaned and closed her eyes. He thought he saw the set of her jaw finally soften. He thanked every Hopi, Anglo and Navajo god and kissed her cautiously.

She would forgive him because it was her nature. She would try to give him warmth because he so desperately needed it. She opened to him because she believed him.

God help her, but she did.

He felt the exact moment when she changed. A spasm passed through her body. Yearning? Regret? He didn't know and couldn't care now. She had come back to him and he needed her heat right now as he had never needed anything in his life.

He was too grateful, too relieved, to try to stop her when she arched her back up from the sand and pressed into him, taking charge again. She twisted from beneath him with athletic grace, and somehow he found himself on his back in the sand again, her lean body on top of his. He caught a hand behind her neck and pulled her mouth down to his.

"Okay," he breathed, "we'll do it your way again. But take your hair down."

"What?" she gasped.

"Your hair." He didn't wait for her to do it. He found the band with his free hand and tugged at it. It spilled into his face, puddling on his chest as she bent over him. It smelled of something like lavender, faintly floral. The scent teased him, barely filling his nostrils, tempting him to want more.

Her mouth moved to his neck and he felt her nails digging little trails across his chest. She was in control, always in control, but he needed that now. He needed to be driven beyond sanity because he was too frightened to follow that road on his own. He had the distinct sense that this time, this second time, was going to change everything, all his remaining fragile rules. He was afraid that if he made love to her again now there would be no pulling back, no pretending that his life wasn't radically altered forever.

He couldn't lead either of them into that. He didn't have the guts. So he followed her.

He let her slide down him, pushing his legs apart, making a space for her body between them. He found the strength to bear the slow friction of her body against his, her nipples, hard and tight, dragging their own little paths across his belly. He was excruciatingly aware of the sensation even through the T-shirt she wore. Then she was tugging at his shorts, and heaven help him, but he lifted his hips to help her. He felt her mouth close over his hardness and he plunged his hands into her hair again, grabbing handfuls of it, thinking he couldn't hurt her, didn't dare hurt her because maybe she wouldn't come back the next time. But then he crossed the line between will and insanity.

When he felt himself losing control, he gave a guttural groan and sat up, dragging her up with him. Her eyes were smoky with desire and he felt an even stronger need of his own crash through him again. He pulled at her T-shirt, her shorts, like a man seeking salvation, finding her mouth again. He sank into her, searching for her tongue with his. She met him, giving, saving him.

He was hard to the point of pain. He needed to plunge himself into her, to feel that sense of joining, of belonging with her even for a few precious moments out of time. But it had been so long for her. She would be tight, sore after their previous night. She would have undeniable needs of her own.

Shadow did. She wanted him inside her again—now—so that she ached with his fullness the way she had before, until that glow came back within, pushing her doubts and fears into the deepest, darkest recesses of her soul. She felt shudders of longing working through her as soon as he touched her, as soon as his fingers slid against her most sensitive flesh, finding entrance, but it wasn't enough. She pushed him back and straddled him again, fitting herself over him before he could protest, before he could try to make her wait.

He gave up then, driving himself into her the way he'd wanted to at the start. He found that she was ready for him after all. It amazed him and he needed—wanted—to examine that, but not now, not here. He caught her hair again and pulled her down to him, seeking her breasts this time instead of her mouth, moving his tongue over her small, tight nipples, closing his mouth over one, then the other, sucking them hard and deep. On some distant level he was aware that she was gasping, a harsh, half-moaning sound that came again and again as she dug her nails into his shoulders as if to hold on.

She felt him plunge into her again and again. She moved to help him, and finally it was everything she needed, more than she could bear. If she had to live a lifetime in these days, then she knew in that moment that it would be enough and the memories wouldn't fade if she grew to be ninety.

Her climax hit her in a stunning, unexpected ambush, as violent as the emotion that had driven him to hurt her earlier. Mac felt it as if he were part of her, felt the clenching and the spasms, then he groaned and followed her, even as something inside him protested, *not yet, too soon.*

But just as she had from the moment she had plunged down the canyon wall to land at his feet, she left him absolutely no alternative.

Chapter 11

They lay quietly for a long time, then something rustled in the darkness. A shadow darted near the canyon wall and Mac felt her stiffen in his arms.

"Just an animal," he said.

His voice sounded strangely unlike his own. He felt changed, altered on some very deep level, but Shadow didn't seem to notice anything amiss.

"Let's move," she suggested, her fingers digging into his skin just a little deeper. "I don't like it down here."

He was about to point out that she was the one who had run to this place, then he thought better of it. She hadn't run. He had driven her.

"It hurt coming out again." He wondered if she would understand.

"I know," she answered softly. "But maybe now you'll be free of it."

He wondered if anything could be as simple as that. In her neat, orderly world where rules were easy, maybe it was.

She slid off him, groping around in the dark for her clothing. He had barely pulled his shorts back on before she was hurrying off down the canyon, back toward the place where their campsites were.

Their campsites. What was he going to do about that? He followed her more slowly, raking a hand through his hair. He stood beside his tent for a moment, then he grimly began dismantling it.

Shadow watched from beside her own sleeping bag. "What are you doing?" she asked finally.

"You're too vulnerable when I'm sleeping in here."

She thought of pointing out that it might be safest if they were *both* in there, but she knew he still couldn't handle that. The deepest wounds were the earliest ones, and he had been protecting his since he was ten. The deep ones took the longest to heal and they had to do it from the inside out.

She lifted one shoulder in a half shrug. "That's no reason to take it down. Just sleep outside again."

"I don't want to leave him any doubt as to where I am."

Shadow scowled. "What difference does it make?"

"If he knows I'm outside, then he probably won't try anything new."

"If he thinks you're inside and you're not, maybe we could catch him."

"Considering what his tricks do to you, it's not worth it."

"You still think it's just someone playing pranks?" she asked dubiously.

He twisted it around in his mind and couldn't come up with anything else that made sense. He nodded.

"Oh," she said absently, still watching him. Suddenly her heart thumped.

He picked up his sleeping bag and moved it, closing almost exactly half the distance between them. Just half. She wondered if he even knew himself what he was doing. She didn't think he was worrying about their tormentor.

She thought he was just prying excuses up from shaky ground the way he pulled the past from the earth, wanting to come closer and not daring to, settling for an alternative halfway.

Her heart thrummed, but then she suddenly felt like crying, although she couldn't even remember the last time she had done that. It would take time, so much time, for him to close that last little bit of distance, and they had so little time left. She wanted that distance gone more than anything in the world, she realized suddenly, more than she had ever ached for anything in her life. And for the first time in her life, there was absolutely nothing she could do about it. It was out of her control. It was something Mac could only do for himself.

She lay down in her own sleeping bag, careful to keep her back to him. But it was a long time before she slept.

When the first new sun speared into her eyes in the morning, she looked immediately to where Mac lay. His sleeping bag was empty. Shadow sat up quickly, feeling stricken, feeling life and love and hope slide through her fingers like sand.

Had he spent the night prowling as he had that first time, unable to bear even this small closeness?

Then she remembered. He had said he would go up the mountain to hunt this morning. She let out a shaky breath and kicked her sleeping bag off her legs.

Her relief lasted only a short time. She looked around the canyon and realized it had an isolated, abandoned feeling without him. Despite the gathering heat, it seemed cold and threatening. She shuddered. She really didn't want to be here alone.

Hurriedly, she pulled on a pair of shorts and socks and boots. At the last moment she hesitated and changed her white T-shirt for a bright red one. If he *was* hunting, then it wasn't smart to move in on him when he wasn't expecting her. She didn't want to leave any doubt that she was of the human persuasion.

She climbed up the slope in the switchback, then she stood, waiting for the sound of a gunshot, for something to tell her where he was. There was only silence, but Uncle Ernie had taught her how to track. It had been a very long time since she'd had need of the skill, but she finally picked up fresh boot prints and followed them up the mountain.

She came up on him from behind, then her heart skipped. His hair was pulled back again, and she realized for the first time that it was a style reminiscent of her ancestors. Navajo warriors had once knotted their hair at their napes because braids got in the way of hunting, raiding, fighting for their lives and their people. But even more startling than his hair was the bow and arrow he held. He aimed silently, tensely, at some deer that were nuzzling the water at a nearby hole.

Shadow gasped just as he shot. He turned back to her sharply, then his face relaxed when he saw her.

"Wh—what are you doing?" she asked hoarsely.

He lowered the bow, resting it neatly against a boulder. "Fresh meat tonight. We had a deal."

He went to the fallen animal. The others had flown when the small buck he had chosen had fallen.

"I know...I mean, I didn't even know you had that thing with you." She motioned at the bow.

"It's kinder, assuming the hunter knows what he's doing. An arrow to the heart is instant death. It's fast and it's silent. This guy never even saw it coming. There was no time for him to know fear, for his instincts to kick in, for them to urge him to run." He worked the arrow out of the buck. "A bullet isn't always as accurate. It can deflect off bone more easily if your aim's half a breath off. Even if it's not, there's less guarantee that death is going to be immediate."

"Wait," she said as he started to pick the deer up.

"For what?"

She felt dazed. The bow and arrow had given her a jolt, still had her pulse moving oddly. In contrast to that was a warm feeling that tried to squirm inside her at the kind of compassion it would take to make a man worry over the way he killed a deer.

She finally closed the distance between them and stooped near the animal, murmuring quickly in Navajo, thanking the animal for his life that they might eat. Then she sent him on to the afterworld as Uncle Ernie had taught her to do.

"Now you go on your way alone. What you are now, we know not. From now on, you are not of this earth," she said, finishing in English. She straightened again and realized that Mac was watching her with a strange expression.

Her chin came up. She more than half expected him to mock her, the way Kevin had always done. It was rare that she reverted to her own heritage in the presence of anyone who wasn't Navajo, at least in spirit.

"You use your arrows, and I make sure he knows his death wasn't in vain," she said stiffly. "It's more or less the same thing. It's just a matter of respecting something that's weaker and dumber than we are."

He didn't answer for a long time. "Can I pick him up now?" he asked finally.

He wasn't being sarcastic, she realized. Something moved inside her. He simply didn't want to do anything that would interfere with what she wanted to accomplish.

Shadow nodded. "I—yes. His spirit is gone now."

He lifted the deer and slung it over his shoulder. "You're not afraid of it, of his *chindi?*"

"Animals don't have *chindis,*" she explained, stepping in beside him as he headed back down the mountain.

"But you said his spirit left."

"Spirits and *chindis* aren't the same thing. A *chindi* is everything that was bad and evil about a person in life.

Animals are pure. Only people have the intellect to be evil. That's why I'm so scared of the dead. It's not a matter of a simple 'boo!' in the dark. That I could handle.''

Mac thought about it and realized it made perfect sense. Her terror at those arrows and at Kokopelli's shadow had been extraordinarily deep. Now he understood.

He had given up on any religion, Hopi or white or otherwise—too many gods had let him down. But he thought that this *chindi* premise might deserve some pondering.

Later. When he was alone again, with only his thoughts for company, he could think about it. Now he felt a driving, totally uncharacteristic need not to squander a single moment of her remaining time here.

They reached the canyon again. He found an unobstructed expanse of wall and lowered the deer to let it slide down. ''Hungry?'' he asked.

''Starving,'' she admitted. The cakes last night had been good, but they weren't filling and she'd barely touched the stew.

''So we'll roast some of this meat now,'' he decided.

She looked at him, surprised. ''Don't you have to start digging in the apartments?''

That was another thing that could wait a little longer, he decided . . . until he was alone again. ''Those rooms aren't going anywhere.''

But she was. He felt a strange, sharp pain in the area of his heart.

Shadow didn't understand what was happening, but as the day unraveled she knew that it was precious and rare. Mac was apparently going to take time off from the dig. There was almost a forced easiness about him—an uncharacteristic laziness as palpable as something she could reach out and touch.

They skinned the deer together and she took the offal back up the mountain for the coyotes. When she returned she settled down beside him to take some of the meat he had cooked. She felt the sun warming her skin—gently at first, then with a burning intensity.

"I thought you Navajo had a grudge against those guys," Mac said finally.

"Against who? Coyotes?" She grinned and shook her head. "Coyote's the Trickster. But he's smart and he's helped us out of more than a few jams. You wouldn't want to *call* a Navajo a coyote—that would be an insult. But we owe the Trickster a few favors, so we provide for his kin when we can."

"What kind of jams?"

Shadow chewed, thinking. "Well, he brought us fire, for one thing. Back in the beginning, when we first came up into this world, we didn't have any. The nights were like pitch and the People were cold and we had to eat our food raw. The fire was up on top of one of the sacred mountains that watch over our land, and it was guarded by birds. So Coyote went up there—we couldn't, I don't remember why now—and he tricked one of those birds into sitting on one of the fires. Its tail went up in flames and it panicked and flew right down to us. One of our warriors caught the bird and we've been warm and cozy ever since."

He cracked a small smile. "Interesting."

"How'd the Hopi get it?" she asked deliberately. From the inside out, she thought again. Perhaps, if there wasn't time to give him anything else, she could give him back what few good memories he'd had.

But Mac's smile faded. "I don't remember. I only lived on the Mesas for a couple of years."

"You remembered the skinny cakes."

"They have a practical advantage. I need to eat. Cheap, easy fixings came in handy almost from the time I left." He stood abruptly, kicking sand over their fire. "I'm going to take a bath, get some of this crud off me."

Shadow looked at his strong, muscled body and felt the urge to touch him again—as urgently as if she'd never had that glory at all.

"You should try the waterfall," she suggested carefully.

"I intend to."

Her jaw dropped. "You do?" He didn't seem the type to wallow in sensual pleasures—at least not of the solitary kind.

Then something shot through her blood, something hot just beneath her skin. He reached down and grabbed her hand, hauling her to her feet. He didn't intend the pleasure to be solitary, she realized.

His hands moved to her waist. He didn't pull her close. He didn't have to. He simply held her, watching her, his rugged face inches from hers.

"I'm not going to let you hog it," he said quietly. "Didn't those Navajo ancestors of yours teach you to share?"

Her pulse skipped. "No...I mean, sure...but you...you could have used it anytime. I didn't even show up until a few days ago."

It had been the wrong thing to say. His face closed down and he pulled away from her. She watched him, something frantic pushing up in her throat as she wondered why her simple words had struck him so hard.

Then she understood and it rocked her.

He hadn't used the waterfall before because he hadn't known then how to reach out and touch pleasure, hadn't wanted to, had closed himself off from everything sweet because it might not be there tomorrow. She was sure he'd had some cold, logical excuse for bathing at the cave side...and she knew that he would probably go back there when she left. But this time, on some level, he would know what he was missing. He would remember that icy spray, the *life* in that tunneling water, and the quiet, tepid stream on the other side would be somehow lacking.

For the first time she realized that maybe the kindest thing she could have done was just to have left him alone from the start. Despite all her best intentions, she *was* giving him something that would be taken away again, if only by his own hand.

When she didn't move, Mac looked back at her. And impossibly, though it blew his mind clear to heaven to realize it, he knew exactly what she was thinking.

He closed the distance between them again, scraping his fingers through her hair on either side of her head. "It was always my choice, Sergeant," he said roughly. "I only let you think you were leading the way."

Then he kissed her again, hard, punishingly, until her knees felt weak and she had to dig her fingers into his waist to hold on. She didn't believe him, but she would worry about it later....

Later. When later came, she thought she would probably have a lot of thoughts that haunted her for a very long time.

But now he was pulling her down the canyon, at first only tugging on her hand, but then they were running. She laughed huskily at the sheer joy of it. Why was it, she wondered, that when you grew up you never simply *ran* anymore unless something was chasing you, unless something was wrong? He felt it too—she could see it in the almost surprised look on his face. Then he grinned and it took her breath away.

He swung her close as they reached the switchback, one arm hard around her waist, holding her, even as he worked at the button on her shorts with the other. He let her go to push them down her legs with both hands. Shadow kicked out of them and yanked her shirt over her head. When she looked again, Mac was naked and he was pulling her into the stream right where they stood.

He wasn't grinning anymore. He wore an intent expression that made her heart chug in anticipation.

The first icy touch of the water was a shock after the sun, curling frigid fingers around her calves. But his skin was warm, so warm.

"Here," he rasped. "Right here. I want you just the way you were the first time I saw you naked, in the water."

Her heart spasmed as she remembered the look in his eyes that day. She dove into him again as she had wanted to from the first, but this time she did it purely for him, all for him, giving what he found it so difficult to reach out and take for himself. Pleasure, she thought, just pleasure, and maybe it would glow inside him long after she had to let him go.

She wouldn't cry.

Her hands framed his face and she brushed his mouth again and again, using her tongue and her lips and her teeth, whatever it took until she felt him tremble with the goodness of it. She bit his lip, holding it as her tongue stroked there, until he groaned her name and his arms tightened around her, urging her down into the water.

They sprawled together with a splash. He lowered himself on top of her and she drove her hands into his hair, taking all his mouth this time. The force of his response was instant and raw.

Suddenly Mac's breath was a hard, painful rock in his throat. Her lips and her tongue slid down his neck, licking up the water, warm following cold . . . she seemed to savor the feel of his body, and she soothed his soul. He realized that no one had ever given to him like this before, and knew that no one would again.

Her tongue found one of his nipples through his chest hair and her teeth dragged at it. Sensation shot through him. He straightened his arms, bracing his weight on them to rise above her. He had to be inside her, had to find that home he knew waited within the wet, welcoming heat of her, but this time she wouldn't let him. Her hands, cold from the water, slid over his waist and belly, over skin that his own blood had heated. The contrast made him shudder…or maybe it was her, only her. Her fingers closed over his rigid male flesh until the heat of him warmed her touch, and then he knew that the trembling inside him had nothing to do with ice and fire at all.

He was going to lose the last tenuous grip he had on control. He caught her hand to stop her but then he only found himself moving his hips against her grasp. Her hand tightened, and something growled from his throat. It might have been her name or it might have been a plea. Everything he knew about life and loving shattered into a million pieces inside him until he found himself enjoying for the sake of pleasure, until he gave himself up to her without wondering how he was going to get away when it was done.

"Now," she gasped. "*Now* take me." Now, when there were finally no defenses in his eyes.

But he didn't, at least not as she thought he would. He didn't slide into her with a groan and a giving in. He thrust hard and fast and completely so that her breath shot out of her, then he lifted her at the same time until he was kneeling.

"Wrap your legs around me. Hold on. That's it."

She did and he got to his feet, taking them, still joined together, the rest of the way to the waterfall. Then he eased her down again without leaving her, covering her, absorbing the freezing spray of the water with his own body, giving her only his heat. Then and only then did he begin moving inside her, penetrating, then withdrawing until she moaned and moved her own hips to capture him more fully.

Maybe he was only letting her think she was leading the way, but it didn't matter, because now they were together and even as she groped for his shoulders, he tangled his hands in her wet hair. This time when she took, he gave. This time as she surrendered, he demanded.

The water crashed over them and she was as she had been the first time he had seen her here, the time he had first wanted her with such sudden force that he had almost forgotten to breathe. He watched her arch beneath him, her head falling back, her hair sleek and streaming and pooling in the water beneath them. Her nipples were tight and hard from the cold and from the fire inside her. Her legs were wrapped unflinchingly around him, so strong and slender. He wanted this time to go on forever, but she gave a rippling, throaty cry of release and the sound tore into him. He felt his own completion roar through him, pulsing, pouring, and he gave himself into her keeping.

Chapter 12

Two more days.

Shadow shifted in her sleeping bag, half rolling over so she could watch him as he slept. He remained just close enough that she could see him despite the impossible light, not near enough to touch. The moon had gone and the sun had not arrived yet, and the sky was thick, dark gray against the blacker canyon walls.

He was snoring slightly, and that almost made her want to smile. How long since she had been close enough to a man, had *wanted* to be close enough to hear him snore? Never, she realized. And she knew with a pang that she never would again.

Suddenly anger closed her throat. It was all so stupid! She wanted to spend all her days beside him, all her nights rolling with him, skin to skin. She knew that he enjoyed her company as well—he certainly seemed to enjoy making love with her. Why couldn't that be enough? Why couldn't she twist this situation, wrestle with it, make it *workable?*

She tried. She thought she could go back to work on Monday and return here next weekend—after all, it was only a five-hour trip. They could spend a couple of days laughing, touching, loving beneath the broiling sun again, then they could do it all over the following weekend and the one after that.

Until he finished his work in the canyon. Until he moved on to continue his quest for She Who Waits.

Sooner or later it would have to end, Shadow realized. She knew it was best for both of them if it happened now—like a Band-Aid being yanked off suddenly instead of by small, painful degrees. He would move on and she would find other broken doves, ones she could truly save. And there would be memories.

Mac Tshongely was who he was, and it could not end any other way than that. She doubted if she would have been drawn to him in quite the same way if he had not been broken, wary, if each of his kindnesses had not been so rare and pure.

She rolled back the other way, trying to sleep a little more until dawn came.

Mac knew the instant she rolled back over, but he cracked one eye to make sure. He fought the ragged sigh in his throat, fought against altering his breathing, against doing anything that might let her know that he was awake.

He didn't want to talk anymore. He'd had enough of moonlight confessions. He couldn't give her anymore. Still, questions tormented him.

He realized that he didn't even know her last name. Where would she go when she left here? Back to what kind of life? He had a strong instinct that she'd be surrounded by family—steady, stalwart people who bolstered her. She'd tried to leave them before, and had ended up running from the man who'd taken her from them.

There was no future for them. He couldn't give her a home. He didn't have one, didn't want one, but she was the kind of woman who needed just that. She had said as much. If she tried to follow him from dig to dig, she would end up leaving him as well, lonesome and aching for all those anchors she had left behind.

He could ask her to come back next weekend, but he wouldn't because he couldn't bear that ultimate ending. Better, he thought, that they just have this time in the sun. The shock of its abrupt ending would shake them both for a while, but then they would go on.

He would go back to a past that endured.

She would go home to a family that loved her, something he didn't trust, couldn't even begin to comprehend, even now that he had found his way into her warmth. After all, he had known from the first that warmth was transient.

He forced his eyes closed, wondering if he would be able to sleep again until dawn.

By the time Shadow woke fully, Mac was already digging again. She heard the sibilant sound of his brush moving against sand and rock and she looked up at the new site in the cliff dwellings. He was already in there, and her skin crawled. He was in the rear of one of the center rooms. *All that lingering evil.* She stood up shakily.

The coffeepot was sitting on top of his flickering, dying fire. Normally she would have taken him a fresh cup. She couldn't bring herself to do it under these circumstances. She couldn't go up there.

She wondered suddenly if he had counted on that.

She thought of a bath and vetoed that idea, too. She didn't want to go back to the waterfall alone.

She gave a choked, hoarse laugh. All things considered, it was better if she left today instead of dragging it out.

She went to his fire and poured herself a cup of coffee, then she carried it back to her sleeping bag and settled down there with her notebook. She flipped through all the pages filled with her notes about what he had taken out of the first dig. Her mouth twisted wryly.

Well, it was about time she admitted that it had just been an excuse. She had been running from Cat and Jericho's baby, from her own lost sense of self. And she had tumbled straight into the arms of a jaded man who vastly preferred to be alone.

She put the notebook down again with a slap. If Mac heard it, he didn't look down from the new dig. She shot a surreptitious glance at him, but he kept working. She started to roll up her sleeping bag and realized her hands were shaking.

Think about practicalities. She would have a hard time getting everything back down the mountain again. Her tent was gone—and with it her backpack frame and the nylon sack itself. But for the first time in her memory she couldn't think how to adjust to the circumstances. Something was choking her breath off, and with it the blood to her brain. Something was burning at her eyes, blurring her vision. It wasn't tears. She never cried. She gave a wretched curse and settled back on her haunches, rubbing them.

That was when she heard Mac give a strange, strangled sound.

She looked up but didn't see him. Her heart plummeted. For one breathtaking moment she had thought that maybe he had seen what she was doing and would try to stop her. But he wasn't watching her because she couldn't even see him.

His voice came again, too quiet, too strained and tense. He was saying something, but she couldn't quite make out his words. She stood again, scowling, her eyes searching over the cliff dwellings.

She saw a spot of blue in the apartment farthest to the right—undoubtedly his clothing. But if it was Mac, he was standing very, very still.

"What?" she called up to him. "What's wrong?" *Chindis,* she thought again, but she remembered that he didn't believe in them before her knees could go weak.

"My gun," he answered quietly. She had to strain to hear. "Snake load. In the chest."

Snake load? They were small, flat-tipped bullets loaded with tiny pellets that would spray upon contact to take out a skinny, sliding enemy. So there was a rattler up there. Her heart steadied. She could handle that.

Except she was going to have to go in there to take the gun to him. She swallowed dryly.

"Hurry," he ordered with more force.

She couldn't think about *chindis* now. With sheer force of will, she pushed them from her mind. He had left the gun near his sleeping bag and she grabbed it as she jogged to the place where his tent had been. She found the bullets in his chest and exchanged them for the real ones, ramming them home. Then she ran back to the opposite cliff wall.

She shoved the gun into her waistband and climbed up. When she reached the first apartment where he had been working, she fought the urge to hug herself against a chill that was surely all in her mind. She began making her way carefully to the right, to the place he was now, then she froze.

Not a snake. *A lot* of snakes. "Oh, my God," she breathed, her blood draining.

Her voice was almost lost beneath the *chhhhhhh* of all their tails. There was a huge, shifting knot of them, heads gliding gracefully up, tongues flicking for a moment before they sank again into the morass. Shadow fought the urge to scream.

She was not afraid of snakes. But this . . . this was too much.

"Shoot," Mac said quietly.

"I . . . I can't."

It was impossible, she thought wildly, and surely he knew it. If she shot from where she stood now, the snake load would spray into his flesh as well. If she moved to aim around him, the snakes would sense her motion and strike him. *Why were there so many of them?*

He would probably survive one bite, she thought. He might even survive two, if she could get him to one of their trucks without moving him too much. But there were easily twenty-five rattlers in there, in an oval depression against the far wall that might once have been a shrine.

A thin cry came from her throat, one of such horror it made him stiffen. He waited helplessly for her to get a grip on herself, knowing she would, sooner or later, knowing she was that kind of woman. But later might not count. Later he might already be dead.

Believe, Shadow thought. All she could do was believe. It was the only thing that might save him. In the end it was the only thing she could truly give him. Life, so that he could move on. Breath, so that he could drink in a solitary sunrise even one more time. If she didn't do something, she doubted if he would ever walk out of this canyon.

She sank slowly down to her haunches, closing her eyes. *Remember.* It had been so long since she had thought of the chant she needed now, an ageless one taught to her by her uncle and brother. Oh, sweet Holy People, how did it go?

Suddenly it filled her mind, seeping into her the way light filled the sky at dawn. She stood again carefully, and in that moment there was not a doubt in her mind that the Holy Ones had heard her, had felt her desperation, were with her, by her side.

Mac sensed her movement and his breath caught. *What the hell was she doing?*

She came up beside him, then moved past him, closer and closer to the nest—but not a nest, he thought in some still rational, functional part of his mind. He was torn between that sudden realization and the urge to grab her back. The need to protect her was suddenly a violent, clawing animal within him, and if he died in doing so, then he died. But something about her stopped him.

Her face. It was so... serene. Her eyes seemed unseeing.

His hands clenched at his sides but stayed there. Somehow he knew that if he moved now, if he shattered her concentration, he would destroy both of them.

She was murmuring something softly, some spell.

"I cast over you the magic formula to make an enemy peaceful. Put your feet down with pollen. Put your hands down with pollen. Put your heads down with pollen. Then your feet are pollen, your hands are pollen, your bodies are pollen. Your mind is pollen, your voice is pollen. The trail is beautiful. Be still. You are at peace."

Gradually, the rattling stopped. Mac stared disbelievingly.

"Go," she murmured. "Find warm rocks to sun yourselves. It is cold here. There is death here. Go away."

She moved again so that her toes were no more than inches from them. A sharp pain screamed behind Mac's eyes, trying to make him shout in protest, but they didn't strike her.

One slid up the wall of the niche, going higher. Another wound its way over the side of the cliff dwelling, heading for the canyon floor. "There is nothing good here," Shadow whispered. A few more split off. Mac felt his heart shift in alarm as one wove its way between his planted feet, but it passed by him without biting.

"I am your friend. I tell you the truth." She moved into them even farther. His eyes bugged as they brushed past her ankles, moving on.

"Goodbye."

They were all leaving now, slithering, bright, beady eyes darting about as they sought some other place to rest. Shadow closed her own eyes, relief making her weak. She sagged against the back of the alcove, adrenaline rushing out of her too fast.

"It's okay now," she began, but then her voice choked off in a scream.

At first he didn't understand. He thought one had bitten her after all. But they were all past them now, and he heard the sharp, grating sound of moving rock. She brought one hand up, grasping blindly at the air, and then she was gone.

Gone?

Mac lunged forward but it was too late. Her scream faded as she fell. Where the back of the alcove had been, there was nothing now but a black, gaping hole.

He roared her name and dropped down beside it, feeling disassociated and dazed. In the next moment, his brain cleared into sharp, cutting clarity. There would be time later to think about what she had just done. Now the pieces of what had happened afterward came clicking together in his mind.

No, the snakes hadn't been nesting. There were too many of them. They had been planted here, like deadly watchdogs. Rage streamed hotly into his blood. They had been meant for him, but she had gotten past them and God only knew what had happened to her now.

"Shadow!" he bellowed again.

He heard her cough and the relief he knew in that moment was like no other emotion he had ever encountered in his life.

"I guess . . . I fell again," she mumbled.

Mac closed his eyes. For an incredible moment they felt hot, and he had the most bizarre urge to laugh. He looked down into the hole again instead.

"Are you hurt this time?" he asked roughly.

There was a long hesitation. "Nothing's broken."

Then Shadow put a tentative hand to the back of her head and it came away sticky. There was a good-size gash there, she realized. She had cracked her head against something when she had fallen through.

She looked around. Blackness pressed in on her, penetrated only by the shadowy light from the hole up above. But her eyes were beginning to adjust to the filmy darkness. She gasped, recoiling, cold terror sliding through her again.

Bones. So many bones.

Mac heard her sharp, indrawn breath. "What is it?"

"I think I've found your midden," she answered thinly.

Her voice was too close to breaking, he realized. What had she found down there?

"I'm coming in."

"No!" Her voice was stronger this time. "You can't. I'm...it's about a ten-foot drop to the floor in here. If you come down, I don't see how either of us will be able to get out." She cleared her throat. "What happened?"

"The back of the niche was just a thin rock, sort of braced upright. When you leaned against it, it slid backward."

"It was covering the hole," she agreed.

"Yeah. Covering something I wasn't supposed to find. What do you see?"

"Just...bodies."

He heard her voice crack again. Given the desperate measure of the snakes, he knew someone had to have hidden a hell of a lot more in there than that.

"Okay," he said. "Just hold on. I'm going to get a flashlight and some rope and I'll be right back. Are you sure you're all right?"

She gave a wild, high-pitched laugh. "Fine...under the circumstances."

She heard a few scratching, thudding sounds as he left. She was alone.

Shadow glanced over her shoulder. There was nothing behind her, just the wall of the . . . cave, or whatever it was. She inched slowly backward, feeling better when her spine touched the cool rock.

Her back was protected now. She shuddered and looked around again. The cave was about twelve feet deep, maybe sixteen feet across. She kept a tenuous control over her panic as she looked at the skeletons.

Not Anasazi, she realized suddenly. They were all sitting up, braced against the far wall, five of them. Some of their hands were bound together in their laps; others had their arms tied behind them. Scraps of decayed cloth showed at their wrist bones and the one directly in front of her had a shattered hole at the front of its skull.

Another scream tried to climb in her throat, but she had no breath to give voice to it. Then it finally escaped, a shriek that tore from her again and again until finally she felt Mac's strong hands on her, *live* hands, gathering her close, pressing her face against his chest so she wouldn't have to look. She clawed her fingers into the shirt he wore, hanging on, gasping.

"Okay, okay, come on," Mac said. "Let's get you out of here."

He pulled her to her feet, guiding her back to the rope he had left dangling from the hole over their heads. She groped for it blindly and tried to pull herself up.

It gave in her hands. She fell again and it came with her, puddling in her lap. There was a grating sound from above them as the rock slid back over the hole. Then they were caught in impenetrable darkness.

Shadow screamed again, a bloodcurdling sound of horror and despair.

Chapter 13

For one stunned moment, Mac was frozen. Then he turned on the flash and a thin beam of light stabbed through the pitch. He aimed it to the side of her, spilling just enough of a glow over her face that he could see her.

She was as white as the skeletons and her eyes were huge and stricken as she stared up at the closed hole. He swore and put the flash down, gathering her close again. Her trembling rocked all the way through him.

He guessed she was probably beyond speech, but he prayed that she would at least hear him. "Listen to me, sweetheart. It's not *chindis,* it's not evil, it's not anything supernatural at all. Sure, there are bodies in here, but they're long past hurting anybody. It's just the guy who's been trying to scare us out of here. We found something he didn't want us to find. That's all."

She didn't answer.

"We can fight something human. We can outwit him."

Nothing.

"I'm going to have to turn the light off again, but I'm right here. Okay?"

He finally felt her nod. He reached down and switched off the flash. "We're going to have to be able to see if we're going to find a way out of here," he went on, "so I don't want to run the batteries down."

He stared at the opposite wall again, though he couldn't really see it now in the dark. Still, the sight was indelibly imprinted on his mind. Five bodies, he thought. Five relatively new bodies. He doubted if any of them was more than a few years old. So much for the legend, he thought, fighting a laugh that would surely come out crazed. He had been right. The stories had gotten started somewhere along the line, then someone had decided to breathe a little extra life into them. But that someone hadn't been playing pranks. He had been protecting a secret. Five people had found it, and five people had died for it.

It wouldn't be seven.

He had to get her talking, had to bring her back to him. She was going to have to work with him on this. He knew she would—she always did—if only she would come out of her terror, deeper this time than it had been yet.

"What did you do up there?" he asked softly.

She shook her head as if she didn't understand his question.

"With the snakes," he clarified.

"Oh." It came out as a breathy little sigh. But then she finally spoke, and he closed his eyes in relief. "I believed."

"*Believed?* In what?"

"In the Holy People. They help anyone who seeks their assistance, if they trust in them enough. I didn't actually talk to the snakes. They did."

It shook him deeply. He had seen it with his own eyes, but he had never believed, had never trusted in *anything* so profoundly that he would walk into a writhing knot of deadly rattlers. That she could, that she had done so, left him awed. Over and over she showed him things, gave him things, that he would have sworn hadn't existed in this cruel, uncompromising world.

Because he couldn't deal with that right now, he changed the subject. "Can you stand?" he asked quietly.

He felt her nod again. "Good. I need you to help me. Two heads are better than one."

She finally loosened her death grip around his waist. "My head hurts," she murmured. "I think I knocked it coming down."

He ran his hands through her hair, over her scalp, and felt the blood. *Too much of it.* His heart staggered. They didn't have a lot of time.

"There's got to be another room," he muttered, helping her to her feet.

"Why?"

"Because I can't see the sense in killing people to protect a few skeletons. I can't see someone wrestling with a bunch of snakes to keep me from stumbling on what we see in this room."

"He's out there," she breathed suddenly, as if understanding had just dawned on her. He figured it probably had.

"No," he answered. "He's gone by now. He thinks we're history."

"He's sealed us in, Mac! He untied your rope and trapped us in here! There *can't* be another way out. He would know about it if there was. He's either waiting for us at another entrance or he knows we're going to die in here!"

Her voice was escalating. *Touch her. Keep touching her,* he thought, stroking his hands up and down her arms, her back, holding her close. Maybe he needed the contact—that sense of life—as much as she did, he thought. What she'd just said made a lot of sense.

But damn it, there *had* to be more than bones!

"Come on," he said.

"Where?" she demanded wildly.

"Think, Sergeant. Use that practical brain of yours. If you were a way out of here, where would you be?"

She clutched him close, shivering, refusing to look at the skeletons. But she thought about it because it beat anything else that came to mind—the terror of being trapped in here with so very many *chindis,* the horror of knowing that she was going to die. Something reared up in her at that, something furious. She wasn't ready yet. Oh, God, she wanted babies and Diamond Eddie's job, she wanted Mac! She wanted to share every lonely sunrise with him for the rest of her life! If only they could get out of here, she knew she could leave the Res for this man because he *was* enough to sustain her, because he was beauty and fire, because he made her think and made her laugh.

"Well?" he persisted.

"I'm working on it." Then she knew. "The wall!" she gasped.

"Which one?"

"Behind us. Where I was sitting when you came down. Why didn't he put the bodies there?"

Mac whistled softly. "Because that moves, too."

"Maybe." Or maybe he had just chosen the other one by chance.

But she didn't want to consider that until she was faced with irrefutable proof. Mac switched the light on again. She pressed close to his side and they moved to the wall.

"We could check it a whole lot faster if we separated," he pointed out.

"No," she answered quickly. "No way."

He found he was just as glad for her refusal. He slid an arm around her waist, pinning her against his side, smelling that faint lavender scent of her hair again. "Okay," he said. "Let's start at the top."

It quickly became apparent that he could reach a lot higher than she could. He skimmed his hands along the ceiling while she pressed against the lower half of the wall.

Nothing happened.

"What are we looking for?" she muttered. "I don't even know what I expect to find."

"Something that gives the way the rock up top did. Push harder."

"What if we die in here?" The words scraped from her throat. But for some reason, she had to say them. Maybe it was just to wrangle an assurance from him that it wasn't going to happen. Or maybe it was because if she spoke the possibility, it was made real. It forced her to face it, to come up with a way to deal with it.

Mac didn't give her assurances. He was quiet for a moment, considering it, then he looked for the goodness she had somehow taught him to find.

"Then I'm going to go out buried inside you," he answered, and she wanted to cry. "It would almost make it worth it."

"Oh, God, Mac, I need that now."

"You'll have it, sweetheart. Just hang in there a little longer and it'll happen in the sunlight. It'll be a celebration of life."

"But—" She broke off at the scraping sound of more rock. For a wild moment, she thought their tormentor was coming back. The sound came from above her. She threw a terrified glance back in the direction of the hole through which she'd fallen but there was still only blackness there. Then she felt a rush of damp, cool air on her neck and she whipped around the other way again.

"You found it!"

"I found something." Mac pushed with all his weight at the upper half of the wall, leaning his body into it. It groaned and slid back, revealing another room.

"Good thinking, Sergeant."

"Don't call me—*oh!*"

They had climbed over the bottom slab of rock. It took her a moment to realize what she was seeing when he moved the flash around inside. At first she thought it was diamonds...millions upon millions of diamonds glimmering in the sharp beam from the flash. Then disappointment rushed at her so fast she felt faint. She looked at his face. It was grim as the dream of years slid through his fingers like sand.

They weren't diamonds. They were pots, easily a hundred of them, all covered with an ice blue glazing. For the most part, they were precious and whole, neatly situated at one end beside the small, fragile skeleton of what had once been a woman. But someone had stumbled into one end of the pile. A few of the vessels there were cracked and broken—shattered.

Finally, too late, Shadow realized where the piece on the trail had come from.

Mac moved to the skeleton and Shadow went with him, close by his side. "She Who Waits," he said, a strange, dull tone to his voice. "It's got to be."

Shadow's breath snagged. Nestled at the skeleton's breast was another tiny bundle of bones. *A baby.*

"He...Kokopelli...came back to her. He gave her a child." She had no way of knowing that. For all she knew, the baby had been another man's. Perhaps Kokopelli had never really existed at all. But she felt Mac's arm tighten around her and she knew that he wanted to believe it, too.

"And then she died," he said quietly.

"Oh, Mac, I'm so sorry." Her pots wouldn't lead him to the place where the Anasazi had vanished to. They had found the end of her trail.

He let her go to kneel beside the bones. "I'll be damned," he murmured suddenly.

"What?"

He motioned her closer. She knelt beside him. There, next to the skeleton's right shoulder, partially concealed beneath her collarbone, was a flute. Shadow felt a shiver race up her spine.

"You were right," she breathed. "Your whole premise was right. She was Kokopelli's woman." She knew it wouldn't be proof enough for the archaeologists, but the flute's implications satisfied her. Mac, too, she realized. He couldn't publish his findings here, but after a moment he nodded.

"There'll be another way to learn where the Anasazi went to, and someday somebody'll find it. I think I'd almost rather know that this woman got everything she wanted and died happy."

Shadow smiled. It was a tremulous reflex at first, but then it grew because she knew the kind of man he was beneath his hard, rocky surface. And that man really would rather think that She Who Waits had died happy, rather than fleeing from some enemy so much stronger, so much more formidable than her own people.

"So," she said on a shaky breath, straightening again. Odd, but she felt no real threat here so close to this particular skeleton. It was almost as if her lingering spirit was pure benevolence, at least as far as Shadow was concerned.

She looked around, and then she gasped again. On the other side of the room there was another treasure trove.

"Mac," she breathed. "Look. Look over there."

He stood again and turned about.

"I don't think our villain was protecting She Who Waits," she murmured.

Mac went to the other pile. His heart jumped. It was, he realized, enough to kill for. It was enough to wrestle a bag of deadly snakes for. It was a lifetime income to be removed from here piece by invaluable piece, judiciously filtered into the general population, slowly enough that no one would be suspicious, steadily enough that a man would be rich for all the rest of his days.

Anasazi pots. Ancient artifacts, tools and whole scraps of leather, a history of a civilization in one sprawling pile.

"But why not She Who Waits's stuff?" he wondered aloud.

"He must be Navajo," she said flatly, moving up close to him again. "No way would anyone who believes in *chindis* touch her or any of her pots, not on purpose. She's still whole. That's worse—" She paused to rub her temples, trying to explain. "That's much worse than isolated bones, a rib here, a skull there. Her whole skeleton is *together*. A *chindi* would be more likely to come back to that than to just a piece of itself."

"And he doesn't need her pots," Mac mused.

"No." The thief hadn't been carting She Who Waits's pots out of here—he had been removing items from his own stash. The shard on the trail must have gotten lodged in the sole of his shoe when he stumbled into her treasures, working out later as he climbed.

The fact that she felt no relief told her how long it had been since she had really suspected Mac.

"This stuff isn't from this canyon," he said suddenly. "I didn't find enough signs of trespass for a dig this big. He must have gathered it from a lot of different illegal sites, then brought it all here to sell as he needed to. The legend would have made Kokopelli's Canyon a perfect place for his stash. Hardly anyone ever comes in here."

"We did," she said tightly. She started looking around again wildly, her fear coming back.

"Give him credit. He tried to scare us off first."

Mac started looking around, too. There was definitely a damp draft in here, he thought. It had to be coming from somewhere. He started moving, following his nose. The air was coming from behind She Who Waits, yet her head was almost touching the wall.

"Good news, sweetheart. I don't think our thief knew there's another way out of here."

Shadow looked at him sharply. "Why? What did you find?"

"Assuming you're right about him being Navajo and not wanting anything to do with our girl's bones, he wouldn't have come close enough to her to find this."

He stepped carefully to the side of her head opposite the pots. Then he pointed up. Shadow followed his gaze and her heart leapt. There was a thin crack at the top of the cave wall.

Sunlight. Just a glimmer, but it was the sweetest thing she had ever seen in her life.

"Thank you, Holy Ones," she whispered.

He had noticed that she reverted back to her heritage when she was most stressed, so he reached behind him and grabbed her hand to steady her.

"Don't thank them quite yet," he cautioned. "There's air. We won't die as long as we stay in here, at least not from suffocation. But it's going to take a lot of hard work to widen it enough for you to get through."

"Me?"

"There's less of you. You'd make it before I would. You can go for help."

Unless the thief is out there. Then she would surely be killed, and Mac would die in here waiting for her to return.

"There's got to be a way we can both go," she said stubbornly. "Lift me up on your shoulders. Maybe the ceiling moves. So far we've found two slabs that have. The Anasazi obviously used these rooms for something—She Who Waits is here. They probably had a lot of hidden ways to get in and out."

"I like the way you think, Sergeant."

"Don't call me—" She broke off again, this time with a little gasp as he lifted her effortlessly over his head. For one breath-robbing moment, she remembered the way he had carried her to the waterfall yesterday, then she pushed the memory grimly out of her mind.

There would be time to remember later. There would be nothing *but* time in which to remember. Now that it appeared they might get out of here alive, all her desperate determination grew shaky again. They weren't going to die, and there was no way to follow him for the rest of her life.

He wouldn't let her.

Her head spun badly as she scissored her legs, helping him to settle her on his shoulders. "Can you get me any closer?" she asked tightly.

He inched them nearer to the fissure. She braced her shoulder against the ceiling and shoved.

There was a shrieking, grinding sound, but no appreciable difference in the size of the crack. "Try putting pressure the other way," he suggested. "You might be pushing it closed."

He moved around, allowing her to try. Shadow gritted her teeth and braced her shoulder against the rock again.

"Ah!" It slid, slowly at first, then more and more as she leaned steadily into it. "Yes!"

"Good. Okay, now come on down from there. I'm going out first, just in case."

So he wondered if their tormentor would be out there, too. It frightened her, but then she felt his hard hands capture her waist. He eased her slowly to her feet again, too slowly. Her body slid down his until her heart pounded painfully.

She closed her eyes, shaken by her immediate response. She had gloried in his touch, in his body, for days now, yet she still hadn't gotten used to it. Still he could make something heat inside her with a simple, unintentional caress. *How am I ever going to live without him?*

She shuddered, then her eyes flew open again as she felt the brush of his mouth over her own.

"Hey, sweetheart, I told you there would be one more time in the sunshine. And I never break my promises."

He always seemed to know what she was thinking. She managed a thin smile.

He moved away from her, looking around the chamber. He found a boulder too heavy even for him to lift, but he managed to work it away from the wall, into the middle of the room.

"Look away," he said tersely.

"Why?"

"Because I've got to do something I don't want to do."

Suddenly she understood. "Wait!"

She looked around wildly for something to wrap the child in. There was nothing. Finally she yanked her T-shirt over her head. Mac made a hoarse sound in his throat as though she had punched him. She looked to find him staring at her bare breasts, then slowly he moved his eyes up to hers.

The pain she saw there took her breath. She knew then that he would go away, but he would ache for her sometimes when the night was at its darkest. He would ache for what they'd shared.

She dragged her gaze away first. "I know it's the only way for us to get out of here," she acknowledged, "but not her baby, Mac. The baby doesn't have to be disturbed, too. It was... it was what made her die happy." *And I owe her this much,* she thought wildly. She couldn't have said why, but she felt some sort of kindred link with the long-dead woman.

Maybe because she would wait, too. She had been right. She would be more like Kokopelli's mate than like the barren, sex-starved maidens he had serviced.

She swallowed carefully and knelt to try to ease the fabric beneath the smaller skeleton. Suddenly Mac was beside her.

"I'll do it."

"No."

"What about its *chindi?*"

"Newborns don't have them either. Life isn't born evil. And I don't think this baby was very old. She might have died having it. I...I have to do this," she insisted. Her throat tightened hard.

Mac watched her chin jut stubbornly. He eased away from her, not understanding, yet afraid that he did.

"Shadow..."

"I've got it," she said tightly. She had the T-shirt half under the tiny skeleton and was sliding it the last little way, beneath its legs. Very gently she lifted it from its mother's breast. When he glanced at Shadow's face again, he saw that her eyes were shining too brightly.

A rush of pain nearly staggered him. She had never cried, not even when he had been trying to hurt her. Yet the skeleton of a long-dead child moved her past control.

He tried to remember all of the reasons he had come up with the night before for letting her go, and she didn't allow him time to consider any of them.

"Go ahead. Do the rest," she said hollowly.

Mac looked grimly at She Who Waits. Somehow, he thought she might understand this travesty. At least he prayed to God that she would.

He noticed that Shadow kept her back turned, unable to watch. He moved the boulder through the skeleton, disturbing it as little as possible.

"I'm sorry," he said gutturally.

Shadow flinched and whipped around, but she knew without looking that he wasn't talking to her and she was right.

She wondered how she had ever thought him to be cold.

He finally got the boulder to where he wanted it. He stepped up on it. It gave him just enough height and leverage to work himself through the narrow hole. Shadow laid the baby gently on the skeleton's chest again and stepped on the rock as well, reaching her hands up to him.

He grabbed her wrists and pulled her. Then she breathed in clean, sweet air and sunlight. They saw not another human soul.

She looked around dazedly. They were back in the initial room Mac had been digging in, the one she had first climbed into with his gun. It seemed a lifetime ago now, and she wasn't sure at exactly what point she'd lost the weapon.

"How's your head?" he asked quietly.

She put her hand to the gash. There was a good-size egg there now, but the bleeding had stopped. "I'll live. I don't think I'll need stitches."

"You're sure?"

She looked at him curiously. A hard, urgent tone had crept into his voice again.

"Relatively," she answered. "Why?"

"Because I figure I can do one of two things now. I can take you to the nearest doctor, or I can keep my promise."

Something hot and liquid pooled at the deepest center of her. "Keep your promise," she suggested.

"Yeah," he said, pulling her to her feet again. "Let's celebrate. It's pretty damned good to be alive."

Chapter 14

Shadow thought they'd move down out of the cliff dwelling. She thought they'd go back to the canyon floor where she could touch him, love him, fill him with herself yet again. And she knew before she drew even a single breath that it wasn't going to be like that, not this time.

He lifted her off her feet right where they stood, bringing her breasts level with his mouth. He licked the tip of first one, then the other, drawing each in, biting gently. Heat burst through her and she clutched at his shoulders.

He drew his mouth away immediately, leaving her empty and wanting.

"Put your hands down," he said roughly.

Confused, she let them slide off his shoulders. But then, finally, his mouth came back and she couldn't think anymore. She gave a broken sigh as he drew her nipple in between his teeth again. Now the heat rushed there, making it so excruciatingly sensitive. She thought she would die if he didn't stop, knew she would die if he did. She drove her hands into his hair.

He pulled away again. "Hands down."

"W-why?" she asked.

"Not this time, sweetheart. This last time we're going to do it my way."

This last time. But she had known that—of course she had known that that was what this was. Tears burned at her eyes; she could feel them trembling on her lashes. But there was at least some small part of her that couldn't cry at something so beautiful. She ached at losing it, and knew she couldn't tarnish this last memory with despair. So she accepted with greedy need, with sweet satisfaction.

He let her slide down his body again until she was molded against him. He pulled the band from her hair and buried his face at her neck, beneath it. His hands were at her breasts now, kneading them, cupping them, claiming them for his own . . . although she knew he'd never do that.

She couldn't stand it. She wrapped her arms around his neck.

"You don't listen, do you?" He disengaged her grip, not quite gently, not quite roughly. "I'm going to take care of you this time, Sergeant. I'm going to pour myself over you without taking anything back for myself. I'm going to make you lose all that control. So keep your hands to yourself."

He wondered if he had ever heard anything sweeter than her low, hitching moan. But he knew suddenly that this was the one thing, the only thing that he could give back to her. She had shown him light and warmth and pleasure. He would make her finally know the release of full surrender. By her own admission, it was something no other man had ever given her. It was something nearly impossible for her to take. He understood that now. But she would take it from him. He would see to it.

He found the button on her shorts and slid the zipper down, but then he stepped back from her again. "Take them off."

She looked at him a little wildly. What was he doing to her?

"Go on," he urged.

She pushed them down over her hips, her eyes searching his. He saw something frantic start to grow there. It wouldn't be easy for her, but in the end she would know it for the gift it was, something wild and vibrant that would stand out in her memory long after the image of those other times between them had faded.

At least he prayed to God that was what would happen. Because those other times were going to stand out in his.

"Panties too," he said roughly, stepping back even more when she would have reached for him. "Boots and socks."

She sat down hesitantly and struggled out of her footgear. Then, finally, he touched her again, but it was only to grasp her hand and pull her back to her feet. He caught his thumbs in the top elastic of her panties and slid them down to her ankles.

She stepped out of them numbly, wonderingly, and hugged herself. They had splashed naked in the waterfall, and groped and touched each other in various stages of undress. Yet this was different. It was the way he just stood there, watching her. It was the way he was still fully clothed. She felt too vulnerable... exposed. As if she were riding a horse and had suddenly lost the reins. As if she were at the mercy of the beast. Her heart raced crazily. The sun was so hot on her bare skin, and his eyes burned her even more as they coasted over her. She felt self-conscious and aroused, embarrassed and hungry for more.

"No," he said quietly. "Not like that."

"Like... what?"

He pried her hands loose from her shoulders, making her drop them to her sides again. Without her arms to shield them, the kiss of the faint breeze made her nipples tighten again, just as they had when they had been in his mouth. Without even touching her, he made her almost unbearably aware of her own body, of each and every inch of her flesh. She felt her bare skin begin to tingle.

"Okay," he said finally. "That's better."

He closed the distance between them again, his hard hands capturing her hips. Then his palms slid upward, into the warm valley between her breasts. He spread his hands wide, capturing them again, lifting them for his mouth. Shadow groaned.

"Yes, please, touch me."

"I intend to, sweetheart. Just stand still."

When she felt the warm wetness of his tongue and his lips on her again, her knees went weak. She understood that he didn't want her to touch him this time, but she had no choice. She had to brace herself against him, and found herself holding his head against her out of some primitive, aching need instead.

He allowed that for a moment, then he slid lower. His rough hands traced her spine, molded her hips, her bottom, her thighs. Then they came up again inside her legs.

"Open to me, sweetheart. Come on. Let it go."

She had no real memory of doing so. Every thought that she had was centered on the feeling of his mouth on her belly, on the rough, velvety texture of his tongue at her navel. But somehow she shifted her feet, opening her legs to him. His fingers tangled into her triangle of midnight hair, sliding, searching, and all of her thoughts shattered.

He would memorize her, he thought. He would remember all of her, always. When the nights got cold, he would pull each recollection out like a cherished snapshot. Then he could get by.

He traced her layers with his fingertips, pushing them inside her until he knew her better than she knew herself. Then, slowly, he withdrew his hand again.

"Come back," she whispered brokenly, suddenly feeling too empty, too hollow without his touch. She thought she heard him chuckle hoarsely.

But finally he did as she asked, and suddenly her world was nothing but his tender penetrations and sliding withdrawals again. Back and forth...in and out. Her legs started trembling. She had no control over them any longer.

She was losing control over everything.

She felt herself sinking, and he let her, easing her gently down onto the rocky floor of the dwelling. But his hand stayed with her, finding the hidden nub at the center of her, coaxing, teasing, until the heat within her burst like a thundercloud, pouring warm rain through her.

It surprised her, left her weak and dazed, but he didn't stop. Even before she recovered she felt his mouth follow his hands. He spread her legs farther and she felt his warm breath as exquisitely as a touch. She couldn't take anymore, yet she needed more. She couldn't bear anymore, but she would die without it.

His tongue probed and sought as his fingers had done. She started clawing for his shoulders, but once again he pulled back, coming up over her, trapping her wrists against the rock above her head. He used his free hand to wrestle out of his shorts, and then he drove himself into her.

He had not meant to take anything for himself, but he knew suddenly that it couldn't end like that. It should end as it had begun, with them together, joined, sharing with sweet simplicity.

Sensation exploded inside Shadow all over again, drenching her, until she cried out. He finally let go of her hands to lift her hips, sliding into her deeper, then deeper still, again and again until he felt her unraveling one more time. Still he stayed with her, rocking, moving within her, until his own control was gone, until there was only a small desperate memory of what he had been trying to achieve when he had started this.

Shadow felt him stiffen above her. His voice ripped from him with a guttural groan. He buried himself within her with one last, final thrust, then he lowered his face to her neck again.

He said something and she turned her face toward him, into his own neck. "Hmm?"

She didn't understand, but then she thought she did. She thought he said, "Remember me."

By the time they got back down to their campsites, Shadow found she couldn't talk. Her throat was a solid knot of pain.

She would *not* cry.

She walked ahead of him to her sleeping bag. It was rumpled and bunched from when she had tried to roll it up far too long ago.

"How are you going to get your stuff back down the mountain?" he asked from behind her. His own voice sounded coarse, strangled.

Shadow shrugged woodenly.

Where there was a will, there was a way, she thought. Then a wild laugh nearly made it past the knot in her throat. Not always, she thought, not always. She flattened the sleeping bag again, throwing her possessions on top of it. She discarded a few pieces that were too bulky to be rolled over. Maybe someday she would come back for them.

Probably not.

She tied the sleeping bag with fumbling fingers, her gear wadded inside, then she finally stood to face him again.

"You don't have to rush out of here like a cat with its tail on fire," he snapped.

"Yes," she rasped. "I do."

It was time now. It simply *felt* as though it was time to go. Her instincts had been right—something had been wrong in this canyon, although it had nothing to do with Mac. They had found it and now her mission—and all that it had encompassed—was over. He had been saying good-bye up in that cliff dwelling, and they both knew it.

Besides, they couldn't stay here now and she was sure he was aware of that as well. Sooner or later whoever had trapped them in the cave would come back. He would expect to find seven bodies inside. When there were still only five, he would be angry and frantic. When he realized what room they had escaped from, he would know they knew his secret. It would be best if they were both as far away as possible when it happened, and there was no way they would be going anywhere together.

She finally got her voice back. "I'll stop... at the Shiprock police subagency on my way home. They've got to be notified now."

Mac nodded. She noticed that he wouldn't quite look at her.

"Where will you go?" she asked, not really wanting to know. She thought if he said the Yucatán, she would probably die.

"I'm thinking about driving down the Baja," he answered, and she breathed again. "I'll roast on the beach for a while and decide what to do next. It might be worth it to go back to all the old sites and try to restructure the life of She Who Waits more completely. I haven't decided yet." He hesitated, then finally glanced her way. "You should see a doctor about that lump on your head."

"I'm going to."

She thought about the baby's bones and closed her eyes. Suddenly she was very, very eager to hold Cat and Jericho's child.

"I just don't know if she'll be in any condition to mend my wounds," she went on with a tight smile. And there would be so many wounds that no one could ever mend, she thought.

She realized that Mac didn't understand. "My sister-in-law is a resident with the Indian Health Service. But she's taken a leave of absence to have a baby. It probably came while I was here.''

Family, he thought. He had been right. She had that, and their numbers were apparently growing. He felt a rare sensation in the pit of his stomach. Envy? He clamped down on it, reaching for the few items she hadn't managed to stuff into her sleeping bag.

"I'll carry the rest of this for you."

"No."

His eyes snapped back at the intensity in her voice.

"No," she repeated more softly. "Just . . . don't. I want to remember you here."

She grabbed the sleeping bag and clutched it against her breasts like a shield, he thought, as if to ward off any more hurt he might give her. He thought he had known pain before, but this was new, a vile, suffocating thing that filled his entire chest.

Stop her.

But there was no way he could. She had family waiting out there for her somewhere, and there was nothing on God's green earth that he could give her to replace that. He'd never considered himself long on virtue, but he found he couldn't do it to her, couldn't ask it of her, just so that he could selfishly fill himself with her warmth a little longer.

He finally moved away from her. "See you," he said shortly.

She took a single step past him. "Yeah."

Finally, he heard her footsteps receding. He jerked around as though some mighty hand had him like a puppet on strings and was pulling him that way.

"Take one of my backpacks," he said suddenly. "Then you can get everything down and it'll be more comfortable."

She kept walking.

Turn around, damn it. Answer me.

She answered, but she did it without looking. She did it with the easy, practical simplicity that had both infuriated him and drawn him to her from the first.

"I can't do that. There's no way I can return it to you."

"So keep it, for God's sake."

"I'd rather not."

And that was that, he thought. She had reached the opposite cliff wall. He turned away again because he found he couldn't stand to watch her go. Then he had to look back because he was worried that she might fall for what—the fourth time?

She didn't fall. She reached the top and looked down at him. He couldn't quite hear her, but he thought he could read her lips.

"Be happy, Mac. Try."

Then, finally, she was gone.

The trek down the mountain seemed inordinately long. Shadow made it blindly, stumbling too often, stopping too often to rub angrily at her eyes. She had known what she was getting into from the first time she had touched him. She wouldn't tolerate self-pity now.

And she had a lot to be grateful for—such a glorious week in the sun. In six short days, she had known more passion than many women ever experienced in a lifetime. It was, she thought, a grand way to see in your thirtieth year, and they were memories she would cherish forever.

She told herself that, but she only felt the loss.

Her truck was where she had left it a lifetime ago, looking just the same, though that somehow seemed impossible because she felt as if she had been changed deeply. The storm that had stolen her tent had left some debris on its hood. She stalled a long time, wiping the stuff away before she got into the cab.

Come after me.

She leaned forward to peer up through the windshield at the mountain trail, but it was empty. She gave a ragged sigh and tucked her hair behind her ears, starting the engine. She jerked hard on the wheel and turned her truck around. As she drove eastward again, she considered that the Navajo had no concept of hell.

They should, she decided. She was pretty sure she was heading into it right now. But she wasn't going to burn for eternity.

She was going to be cold and empty for a very long time.

Chapter 15

This time Shadow brought her truck to a full stop at the intersection in Shiprock. Cars began piling up behind her and someone bleated his horn irritably. The sound scraped along her nerve endings after the sweet quiet of Kokopelli's Canyon.

"Oh, *shut up!*" she snapped into the rearview mirror.

She would go straight to Jericho's house, she decided. For once in her life she needed him—needed *everybody*—more than they needed her.

She turned hard and suddenly onto Route 666. The police subagency could wait, she thought, and so could the museum. She would go back to both places when she was strong, steady—when she was in control again. The police would probably still be reluctant to investigate what she and Mac had found anyway.

Oh, they would send a cop out to the canyon all right—and he would be one mighty unhappy camper. But he would battle back his inherent Navajo fear of *chindis* just as she had done, and he would go into the cave to find She

Who Waits, the remains of five other unfortunate people, and a stash of pots and artifacts. He would report back to his supervisors and finally, eventually, some kind of surveillance would be set up to try to nab the thief. Maybe they would catch him, and maybe they wouldn't. But in the meantime her heart felt as if it were bleeding, as if everything good inside her were ebbing more and more, the farther she drove from that canyon.

She certainly had a responsibility to tell them what she and Mac had found. And she would do it. Later. For the first time in her memory she felt no urgency to act expeditiously and responsibly, to tackle the problems of the world. She just wanted to be home.

She turned onto the side trail that led off Route 666 and wound up the side of Beautiful Mountain. Jericho's house was halfway up the slope. She reached it, then simply sat in her truck, the engine idling, staring at the place.

Her brother's carport and the small clearing in front of the house were clogged with vehicles. There was Uncle Ernie's shocking purple Bronco and a rental car that undoubtedly belonged to Catherine's father. Her own father's old Dodge Ram was there, as well as Ellen Lonetree's rust-ravaged Toyota. *That* raised Shadow's brows. If not enemies any longer, then Catherine and Ellen certainly weren't friends. Ellen had once had some pretty healthy grudges against Jericho's wife—for that matter, she had been in love with Jericho herself. Cat's arrival on the Res had forced Ellen into some painful self-discoveries, and Ellen was notoriously slow to relinquish such grudges.

Still, she and Catherine worked well together, with a certain professional distance and mutual respect. Ellen was the nurse at the Shiprock health clinic—she was also clan, which made her closer in some respects than immediate family. Suddenly Shadow understood. Cat must be having the baby *now*. She *hadn't* gotten into Gallup or Albuquerque in time.

Guilt surged inside her that she hadn't been here for such an emergency. Panic welled in her throat that something had gone wrong after all. She pushed fast out of the truck and rushed up the steps to the front door. She knocked once, got no immediate response, and barreled inside.

Six pairs of stunned eyes turned to her. For a long time she only stood there, breathing hard, looking around at them.

"The wind has returned her to us," Uncle Ernie said mildly. "It is as I told you."

Jericho finally closed his mouth. "Where have you been? And what happened to your hair?"

Shadow ran her fingers through it absently. It was loose, spilling down over her shoulders. Only then did she realize that Mac still had her hair band.

She wondered what he would do with it and her throat closed painfully.

"I'm okay. I just...I took a vacation," she asserted. "Catherine?" she asked. "The baby?"

"We're fine, but what about you?" Catherine's soft, quizzical voice came from the doorway of one of the two bedrooms Jericho had added on when they'd gotten married and had realized that Cat was pregnant. Shadow's eyes flew to her.

Her sister-in-law stood cradling the infant in her arms. It—*he,* Shadow realized—was wrapped snugly in a blue receiving blanket. The room started moving oddly, in and out of focus.

The baby was fine, she realized. Catherine was fine. But Jericho's jaw was clenched the way it got when he was suppressing his temper. Her mother stood behind the counter of the kitchenette, wiping her hands on a towel, and her eyes were too shiny. Her father and Uncle Ernie were trying to smoke a pipe near the fireplace—her father was grinning broadly but Ernie's ancient, wrinkled face was bland and knowing. Catherine's father looked from one face to another as if he were trying to decide what he should say or do now.

Ellen sank weakly into a rocking chair near the big bay window. "You're alive. You've never done anything like this before."

And then Shadow understood. They weren't here because of Cat and the baby. They were here because of *her*. Ellen would never say so outright, but as usual, her heart was all over her face. There was amazement there, and consummate relief.

Shadow held her arms out to them and they rushed at her. She would be all right now. For the first time in her memory, she buried her face against the nearest neck and she cried.

Madeline Bedonie finally pulled away and began organizing everyone like a drill sergeant. "Catherine, give me that baby before he gets crushed. Jericho, get her a glass of water. Ernie, put that pipe down *now*. The smoke's not good for the baby. Martin. Where's Martin?" She shot a glance around the room and made a harrumphing sound when she realized that he was already digging in the freezer for food. After forty years of marriage, he had finally learned how to get one step ahead of her.

"Ellen," she said more quietly, "get the dishes."

Ellen shook her head. "I don't think food will fix this."

"Food fixes everything. Paddy? Where's that Irishman?" She whipped around to find him behind her.

Catherine's father took a wary step into the room. It was readily apparent that he wasn't accustomed to having a woman push him around, though he had raised six daughters. "I guess I'll be having that smoke for you, Ernie," he muttered.

"You will not," Madeline snapped. "You'll be going out to the carport with him to bring in that big table."

Shadow watched them all dazedly, then she rubbed a shaky hand over her eyes. "Stop."

No one paid her any mind. Madeline had set them to marching.

"Stop it!" she shouted.

They all froze again to look at her, but her eyes were fast on her mother. *Was she like that?* She heard Mac's voice again. *Sergeant.* She closed her eyes and swallowed carefully. It was the Navajo way. Their women were their matriarchs. But Mac wasn't really Navajo and he wouldn't understand that. He would just have thought that she was bossy and high-handed.

No wonder he had let her go.

"I don't want food," she said. "I want...I need a Blessing Way. I've been exposed to *chindi* bones and...and sadness." She ignored her mother's gasp. "And please, I need to see the baby."

Catherine took him back from Madeline and laid him gently in Shadow's arms. Shadow felt something tremble very deeply inside of her.

He was so small, so perfect, so *alive*. He opened his eyes briefly to peer up at her and they looked green—Catherine's eyes. But his hair was a thin thatch of black—Jericho's. His tiny fingers closed over the edge of the receiving blanket, and his little mouth puckered as if he were considering either crying or eating and couldn't figure which would bring more satisfaction.

"Did you..." She finally looked up at Cat. "I guess you made it into Abuquerque on time."

"Uh, not exactly."

Ellen made a snorting sound. "More like the windmill," she clarified.

Shadow's jaw dropped. "The *windmill*? Lance's windmill? Where he goes to get drunk?"

Catherine shrugged and gave a surreptitious look at the others. "They were driving me crazy," she said in an undertone. "Jericho was watching me like he expected me to change color, Ernie was chanting, and my father jumped out of his skin every time I sneezed. So I took a walk down the mountain to get away from them all."

"And got as far as the windmill before she realized she was in labor," Ellen said. "By then she was too far gone to make her way back *up*. Isn't it great what Anglo medical schools teach you?"

Catherine stiffened. "You can't *teach* a woman what it feels like to be in labor."

They were going to start again, Shadow realized. Ellen had gotten her nursing degree only so she could legally work the clinic. She was much more devoted to Native cures than Anglo methods of healing. It was another point over which she and Cat occasionally clashed—though for the most part they each conceded that there was as much a need for the other's skills as for their own.

Shadow interjected quickly. "Good thing Lance wasn't there, I guess."

Ellen and Catherine looked at each other and the tension between them dissolved. "He was," Cat said. "He took off real fast though when he realized what was happening."

"He came to get me," Ellen explained.

"I'll never understand how he can drive in that condition," Catherine muttered.

"Not much to hit out here," Shadow guessed. She looked at Ellen. "So *you* delivered the baby?"

Ellen looked very self-righteous, but then she gave a small smile. "Fleabane and untying medicine. Works every time."

Shadow looked curiously at Catherine. "Did it work?"

Catherine's face took on a fresh look of amazement. "You know, it really did."

Impossibly, tears burned at Shadow's eyes again. For the life of her, she couldn't control them anymore. They spilled over again. It wasn't just that Ellen had saved this tiny, precious life or that Catherine possessed the magnanimity

to admit it. It was the way that everything . . . went on. She
had been gone a week and it felt like a lifetime, but everyone here was unchanged. Ellen and Cat were still squab-
bling, and everyone was still smiling the same smiles. They
were the same, constant, these people who were all, in some
measure or respect, her family.

Oh, Mac, you were so wrong. Life endures.

"What the holy hell is going on here?" Jericho demanded again.

Ellen and Catherine spoke in unison. "A man," Cat
said.

"It's got to be," Ellen agreed.

Jericho looked at them dumbly. "A man did this to her?
Shadow? But she's not—she doesn't—"

He broke off in a grunt when his mother punched a finger into his ribs. "She's a woman," Madeline said. "And
for as long as I can remember, there's been a connection.
Now don't all you *men* have somewhere to go?"

When they left, she looked at her daughter again. "So
what are you going to do about it?" she asked bluntly.

Mac slammed an empty beer bottle hard enough on the
bar to make it shatter. If he was startled, then his expression didn't show it.

"Sorry," he muttered.

"It is no problem, *señor.*" The bartender, a small, dark
Mexican named Juan, came to pick up the pieces. But he
kept one eye on his solitary customer as he worked.

"Another," Mac said.

"Now *that* is a problem."

Mac's eyes narrowed dangerously. "I'm not drunk."

No, he wasn't. But he *should* be. He had come here the
previous night after arriving in town, looking as if he had
driven for days without stopping. He had returned early
this morning, and since then he had put away one beer after another with steady, unwavering intent. Mac had a fire

burning inside him that would take more beer to put out than there was on all of the Baja peninsula.

The bartender lifted one bony shoulder in a shrug. "There is no more Corona," he explained. "This is not a big tourist spot. We do not stock so much."

"A Sol then."

"That I have."

Juan popped the cap and placed the bottle neatly in front of him, but Mac didn't touch it. He went to the edge of the veranda and stood among the palms and the eucalyptus to stare out at the rain.

He'd wanted civilization, Mac thought. He'd told himself he just needed a change. Something so radically different from Kokopelli's Canyon that thoughts of that place would be an absurd intrusion. He'd thought he'd tried. He wore jeans instead of shorts. The rough denim scratched his legs, irritating skin that had spent several long months uncovered. He'd stopped in San Diego and had his hair cut off. His neck felt bare and exposed. But in the end, he had only come here, to San Jose del Cabo, Mexico. An isolated scrap of a town, a spattering of white buildings in the hills overlooking the Pacific, a few forlorn boats bobbing at the shore, as far south on the Baja peninsula as he'd been able to drive. Beyond the palms, the narrow streets looked empty now—except, incongruously, for a cow that trudged by as if it had nowhere in particular to go. It probably didn't, Mac thought. It was noon, time for a siesta, and the rain drummed down.

In the end he had done what he had always done, he realized. He had gravitated to a place where he'd be alone. And loneliness ached inside him like some kind of spreading cancer.

Guadalajara was as close as a ferry ride from nearby San Lucas. There would be tourists there, sunshine and browning bodies beside a pool. Mac went back to the bar instead and drank half the Sol in one long swallow.

"Do you stock tequila in this place?" he snarled.

Juan nodded cautiously. He poured the tequila and found him a sliver of lime. "It is a woman, no? It is always a woman."

Mac made an ugly, snorting sound. "There's not another woman in the world like this one."

"I have heard that said many times before, over this very same bar."

"Yeah?" Mac tossed back the tequila. He hadn't intended to talk and found himself doing it anyway. "You've heard that she controls everything in her world with an iron fist? That she makes you want to choke her and instead you find yourself loving her?" He heard his own words and they shook him. They shook him *badly*. But he kept on.

"She's organized and practical and you'd think she wouldn't have patience with anything so untenable as emotion. But she could make a rock laugh and the sand weep. She can feel time in a bone and she respects silence and she *believes*." God help him, but she had believed in him. And to what end?

"So where did she go?" Juan asked.

"Home. She has family."

"We all have family, *señor*."

Mac's face turned mean. "No."

The bartender pushed on anyway. "That is where you are wrong. Me, I'm an orphan. I have no mother, no father. I have no wife. But down there near the boats there is a cabin. A woman lives there who can make me warm. She is my family, my home. It does not necessarily have to be blood or legal ties."

Warm? Home? His choice of words jolted Mac.

"So why don't you marry her?" he demanded.

"Ah, *señor*, she has a very big, very mean husband already, one who will not let her go."

Mac didn't know whether to laugh or to cry. He raked a hand through his hair and felt momentarily lost to find so little of it.

He hadn't changed anything. She had. She had changed everything.

"Even so, she will be there for me forever," Juan went on. "This I know. I know it here." He slapped a hand against his heart. "Her love for me is as strong as the sun and no matter what Jorge does to her, it will endure."

Endure? "Who the hell are you? Some kind of Navajo Holy One?"

"Señor?"

"I love her," Mac muttered wonderingly. "Good Lord."

His eyes ran up and down the empty street again. The cow was gone. Fear caught his throat. He had no doubt that it was every bit as strong as what she had felt when those arrows had started flying.

"That is good," the bartender said from behind him, "but *señor,* you are here alone. Perhaps you should go find her."

"I don't know where she is." But a good place to start looking would be the Navajo reservation, he realized. Somewhere east of the canyon. Shiprock. She'd said she'd go to the subagency there. But he still didn't even know her last name.

"I might never find her," he admitted aloud.

The pain came back, burning a hole right through the middle of him. He winced. "I love her," he said again, and it didn't shock him quite as much this time.

"Well, *señor,* I think you should do something about it."

Three days later, Jericho's house finally emptied out. All the clan relatives had left. The sing was over and Shadow's parents had gone home. Paddy had finally been convinced to go back to Boston and Uncle Ernie was out in the carport, singing for her spirit.

Shadow sat at the kitchenette counter and sighed. She hadn't told the old shaman all that had happened. She hadn't told any of them. In the end, it had just felt too private. And knowledge of the thief's cache wasn't something she needed to burden them with anyway. It was her own problem.

Still, one mention of Kokopelli's Canyon had been enough to convince Ernie that Jericho's Blessing Way wasn't nearly all the medicine she'd need. But it had been. Shadow felt purged inside, clean, strong. Restored.

But maybe that was only because she had made a few decisions while Jericho had been singing the ghost poison free of her soul.

She looked up when Catherine settled on the stool next to her. Ellen hovered behind her, watching Shadow critically. For all their differences, the three of them were a sort of necessary sisterhood. This isolated Navajo land made friendships vital and necessary.

"So what *are* you going to do now?" Cat asked. "You never really did answer your mother."

"I'm going to take a leave of absence from the museum, for starters."

Ellen looked aghast as only a Navajo could. "You're not going back to that *chindi* place!"

Shadow shook her head. "No. I guess I'll start with the Baja."

"You're going to *Mexico?*" That seemed to shock her just as much.

Shadow shrugged. "I don't know where else to look." Something constricted in the area of her throat. "I may not ever find him," she admitted on a whisper. "But I have to try."

And when—if—she did, what would he do then? Perhaps he would call her Sergeant again and send her packing. But in the meantime, only one thing felt clear in her heart now. She had been wrong when she'd thought she could simply walk away. In the end, she found she couldn't succumb to this pain, this loss, this emptiness inside. She couldn't withdraw into the hollow shell of her heart and live each day as something to get through, as a prelude to dying, and tell herself that she was lucky to have had that one steamy week in the sun. She wanted more.

Maybe she was bossy. She'd even accept high-handed. But, damn it, she wasn't going to walk away from him just because he thought she should. It simply wasn't her nature.

She realized that Jericho had come to stand behind Catherine. "How long a leave of absence?" he demanded.

"That depends."

His brows went up in a look that was uniquely his. "You're thinking of leaving the Res?" he asked incredulously.

Shadow swallowed carefully. "If I have to."

"Oh, Shadow," Catherine gasped, "who *is* this guy?"

For the first time since she had come home, Shadow felt her mouth pull into a smile. "He's...hard. A loner. He doesn't think he needs anybody or anything. But he won't shoot a deer with a gun, because it might somehow know it's going to die. And he apologized to a bunch of seven-hundred-year-old bones." She saw them exchange a look. "He holds forever in his hands."

"You love him," Catherine said quietly.

Shadow felt her heart punch into her ribs. "Yeah. I guess I do." She had thought so before, but now that she had left him she felt it so much more strongly, like something irrefutable she knew she would never escape from.

"You thought you loved Kevin," Jericho pointed out harshly, "but it wasn't enough."

"Then that wasn't love," Catherine interrupted calmly, tilting her head back to look up at her husband. "When it's the real thing you can leave everything you know and dwell on the moon, if that's where your man wants to be.''

Shadow saw something hot flare in her brother's eyes and she looked away, feeling as if she were intruding. But she knew Catherine spoke from deep within her heart. She had been born and raised in the East, but she had turned down a residency with the Center for Disease Control in Atlanta to remain on the Res with the Navajo shaman she loved.

Inadvertently, Shadow's gaze fell on Ellen. That woman's face was as pained as Catherine's was loving and satisfied. Shadow knew she wasn't thinking of Jericho this time, but of a love that *hadn't* been the real thing and the hearts it had broken.

Shadow stood. ''The baby's crying. Better go take care of him and stop looking at each other like that or you guys are going to have twelve kids.''

''There's a thought.'' Catherine laughed, but Jericho was already gone, hustling into the bedroom to see to the baby. Cat looked back at Shadow. ''I hope you'll be here when we name him.''

Shadow was startled. ''I thought you were calling him Ryan.''

Catherine laughed again. ''That's his Irish name. He'll be a little bit of both, I guess.''

Shadow nodded. It was Navajo tradition to hold off on a naming ceremony until a child said or did something indicative of his spirit.

''I'll be here,'' she vowed fervently, ''if I have to travel a thousand miles to get back.'' How far was the Baja? she wondered wildly. About that, probably. ''Can you convince your husband to leave his son long enough to give me a ride to the airport?'' she went on.

''I can do it,'' Ellen volunteered, but Cat shook her head.

''You need to get back to the clinic. I'll get Jericho to go. He won't like it, but I'll just threaten to do it myself.''

"Thanks." She hugged her quickly. "I've got to go talk to Diamond Eddie. Tell Jericho to meet me at the museum." She glanced down at her watch. "In about an hour."

What the hell was he supposed to say to her when he found her?

Mac drove north again, scowling hard. *I love you.* In all his memory, he had never spoken those words to another living soul, although he imagined that at some point he had probably said them to his mother. A lot of good that had done. *Come with me. Give up everything you love and tag along. I like camping with you.* He gave a raw, ugly laugh at that one.

The hell of it was, he was pretty sure she'd do it. More incredibly, he was beginning to think she might even stay. For so long now, he had mistaken selfishness and coldness for strength in the women he had chosen to touch and leave. Until Shadow, he had never understood that it took passion and caring to make a woman strong.

Mac took one hand off the wheel to rub his eyes, grainy from too little sleep. Somewhere in this world, he figured there was probably a man who could handle this situation with charm and finesse. But he wasn't that man and he decided he needed an excuse. Some reason for finding her again. Then, later, they could tackle the rest, whenever he figured out what that might be. Right now, he only knew that he needed to be with her. Without her, the world was too cold.

He could go to that Shiprock substation, he realized. *He* could report the cache in Kokopelli's Canyon. He could ask if a woman had already been by to tell them about it. They would probably have taken her full name, maybe even her address. Then he could find her and tell her that he just wanted to make sure she was okay. That he wanted to assure himself that their thief hadn't tracked her out of the canyon.

He crossed from California into Arizona again and pressed down on the accelerator a little harder, his heart skipping a single, cautious beat. *Had* the guy tracked her out of the canyon? God in heaven, he had been so preoccupied with her leaving, with what he was going to do next, that he'd never even considered that she could be in danger.

He swore violently and shook the possibility out of his head. But it came back, nudging him, haunting him.

No. If the thief had hung around after closing them in the cave, then he would have been witness to their last love-making on the cliffside. If the thief had been around, what better way to dispose of them both than when they were both so completely absorbed in each other? Shadow was safe. She was home somewhere, maybe right there in Shiprock.

Safe. Except . . .

Suddenly he pulled the Explorer off onto the side of the road, its breaks screaming. *Why had he not realized the connection before?*

Because his senses had been filled with her. Because he had been too busy wanting her and not touching her, then too busy losing himself in her heat. Because he'd really given relatively little thought to their prankster until now, until he needed to use him to find her again.

And now he realized that the thief hadn't started tormenting them until *after* she'd arrived. Not one suspicious occurrence had happened before she'd plunged down the canyon wall to land at his feet, and he'd already been there for three weeks at that point. But no one had been trying to scare him away then because no one had known yet that he was there. No one had known until she'd told them where she was going and why.

His blood turned to ice. Could it be one of her *family?* He thought that would probably destroy her, although he had no trouble accepting such an idea.

He hauled on the wheel of the Explorer and aimed it back onto the road, burying the speedometer needle.

Chapter 16

Shadow's thoughts were working hard and fast when she pushed through the museum door. Her truck needed a tune-up, so she would leave it down the street at the Exxon station while she was gone. When Jericho came for her, they could swing by her hogan—it was right on the way to Albuquerque. She could grab some clean clothes and her bank card. She had no use for credit cards on the Res, but she could take cash from her bank account through one of those nifty machines in the airport.

It would all work out very expeditiously, she decided. She headed for her own little office to call the airlines and shouted into Diamond Eddie's room as she passed it.

"Hey, when you get a minute, I need to talk to you about something."

There was silence, then a resounding crash from inside. She hesitated, frowning. "Eddie? Are you all right?"

There was no answer. His door was open a crack and she leaned forward to peer through it. As soon as she did, he yanked it open from the other side and she reeled backward.

"Oh! You startled me."

He was looking at her strangely. His mouth was half open, making him look like a small pinch-faced frog. His breath was coming too fast and he was pale. She reached a hand out to him.

"Eddie, what's wrong? Are you sick?"

His expression cleared slowly and he closed his mouth. "Not now that you've returned. But what are you doing here? I thought you were taking time off, beautiful one."

"I did. I'm back. I'm leaving again." She turned away from him and headed into her office. "And don't call me that."

He followed her. "Shadow, Shadow, you've used up all of your leave time. I can't give you any more. Don't tell me you're going back to that canyon?"

"No—oh, that reminds me." She sat down at her desk and reached for the phone.

"Reminds you of what, *señorita?*"

"Would you stop with the Spanish? I've got to call over to the substation. You would not *believe* what we found up there."

"I can imagine."

"No, I'm not kidding. There's a cave up in one of the cliff dwellings and—" She broke off midway through the number she was punching out when a familiar clicking sound came from behind her.

It was the sound of a revolver being cocked. Shadow looked over her shoulder at him, confused, and her heart went suddenly still.

She stood slowly to face him. He kept the gun level on her chest.

"Eddie," she whispered disbelievingly. *"You?"*

"You were supposed to be dead by now, little one. For a moment, when you came in, I thought I was hearing a *chindi*. You and your friend should *both* be dead. Where is he?"

"I . . . don't know."

He looked genuinely pained. "You lie to me, *señorita*. I watched you together. Neither of you was going anywhere without the other."

"You *watched* us?" Suddenly she felt as if she were going to throw up. He had managed to do what all of Mac's cynicism had not achieved. He had taken something beautiful, something sweet and good, and had made it sordid and vile.

Diamond Eddie only shrugged. "Don't look at me that way. If I were coldhearted I would have shot him in the back while you were cowering there in your sleeping bag, afraid of old Kokopelli. Did you like that trick?" He didn't allow her time to answer. "That's when I should have shot him," he mused aloud. "But I was too curious to find out if you were really made of ice or if it was just me you didn't want."

"Now you know," she retorted and regretted it immediately. His finger curled tensely around the trigger.

"Now I know," he agreed bitterly. "I was waiting for an encore, but you didn't cooperate, at least not while I was there."

That brought her breath back a little. Her stomach settled. He hadn't seen everything then. He hadn't ruined and tarnished the whole glorious time.

"Shadow, my friend, you are simply too hardheaded for your own good," he went on. "Why didn't you run? I gave you so much opportunity. Do you care for him so much that you couldn't bear to part with him even in the face of *chindis?* That's really too bad. I hope you love him enough to die for him." His finger tightened.

Shadow stared at it. "Jericho's coming!" she burst out.

His eyes narrowed suspiciously. "I think you're lying again."

Shadow shook her head hard. "No. No, I'm not. He's going to meet me here, to take me to the airport. That's what I came to tell you. I'm leaving—with Mac. I quit, Eddie. I'm going away. And I haven't told the cops yet what we found. Don't you see, you don't have to kill anybody else! You certainly don't have to kill *me*."

"Ah, *señorita*, that's a risk I can't take. This is my whole life we're talking about here. You saw my treasure. I can live off it forever. But I wouldn't live happily if I thought maybe you could come back and ruin it all."

"Eddie, for God's sake, you don't want to do this!" For the first time she felt true fear, thick and black, rolling through her. It took her breath; it made her legs feel light and empty.

He shook his head. She wasn't reaching him.

"No," he agreed. "I don't. I would really have preferred it if you had just stayed in the cave. I truly do think you're beautiful, you know, and I hate to mar a work of art. But since you didn't stay put, we can't take chances. If you say your brother's coming here, then I must believe you and take you back to the canyon. That's best, anyway. They won't find your body there. People will think what they've been thinking all week—that you've just suddenly gone crazy and now you have disappeared."

She thought wildly of trying to fight him. If she hurled herself at him fast enough, suddenly enough, maybe she could take him by surprise. Maybe she could knock the gun from his hand without it going off. He was small....

But then she remembered the rock he had used to hide the hole in the ground that Kokopelli's cutout figure had made. Yes, he was small, but he was also strong. She'd had no idea he was that strong.

She moved unsteadily away from the desk and let him catch her arm, propelling her back toward the door. Surely she would find some opportunity to get away from him on the mountain.

She closed her eyes, feeling a horrible, impotent helplessness. It was a long shot. Her memories of Mac wouldn't grow old and fade after all. She'd never have a chance to find him. She could only pray that he was long gone from the canyon himself by now, that he was in the Baja or at another dig, somewhere where Diamond Eddie could never find him.

Mac ground his foot down on the brake again, downshifting hard, as he came upon the turnoff to the mountain. Every instinct he possessed told him to turn, to go back to Kokopelli's Canyon, to find the bastard who was doing this and kill him with his bare hands. But a more practical voice hissed sanity at him.

The odds were a million to one that the thief would actually be there at the same time he arrived. In the meantime, God only knew where Shadow was. There was a much more reasonable possibility that she could actually be *with* the man right now, maybe sharing coffee with him, with some relative or friend, never knowing that he was the one who had tried to kill them.

Until he made his move. Until it was too late.

Mac made a choking sound. It made more sense for him to keep driving straight, right down U.S. Route 191 into Chinle. It made more sense to pray like hell that there *was* a police substation there. It made more sense to enlist the help of the authorities whether he had any respect for them or not, because they presumably had radios and telephones that would link them to other cops all over the reservation. They could put out an alert, find her, protect her, while he tried to put the missing pieces together and figure out who she might have told.

He growled another inarticulate sound and hit the accelerator again. Twenty minutes later, he reached the small town of Chinle. He found the subagency almost immediately, logically situated near the entrance to historical

Canyon de Chelly. Behind the front desk was a pretty Navajo girl who was almost certainly too young and inexperienced for what he was about to hit her with. And he was in no mood to coddle her.

"Get on the phone," he snapped at her. "Call your substation in Shiprock. You need to find out if a woman reported a pot hunter in Kokopelli's Canyon. Find out who she is and where she might be found, and we'll take it from there."

"I—what?" The girl gaped at him.

"Do it."

She picked up the phone and began tapping in a number. "I should get my supervisor," she tried.

"That'll be next. Talk to Shiprock first."

A few minutes later, she covered the receiver with her hand. "I'm sorry, but there's been no such report."

He had already gotten to her. Mac felt as if he were strangling, dying inside. The colors in the room faded.

He pushed away from the counter. "Then find your supervisor. You need to send some men out to that canyon—fast. No horsing around with Indian *chindi* voodoo first." She looked horribly insulted. He couldn't care. "There's no time," he went on, "and there's no *chindis*. Just a very real, very nasty character who's left five bodies in a cave there and who's about to add a sixth if we don't find him." *Pray God he hadn't done it already.* "Get Shiprock to try to locate the assistant curator at your museum over there."

The girl looked as if she was going to cry. "Why?" she breathed.

"Because that's who he's going to try to kill. And when you find her, I think you'll find him as well."

"Wait! We need more information!"

But Mac was already gone. He should have trusted his instincts. He should have gone straight to the canyon. But if the thief had gotten to her on her way down, then it wouldn't matter anyway. Then it was already too late.

For the first time in his life, Mac knew emasculating, breath-robbing terror. He knew this was a horror he'd never be able to isolate himself from, not if he lived a hundred more years.

Jericho stood in the doorway of the Navajo Nation Museum, scowling irritably. "Hello?" he called out a second time.

Nobody answered.

"Shadow, damn it, come on. I don't want to waste all day with this." His own voice seemed to echo back at him in the silence. Yet the door had been unlocked.

There was too *much* silence, he realized. The wrong kind of silence. It was more like an emptiness, as though all life had gone from the rooms. His shaman's instincts prickled the hair at his nape. The strange sixth sense that was as much a part of him as it had been of his ancestors twisted his gut.

He took a slow, cautious step into the building. He avoided the display room with its *chindi* artifacts and went to the back hallway where the offices were. He poked his head into his sister's room.

The light was on, but nothing was disturbed. Except . . . her chair was pulled back from the desk. It had rolled on its little coasters halfway into the room. He stared at it. It was such an inane little thing, but his sister never left a room without putting everything in order first. That chair should have been neatly flush with the desk.

She had been gone for a week. Maybe someone else had used her office and had left it this way, but Jericho didn't think so. He went back up the hall to Diamond Eddie's room.

He felt as if he could actually *smell* the man here, though he knew that was impossible. It was just his instinctive antennae again—that, and the fact that he had never liked the man. He had never quite figured out how anyone living on the Res could find the money to wear three diamond ear-rings. The room stank of him—of something sour like fear, of something dark like anger.

Jericho didn't like that at all. But he liked the toppled filing cabinet even less.

He crossed to it and looked down at it. The fear smell was stronger here. He knew beyond a doubt that Diamond Eddie had been standing right here at this place when something had scared him badly enough to make him reel into this cabinet and knock it over.

What? More importantly, where was Shadow?

He moved around behind the desk and looked out the window at the parking lot. Her truck was there. Diamond Eddie's Cadillac was not.

That Cadillac had always bothered Jericho as well. Excess in anything was not the Navajo way. Anyone who disregarded that doctrine was suspect. They had either converted to Christianity or they were a wolfman—a Navajo witch. But Jericho didn't think Diamond Eddie was a witch and he had never heard that he'd converted to Christianity. He just got the impression of gluttony, of a man who had wandered a little bit off the Navajo path to *hozro,* to balance with the universe. Eddie was an oddity, someone to be watched with one careful eye, but Jericho had never been more suspicious of him than that.

Until now.

He picked up Eddie's phone and punched in the number for the mobile unit he had bought for his house while Catherine was pregnant. She picked up on the third ring. He could hear Ryan fussing in the background and it was almost enough to make him smile.

"Shadow been there?" he demanded without preamble.

"Well, hello to you, too. Where are you?"

"The museum. She's not here."

There was a long silence. "Did she decide to drive into Albuquerque herself?" It wasn't like her to do that without letting them know, Catherine thought, but Shadow had been anything but herself lately.

"Her truck's here," Jericho responded.

Catherine was quiet again, thinking. "I don't like the sound of this," she said finally. In the year she had been on the Navajo reservation, she had learned a certain healthy wariness. Strange things could happen here, things she had never before believed in. Moreover, the Res was big enough, empty enough and remote enough to occasionally attract an unsavory character or two.

"I don't like it either, Cat Eyes," Jericho answered on a long, drawn-out breath.

"Do you think you and Ernie missed some of her *chindi* poison?" she ventured.

"No. I think this is a threat of the real flesh and blood kind."

Up on the mountain, Catherine's breath caught. That scared her. That was never her husband's first suspicion. Why now?

"It has something to do with that canyon," she said impulsively. "She was fine until she went up there that first day to look into the pot hunter. Then it was like everything went to hell in a hand basket."

"You're saying I ought to drive out there."

Cat knew it was probably the last thing in the world he wanted to do. He was the strongest man she had ever known—yet anything supernatural touched the deepest, darkest Navajo part of him. He was also the most protective man she had ever known, when it came to the people he called his own.

"Jericho, you have to. It's what you do. You help people. In this case, it's Shadow. And for some reason, that canyon is the most logical place to start looking for her—or at least for some clue as to where she's gone."

She heard him give a rough sigh. "You're right. Okay, I'm going. But I don't know when I'll be able to get to a phone again."

"You don't have to worry about it. We're here and we're fine. Shadow's the one who's missing. I'll see you when I see you."

Jericho held the phone away from his ear to look at it a moment. "I love you," he finally answered. "Have I told you that lately?"

She laughed huskily. "Just don't bring me any more flowers. My system can't handle it."

"Wouldn't dare," he muttered. "I'll be in touch as soon as I can, as soon as I know something."

Catherine started to hang up, then she hesitated. "Be careful."

"Yeah," he answered quietly. "I have that instinct, too."

Chapter 17

The sight of the mountain hit Shadow hard—like a sweet dream that had somehow plunged into nightmare, memories of glory and pain flashing at her out of sequence. She had only been gone from it for a few days, yet it felt like a lifetime.

Even worse was the way Diamond Eddie had tied her wrists together. It reminded her of the skeletons in the cave. They laid in her lap as his Cadillac bumped up the trail to the first foothill. *Please, Holy Ones, let Mac be gone from here*. The prayer was a litany in her head and her heart, sounding over and over as they left the car and struck out up the mountain on foot.

The biggest problem with dying, she thought a little crazily, was that she would never know if Diamond Eddie had found Mac. Surely it had occurred to the little weasel by now that she wasn't the only threat to his cache. Mac Tshongely knew about it, too. Of course, Mac probably wouldn't do anything about it. She had told him that *she* would go to the subagency. Why would he bother? No, he would probably go on his wandering way, maybe thinking of her sometimes, aching for her once or twice, but he would never open old wounds by stopping to inquire about a pot thief if he happened to be passing a Navajo tribal-police subagency.

So if Diamond Eddie disposed of her, he would be relatively safe. Shadow stumbled and Eddie pushed the barrel of the gun into the small of her back.

"Oh, stop it!" she snapped. "You're no more a tough guy than you are Spanish! I *hate* your airs. Did I ever tell you that?"

"I could kill you right here, *señorita,*" he reminded her.

"But you won't," she retorted.

"And why do you think that?"

Shadow had no idea. She was just talking, irritating him, because it made her feel better, because it was infinitely preferable to going docilely to her death and never knowing what had happened to Mac.

Please, Mac, be gone, she prayed again. She noticed that Eddie was huffing badly from the physical effort the steep trail required. Then she heard the misstep of his feet as he skidded on a rock.

It was almost impossible to climb this trail in regular shoes, she thought. She hesitated just enough to glance down and behind her. He wore loafers.

Now.

Shadow ran. She took in a healthy breath of air and scrambled while he was still trying to reclaim his balance. He was behind her so she went up, crashing into brush, a cry of frustration catching in her throat. He would probably shoot, she knew that, but his arrows had been wild and maybe he couldn't aim a gun any better. It was a chance, only a chance, but it was the only one she had.

She stumbled onto clear trail again and kept running, but her own balance was off with her wrists tied together. She brought them up to her mouth and pulled savagely at the rope with her teeth, finally getting it free. Then she heard one of his bullets ping off a rock to her left and she screamed.

That answered one question, shattered one distant hope. He wasn't so infatuated with her that he wouldn't kill her.

She didn't dare look back. She shoved past obstacles when the trail narrowed and leapt rocks where they would have impeded her. She ran blindly and came to the top of the trail long before she expected to.

She skidded to a stop, teetering dangerously, and looked wildly down into the canyon. *Mac was gone.*

She hadn't been prepared for the relief. It drained her. She wasn't expecting such terror. She was truly alone here. Until this moment, until she saw it with her own eyes, she hadn't dared allowed herself to believe it.

She was on her own...and Diamond Eddie was right behind her.

She took a deliberate step over the rim and plunged. This time her shoulder crashed hard against an outcropping. She shrieked with the impact and with the shattering pain it brought. When she hit the bottom she rolled out of habit and felt her bones crunching against each other. But there was no time to acknowledge the agony it brought. She lunged to her feet again, running.

The cave. Of all the places to go, that would be the worst—she would be trapped there. But for some reason the image of it filled her head, demanding that she run there. And in the end, there was nowhere else for her to go anyway, she realized. She didn't want to face him in area she was unfamiliar with. At least she *knew* the cave—the only other places she had spent time in were the switchback and the open canyon floor.

Besides, Diamond Eddie was afraid of She Who Waits.

She reached the cliff dwellings and hauled herself up, even as another gunshot sounded from behind her. She clung to the wall of rock and craned her neck to look back.

Eddie was halfway down the cliff face she had plunged over, almost exactly level with her, and he was shooting down the canyon in her direction.

Two shots gone. Depending upon the make of his gun—she hadn't noticed—he could have as many as seven left. She kept going.

Her shoulder throbbed and shot white-hot pain down her arm. She reached the first apartment room and the wide fissure she and Mac had crawled out from. She wriggled her way into it and dropped, rolling again. Pain took her breath and siphoned her blood, leaving her momentarily dizzy. She lay on the floor beside She Who Waits, groaning.

"Help me," she whispered to her. "Please, please help me."

She got to her feet again and climbed over the low wall into the other room. It was so dark, too dark, and she didn't have a flashlight this time. She dropped to her knees and skimmed her good hand over the floor, groping for Mac's gun in the blackness. She was pretty sure she had lost it when she had fallen in here a lifetime ago.

When her fingers actually closed over it, she was almost shocked. She hadn't really expected to find it. She picked it up and looked down at it dumbly. Finally, for the first time, she felt a surge of adrenaline, of something like optimism. Things were going her way. With just a little more luck, maybe she could get out of this.

The rock above her head shrieked and scraped. She gasped and looked up just in time to see it open and Diamond Eddie's face appear in the hole.

No more time.

She got up again and vaulted over the low wall into the other room. He shot the gun behind her. The bullet ricocheted wildly with echoing pings that filled her head. The dying reverberations made her ears ring.

Three bullets gone now.

She hurried back to She Who Waits and crouched in the small area beside her head, near the boulder she and Mac had climbed up on. She had the gun aimed at the upper moving wall by the time Diamond Eddie appeared on the other side.

"Okay," she gasped, "okay. I'm armed now, too, Eddie. If you pull *your* trigger, so will I. Only mine's snake load. I don't even have to aim and you'll be hurt enough that you'll never get out of this canyon alive."

He hesitated. "Shoot one. Prove it."

Shadow laughed wildly. "Like hell. I've got six left. How many do you have?"

Slowly, carefully, he came over the wall. He started to push the top rock closed behind him. Scant sunlight slanted down from the fissure over her head, and more thin light seeped in from the other room and the hole there. If either place were sealed off, it would take a long time for their eyes to adjust to the altered meager light that remained.

She decided to shoot one of the snake load bullets after all. The pellets spattered the rock over his head, raining down on him. Their impact was deflected, but she knew they had to hurt. He threw his hands up with an odd stricken sound and backed away from the moving wall.

"Leave the wall where it is," she ordered. "I want to be able to see your finger on that gun."

Actually, he had closed the wall just enough that she could barely see his gun at all. And surely he knew that. His own eyes told him how dark it was in here, and he probably couldn't see her weapon either. But she thought he was nearing a stage of full-blown panic.

His breath was still coming fast and hard. He wasn't so out of shape that he shouldn't have recovered from the mountain climb by now, even if he'd chased her at a run across the canyon floor. It was the only true edge she had. She had to use it.

"So when was your last Blessing Way, Eddie?" she asked conversationally.

"What?" Even with that single word, she heard his voice trip. *Thank you, Holy Ones, thank you.* She had been right. He was scared in here.

"Your last Blessing Way. You know, to keep *chindi* evil off you. I had one this weekend. How about you?"

He didn't answer.

"That long, huh? Too bad. I think I can feel her. Of course, she's not going to come after me. *I'm* covered, and you know how that goes. *Chindis* prey on the weak. Sort of like wolfmen. They can't hurt you if you're well protected. So I guess She Who Waits will be coming after *you*."

"*Shut up.*"

"Oops. I said her name. Sorry about that. Between that and her whole body lying here, hardly disturbed at all—"

He shot the gun again. *Four gone.* Shadow cringed back as the bullet caromed wildly, waiting for it to tear into her flesh. But the Holy People were with her—maybe it was even She Who Waits who was protecting her, thanking her for taking care of her child. Shadow didn't know, but it was Eddie who grunted in pain. Her head spun.

Then she froze.

A thud and a muffled curse came from the other room. The voice seared through her, changing everything, rocking her with terror again, but not for herself this time.

The voice was Mac's.

It would be a long, hard fall without a rope. In the small space in his heart that wasn't filled with panic, Mac marveled that Shadow had done it. He finally lowered himself full length through the hole in the first chamber, hanging on to the edge with his hands. He had three extra inches on six feet, but when he let go the impact still shot pain up through his ankles, driving the sensation out of his legs.

He let himself fall, intending to roll right back to his feet again, but his legs were too numb and wouldn't cooperate. He swore, sitting where he was for a moment, looking around warily.

He wasn't sure what he had expected to find in here. Shadow's body propped beside the others? It wasn't there. *Thank God.* He realized that relief would have kept him from moving temporarily even if his legs hadn't gone lifeless. It almost literally rocked through him.

But it was short-lived. He had heard a gunshot when he was up above in the dwellings, a sharp report that had echoed oddly beneath his feet. And the upper half of the moving wall was pushed almost shut now. They hadn't left it that way, so somebody was in here.

He started to roar her name, then he choked on it as the hairs on his nape lifted. He had the certain sense that someone was watching him. He looked back up at the hole above him.

A man looked in at him.

A Navajo man. Mac needed no more proof than that.

Rage rocketed through him and he staggered to his feet again without any thought that his legs might not hold him. They did, barely, but pain shot up to his hips with the effort. He ignored it with sheer force of will and went for the hole.

"Where is she, you son of a bitch? What did you do with her?"

Jericho reacted with primitive instinct. It flooded his blood—the blood he had inherited from his warrior ancestors. Here was danger, here was an enemy, and a boiling need rose in him to attack. He didn't register the man's words. He dropped down through the hole to meet him without any thought for *chindis* or common sense. It never even occurred to him that the man couldn't reach him if he stayed up on the roof. He never remembered that he had promised his wife he would be careful.

He landed hard but rolled with the impact, coming up on his feet again, ready—and the man's fist crashed into his face, stunning him.

Pain exploded and blood flew from his nose. He tasted it at the back of his throat as he reeled. He spat it out in the fraction of a second it took him to recover, to lower his head and barrel into the stranger.

He heard the harsh *whoof*ing sound of the man's breath being driven out of him. But the stranger recovered fast, too. They staggered together into skeletons, arms locked, too equally matched for either of them to get in a good blow.

Then another primal rush of adrenaline finally gave Jericho an edge. He felt the bones of the skeletons dig into his back as they rolled over them, grappling, and he feared them more than he could any mortal enemy. They made him wild.

He got his hands up to the other man's windpipe, grasping. His grip slid away as a fist rammed its way into his kidney, but he groped back and pressed his thumbs in hard.

Mac felt his vision darken. Then, blessedly, the Navajo's grip loosened, because they both went still at the same time.

A scream echoed through the chambers, coming from the other room. They both knew the voice. It was Shadow.

Shadow stared, stunned, at the top half of the moving wall. Impossible sounds came from that room now. Someone was *fighting*. Mac...and who else? *Who else could possibly have come here?* What was going on?

Did Eddie have an accomplice?

Terror made her sway. She had been handling Eddie okay, gaining an edge over him. But in that moment the odds escalated against her with dizzying speed. For one lethal moment she lowered the gun. Then, out of the corner of her eye, she saw Diamond Eddie move fast while her attention was diverted. It was all the opportunity he thought he needed. She screamed as he lunged for her, flinching back, the gun dropping from her suddenly nerveless hand.

Eddie grabbed for her, but he was off-balance and his hand swiped at air. Suddenly she understood. He was trying to attack her from *across* She Who Waits without touching her bones.

Blood seeped from a wound at his thigh where the ricocheting bullet had struck him. Shadow knew then that that was why he was trying to grab her. He didn't want to risk shooting in here again.

In a burst of inspiration, she stopped trying to recoil from him. She reached across She Who Waits and grabbed hold of his arm with both her hands. She pulled with all her strength, her shoulder screaming in protest at such abuse. But she managed to drag him into the bones. Eddie went crazy.

Her breath left her as one of his swinging fists caught her in the midriff, seeming to drive her stomach clear up into her throat. Fresh pain blazed from her shoulder as she groped blindly for She Who Waits. Her fingers closed over a long leg bone and she brought it up, cracking him solidly in the head with it, again and again and again. It finally shattered and she made a startled mewling sound, but then she only grabbed another, an arm this time.

When he realized what she was striking him with, Diamond Eddie howled and started gibbering. A chant, she thought wildly. He was trying to sing a chant.

"They won't help you," she gasped. "You're too far gone, Eddie. The Holy People won't help you. You left the Navajo way."

She backed up from him, shaking, and scurried around the remaining skeleton into the room. *Mac*. She had to get to Mac, had to find out what was going on out there in the other chamber, but she was afraid to take her eyes off Eddie. He still had the gun, although he was sobbing now,

moaning and shoving at the bones he laid sprawled upon.
Frenziedly, he tried to push them away from him. On the
other side of She Who Waits, her pots crashed and shattered as his legs thrashed through them.

Finally she saw the gun drop from his hand. She turned
around just as the wall slid open again.

"Jericho?" Her jaw dropped and she felt her breath
leave her body all over again. His face was smeared with
blood.

Her amazed eyes moved past his shoulder and she finally found Mac. He was gathering himself to fight Jericho again, his fist cocked back.

"No!" she screamed. Her voice echoed.

She staggered as Jericho vaulted over the wall, shoving
past her. Then Mac came over as well, moving more slowly.
She grabbed at him instinctively, still thinking he would go
for Jericho again, but then she watched dazedly as they
both looked at Diamond Eddie.

Finally, they each caught one of Eddie's arms.

"Here's the bastard I think you're looking for," Jericho
said harshly.

Slowly, lifelessly, Shadow slid down the wall to sit on the
floor. Together Mac and Jericho dragged Eddie to his feet,
shoving him up hard against the other side.

"Do you want the first shot at him," Mac asked tightly,
"or can I have it?"

"Don't," Shadow gasped. "Just...don't. He's not...
worth it."

One of them threw Eddie back down on his stomach
again—she couldn't tell who. She finally noticed that Mac
was limping badly, almost hobbling, as he went into the
other room for the rope they had left there so long ago. But
he was alive. He was alive...and *here*. Had he ever left, or
had he come back?

She hadn't seen his tent or any of his stuff out in the
canyon, so he must have come back.

Why?

Mac brought the rope, and Shadow's eyes were huge as she watched him tie Eddie. Jericho rolled the little man up against the wall and dragged a hand beneath his bloody nose. Then he looked at his sister.

"You want to tell me what's *really* going on now? What the hell have you gotten yourself into?"

Shadow hugged herself. Where to start? she wondered wildly.

"Mac, this is my brother," she said thinly. "Jericho, this is the guy you were taking me to the airport to find."

Chapter 18

For a long moment, the two men only looked at each other. Jericho finally nodded, but Mac was clearly confused.

His face hardened in that stony, wary way that made Shadow's heart skip a beat. She had never thought she'd see that look again. Now it was the most beautiful thing she had ever witnessed in her life.

"Your brother?" he repeated.

Shadow nodded.

"So who's this?" He thrust a thumb over his shoulder.

"Diamond Eddie."

"Your *boss?*"

"As of yesterday, anyway. I wouldn't put any wagers on tomorrow."

"I guess you got his job." Mac needed to think about that, about its implications, but at the moment there was too much else to absorb.

"I guess you could be right." But Shadow couldn't think about that now. Shock and disbelief were only starting to filter out of her.

Mac looked at Jericho, at his bloody nose. "So how do you fit in to all this?" he demanded. He still didn't entirely trust him. "How'd you get here?"

"At about a hundred and ten miles an hour," Jericho responded. He tilted his head back, pinching off one side of his nose to stop the bleeding.

"Speed limits don't pertain to him," Shadow explained dryly. "Fifty-five is for the rest of the Res."

"What airport?" Mac went on.

"She wanted to go to the Baja." Jericho lowered his head again cautiously. "I guess you'll fit in all right."

"Fit in with what?" Mac asked warily.

"With the family. We tend to be a bunch of hardheaded survivors. Hell of a punch you've got there."

The family. Mac felt panic swim through him, cold and clammy. He wasn't ready for this, hadn't even figured out what he was going to say to her yet. He looked around at her.

She had been headed for the Baja.

"You were coming after me? Why?"

Shadow tried to shrug. She flinched with the pain the movement brought, but although Mac was staring at her hard he didn't seem to notice. She wasn't ready for this discussion yet, not here, not with her brother watching like a hawk.

"Damn it, Sergeant," Mac snapped. "Every once in a while you've got to let someone else lead the way."

"I thought I had," she answered softly, and saw his eyes flare with the memory. Then a faint, cautious voice called down from the hole in the other room.

"Hello? Anybody in there?"

Mac swore. "There's your reservation cops. Good thing we didn't really need them."

Shadow started to her feet again. He reached a hand out to help her but she shook her head, blanching at the very thought. She hugged her arm against her midriff and struggled up on her own.

"My shoulder," she explained. "I didn't fall quite right this time."

She was injured. Mac finally realized it and felt something painful claw through his own body as well. For the first time it really hit him how easily she could have died here. Up until now, there had been mostly panic, rage. He felt it leave him with only something shaky inside.

He wanted to hold her and was afraid he would hurt her. He wanted to bury his face in her hair and let himself love her, and was afraid he would hurt himself. He never wanted to let her out of his sight again, and he still had no idea how he was going to go about it.

"Ah, Sergeant," he said finally.

There it was again. *Sergeant.* But at least he wasn't sending her packing, Shadow thought. Yet.

He put one hand cautiously around her waist and drew her just close enough to rest his chin on the top of her head. For now, it would have to be enough, he thought, to assure himself that she was warm and alive, even if she wasn't completely unharmed.

"You're shaking," she breathed against his chest. He felt so good. For the first time in days, the world seemed truly right again.

"So are you," he answered.

Jericho watched them a moment, then took a single step toward the other chamber. "I'll talk to the cops," he volunteered, then he stopped cold. "I have no idea what to tell them."

"We'll do it," Mac answered. "Then we need to get Shadow to a doctor."

"I've got one who should just about be itching to get back in the saddle by now."

They went into the other room. The tribal police were peering down through the hole there.

Reluctantly, Mac let Shadow go. Reluctantly, she allowed all of them to help her back up into the dwellings.

Darkness was gathering in the canyon before they finished telling the authorities everything they knew. The story came out in fractured bits and pieces as Mac and Shadow remembered details. Jericho listened with his brows high. Shadow noticed almost absently that he rubbed his arms more than once against a chill that no one else seemed to feel.

Diamond Eddie's cache itself was a federal offense, so they had to wait for the FBI and the state boys. But the skeletons in the cave were the responsibility of the tribal police, and Shadow began shaking again as they grilled Eddie about them. She listened as they badgered him into admitting that he had killed each and every brave soul who had risked the legend to camp in the canyon. Finally, fully, it hit her how lucky she was to be alive.

She eased away from Mac where they were sitting against the wall beneath the dwellings. She went down the canyon to the stream and threw up, then she hugged herself. But even after she had splashed cold water on her face, she still felt sick...and a little crazy. His crush on her had had some merit after all, she thought wildly. If not for that, she was sure he would have killed both her and Mac immediately.

She finally went back to rejoin the others.

"I never guessed," she breathed to Mac, settling beside him again. "All this time I've worked with him, and I never knew he had that kind of evil in him. I just thought he was...weird."

One of the cops came back into the canyon from the mountain. "I called Chinle," he informed them. "They're sending a helicopter to get you folks to a hospital."

Shadow looked around at them. They certainly needed medical help. She couldn't bring herself to care about Eddie, but Jericho's nose still spouted occasionally and without warning. Mac's calves were swollen badly and she didn't even want to think about her shoulder.

Jericho finally spoke. "We don't need a hospital," he said tightly. "Just fly us across the Res to Beautiful Mountain. As soon as possible." He looked around the canyon warily as the night began to push in on them.

"It's okay," Shadow assured him. "I'm absolutely sure now that there isn't any evil here. Spirits, maybe. But no *chindis.*"

Her brother's eyes narrowed on her. She felt Mac look down at her sharply.

"Why?" they demanded together.

"Because only good things have happened here."

"Good?" Mac said incredulously. "You call that nutcase *good?*" He thrust a thumb toward Eddie again. "He was going to kill you."

"But he didn't. I don't think She Who Waits would let him. The one shot that *should* have gotten me ricocheted right back at him."

The men looked silently at the pot thief. Mac shrugged. Jericho looked dubious.

"There's still one thing I don't understand, though," Shadow went on, looking at her brother. "How did you know to look for me here? I never said anything to any of you about Eddie's cache."

"It was Cat's idea. Woman's intuition, I guess." Jericho paused. "That, and the damned chair. I knew something was wrong as soon as I saw the chair in your office. It wasn't flush with the desk. You wouldn't have left it that way."

Mac gave a snorting kind of laugh. She elbowed him in the ribs with her good arm.

"In twenty-nine years," Jericho went on, "I don't think I ever saw you walk away and leave something out of order."

"Thirty," Shadow amended.

"What?"

"Thirty years. My birthday was last week."

He looked horrified. She had known he would. But now she was finally able to grin about it.

"Oh, hell," he muttered. "I'm sorry. I was so wrapped up in Cat and the baby—"

"I know," she interrupted.

"I'll make it up to you."

"You already have."

He shot her a doubtful look.

"You're here," she said simply. "You came to my rescue. Not to mention the fact that by forgetting you sent me barreling out here to the canyon in the first place." She glanced at Mac and left the rest unsaid.

So *that* was what had set her off, Mac realized. He suspected it wasn't so much that her family had forgotten—she would have been able to handle that just fine, with little more than a practical shrug. But the idea of hitting the big 3-0 itself had obviously hit her hard.

Seven years, he remembered, and realized he wasn't at all sorry that things had unfolded the way they had.

They heard the faint *cht-cht* sound of chopper blades in the distance. Something squirmed uncomfortably inside him again.

"Where did you say we were going?" he asked Jericho warily.

"To my house. There's not a thing wrong with any of us that my wife can't fix, and to tell you the truth, I just want to get home now."

"What about our vehicles?" Mac demanded, grasping at straws. Suddenly he felt himself sinking, being drawn into something that made him feel both warm and cold. *Her family*.

"My truck's still in Shiprock. We can bring that back to get the others later," Shadow decided. "It's just not practical to worry about them now. Besides, where are you going to stay tonight? Neither one of us is in any condition to hike down and get your tent. So sleep under a roof for one night and—"

And what? she wondered, choking off suddenly. What then?

"Yes, sir, Sergeant," Mac muttered.

"Get used to it," Jericho drawled, closing the discussion. The helicopter was landing. Whether it was *chindis* or benevolent spirits who dwelled here, he still didn't feel comfortable among them. He made a beeline for the chopper.

Catherine called Ellen to bring supplies from the clinic. By eight-thirty, Mac's bruised tendons were bandaged, Shadow's collarbone was set and Jericho wore a shocking white bridge over his nose.

By nine-thirty, Martin and Madeline had returned.

By ten, Uncle Ernie reappeared and other clan relatives wandered in and out. Shadow's discovery was the most exciting thing to happen in this corner of the Res since Catherine had isolated the Mystery Disease—and some said the wolfman—that had been systematically killing the People. Nobody intended to miss any of the details.

Voices tangled, rose and fell, and occasionally there was a burst of laughter. Jericho sat on the sofa with Catherine nestled beneath his left arm and his son against his chest, looking around at the small house almost dazedly. Once, little more than a year ago, this place had been his haven, a single empty room where he had dwelled with his own ghosts. He could scarcely remember now when it had been that quiet here.

His gaze swept to Mac Tshongely, who had found a seat at the kitchenette counter. The man looked vaguely alarmed and a little overwhelmed. Jericho thought he understood. It wasn't easy to come face-to-face with raw emotions you never expected to feel again, for someone you never expected to feel them for. He knew. He had been there. His arm tightened around his wife, and he thought of going over there to commiserate with the man. But in the end he didn't get up. For starters, he hated the way his voice sounded with his nose all packed with gauze, and as he watched, his sister went to sit beside Mac anyway. Better to let them sift through all this themselves.

"Are you all right?" Shadow asked Mac quietly.

His gaze finally left all the people to swivel to her. "Sure," he said guardedly.

"You look like you're about ready to run for your life."

"I was thinking that I can't remember the last time I've been in a room with so many people."

"Does it hurt?"

"It feels like a pair of new jeans." Shadow thought he almost smiled.

"Jeans break in," she pointed out.

"Eventually."

"It's only for one night." And then what? she wondered, her heart thumping.

One night, he thought. And where would he sleep the next time the sun fell? It wasn't anything that had ever concerned him before. Whenever dark had come, he had settled wherever he happened to be at the time. Alone. Now he wondered how he would make sure she was with him. Now the prospect of being alone seemed intolerable, but Diamond Eddie had trashed all his neat, contrived excuses.

"Who is that guy?" he asked her suddenly, needing to change the subject. "How are you related to him?"

Shadow followed his gaze to Uncle Ernie. The shaman was wandering about the living room now, waving his bird fetishes and chanting quietly, restoring everything, all of them, to *hozro* again.

"By clan."

"Does that mean there aren't any actual blood ties?" he asked her.

Shadow flashed a grin. "Why? Does that worry you?"

"Somewhat."

"It's hard to say. I don't really know. Clans are lineage things that started centuries upon centuries ago, to give some structure to groups of the People living together. We're born to those our mothers belong to, born for the ones our fathers belong to."

"You said something about it being incest to get involved with someone who's related to you that way."

"It is." Something inside her stiffened. Suddenly she wondered what *his* clan affiliation was. His mother had been part Navajo.

Once again, he seemed to read her mind. "Is there one about talking funny?" he asked. "That seems to ring something in my memory. Maybe that was what she was."

Shadow breathed again. "The Slow Talking Diné." She shook her head. "We're Towering Rock."

He was watching her closely. "It really matters to you."

She tried to shrug—unsuccessfully. "It's a taboo. If you break too many of them, you end up like Diamond Eddie."

"Yet you didn't think about it before."

She hadn't. It shook her more than anything else had yet. She wondered if he could understand the magnitude of what she had done.

"You made me too hungry to think about it," she said simply.

He looked at her face, at the wonder there, and felt something hot pool inside him. If they had been alone, he would have known just what to do next. He would have touched her, would have *shown* her that he was glad that had happened. But they weren't alone, so he was left with only words. He opened his mouth and closed it again. He cleared his throat and tried once more.

"Why did you go back to the canyon?" she asked suddenly. "I thought you'd be halfway down the Baja by now."

A coarse, short laugh escaped him. Halfway? He had driven its entire length twice in four days. Because of her. Running from her, chasing after her. But he didn't know how to tell her that either.

"I—"

Suddenly Madeline barged in on them. "So where are you from?" she asked.

Shadow felt her heart sink hard at the interruption. Mac's look was a little wild as he glanced at her mother. Nowhere, he thought, but he doubted if that was what she wanted to hear.

"Everywhere," Shadow responded quietly. "He's an archaeologist. He moves around a lot."

"Moves around?" It wasn't something Madeline could comprehend. "Where do you go when you're not moving?" she demanded. "Do you have kin? Where are they?" She looked at her daughter. "Is he Navajo?"

Shadow sighed. "And Hopi and Anglo."

"What's your clan?"

Shadow answered for him again. For once, he was glad that she took charge. "Slow Talking."

Madeline harrumphed. "They live all the way west. Near the Hopi Mesas. Are you going to take her away from us?"

Mac was definitely looking like a hunted animal now, and there was no way she could answer that one for him. She felt her own sense of panic climb up in her throat. *Are you?*

"Mom, you're just assuming..." Then her gaze flew gratefully to her brother as he approached.

"I hate to break up the party," Jericho interrupted, "but I've got a week-old son who needs to sleep and a wife who's too stubborn to admit she's tired." He looked between Shadow and Mac noncommittally, without his eyes really resting on either of them. "Ryan's still staying in with us, so his room's empty. There's a futon in there and some blankets. You're welcome to them."

Mac risked a glance at Madeline. "What about everyone else?" he asked warily.

Madeline finally turned away. "We're going home. It's just down the bottom of the mountain. Martin!"

Shadow saw that Ellen was looking for her purse. "I'll see you in the morning," she said neutrally to Catherine.

Another burst of conversation rang out. There was a brief escalating argument about Catherine going back to work so soon. Catherine won with a valid point about the Snugli carrier that would keep Ryan comfortably nestled against her chest while she saw patients. Even Shadow felt slightly overwhelmed by the time the place cleared out— except for Uncle Ernie. But even he had finally put away his birds.

"What about him?" Mac asked. "Shouldn't he have the bedroom?" He knew enough about family to respect his elders, but Jericho only shrugged.

"He'll sleep on the roof."

Shadow looked to see Mac's jaw drop. She squirmed a little uncomfortably on her chair, only wondering what he could possibly think of all this.

"Uncle, are you okay?" Jericho called after the shaman.

"I am well, thank you," the old man answered.

"Need anything up there?"

"No. *Hozro* is restored. I will have the stars."

Jericho nodded, satisfied. "Then I'm going to bed."

He left them, disappearing through one of the doors at the back of the room. Ernie slipped outside. The silence they left in their wake was absolute.

Shadow fought the urge to shiver. She wondered what Jericho—what *any* of them—would think if they knew she wasn't even sleeping with Mac, at least not in any literal sense. They had assumed so much. She risked a glance at him.

"You can have the bedroom. I've always just crashed out here on the sofa."

Mac nodded but didn't move off his chair.

"Don't worry about them," she said awkwardly. "They...get something in their heads, see what they think they're seeing, and then they just run with it."

"So you come by it honestly."

Shadow flushed. "I guess."

She stood quickly. "I'll just check the bathroom and make sure there are clean towels and stuff in there for you." She couldn't imagine Catherine overlooking such a thing, but it was a handy excuse. She took two steps when Mac's voice stopped her.

"Shadow."

She paused and looked back at him.

"What's your last name?"

She was startled. After everything, it seemed so impossible that he didn't know something that fundamental. "Bedonie."

He nodded. She started to move again, then his next question rattled her all over again.

"Why were you coming to the Baja?"

"Because it just didn't make any sense not to ever see you again."

She hated the answer as soon as it came out of her mouth. It was so much more than that, yet for the first time in her life she felt tentative, uncertain, afraid to take a single step forward. Everything that laid out there in front of her was uncharted ground. And she didn't know yet why he had gone back to the canyon. And this mattered so very, very much. Now, when they were finally alone and could talk about it, she felt utterly and completely lost.

His next words threw her even more.

"On the Hopi Mesas, when two people get married, they just...sleep together. You wake up one morning and Sallie's over there in Joe's place, or vice versa. And that's that."

She swallowed carefully. *What was he saying?* She wanted to ask, and found herself saying instead, "We Navajo have always thought you guys had an overly simplistic way of doing things."

He laughed roughly. "I guess so. Those ties don't really bind. That's how my parents got together. Or so they say."

She nodded carefully. He finally got up off his chair.

"Don't worry about the towels. I'm too wrung out right now to worry about a shower, and the sound of the water would probably keep everyone awake anyway. I'll catch one in the morning."

He went to Ryan's bedroom. Her heart skipped a beat, then plummeted.

He closed the door behind him.

She closed her eyes.

The silence stretched out. Finally she moved slowly back to the sofa. She took the throw pillows scattered at the back and piled them at one end for her head, then she laid down.

Above her, the faint stirrings and thumps of Uncle Ernie sounded from the roof. She thought she heard Jericho snore distantly through his own closed door. Familiar sounds of life, as it should be, as it always had been. She tried to let them lull her, but her eyes remained wide and fast on Ryan's closed door.

Suddenly it opened again. Her heart leapt, cramming hard into her throat. Mac stood there, a murky silhouette in the thin light from the window behind him. She sat up quickly.

"What's the matter?" she whispered. "Is Uncle Ernie keeping you awake?"

He looked up at the ceiling. Then she thought she saw him shake his head.

"It's a double futon," he said finally. His voice sounded hoarse. "Room enough for two, but I'm only one. Why don't you come on in here?"

As soon as he got the words out, he breathed again. They weren't so hard after all.

Chapter 19

Shadow floated to him. Later she would have no real memory of getting up from the sofa, of her feet moving. She still felt hesitant and uncertain, but then she stood beside him. She laid her palm flush against his chest and breathed again. As always, that felt *right*.

"I'm here," she said quietly.

He caught her hand in his own. She turned her face up to his with every expectation that his mouth would find hers, that he would fill her with fierce, strong loving again. That had been their most common ground from the first. It was when he allowed her close, when he didn't try to shut her out, and she was sure that that was what he wanted now. But he only pulled her into Ryan's room and shut the door behind her.

He went back to the futon and dropped down there with a little sound of pain because of his legs. Shadow remained by the door, staring at him.

"Well?" he said finally. "Are you going to stand there all night?"

Her heart plummeted, leapt, danced. "What do you want me to do?" she asked uncertainly, not entirely willing to believe.

There was a long silence. "Come here," he said from the darkness. She heard him pat the futon beside him.

She took a few steps closer. He caught her good arm and pulled her down. Then he gathered her against his chest, tugging the blankets over them. She thought she heard him sigh, but her heart was thudding in her ears and she couldn't be sure.

Shadow laid rigid, aware of every inch of her body that was pressed close to his. Her back was tight against his stomach and chest and, as always, she could feel the warmth of him through the clothing she wore. Hard to believe she had once considered his skin to be as cool as the canyon rocks at night.

She was afraid to move. Then she felt his warm breath at her nape. She groaned and rolled over into his arms.

It didn't mean anything, he thought as he finally kissed her again. He swept the warm recesses of her mouth with his tongue and told himself that they weren't on the Mesas, and that he fully believed what he had told her. Hopi ties didn't bind. He just needed her close now after the nightmare of the past few days. He needed to feel her, smell her, know she was safe.

That was all. It was nothing more. But in his heart he didn't believe that any more than he believed he was truly bone tired and wanted nothing other than to sleep.

Her hands slid up his back and she pressed herself into him. He felt himself harden again.

"Just sleep?" she whispered.

He made an inarticulate sound, which was supposed to be agreement but could have left the door open for discussion. Somehow he found his hands under her T-shirt, sliding up, covering her breasts, cupping them. Without really intending to, he sought her nipples with his thumbs and felt a shudder go through her. Her hand slid down to his hardness.

"It seems a shame to waste this," she whispered. Especially since she still didn't know when—or *if*—she would be able to touch him, love him, hold him again. Nothing had really been settled between them. No matter what her family thought, they had come back together by chance.

But there would be time to think of that later.

"It does, doesn't it?" he answered after a moment, lifting his mouth from hers.

"It wouldn't be very practical. Waste not, want not."

"I agree."

He moved a hand down to her leg, catching it to pull it over his hip, to open a path for himself. Then he slid into her again effortlessly, completely.

Her warmth closed over him and he went still for a moment, just feeling. Finally, he was home again.

Shadow woke in the morning feeling disoriented, half expecting to find the canyon walls looming up around her, the new sun blazing over its rim. But there was only a single shaft of light coming in from the baby's bedroom window behind her. It did little to illuminate the shadowy room.

Mac was gone.

Her heart squeezed hard and she touched a hand to the bare futon where he had lain. Had sleeping together proved too much for him after all? She got to her knees, groping around for her clothing. Then she went still, cocking her head.

A burst of laughter came from the living room. Mac's? Whatever had happened, he wasn't prowling around like a hunted animal this time.

She dressed quickly and hurried out there. Her gaze swept about. The first thing she noticed was that the clock over the kitchen sink read ten-thirty. Ten-thirty? She hadn't slept this late in years.

The second thing she noticed was that Mac and Jericho were on the sofa, sprawled side by side, their feet up on the coffee table. Glasses and plates littered it, along with the remnants of what once must have been a fairly substantial pile of sandwiches. The volume on the television was turned low, presumably in an effort to keep from waking her. They looked her way, then back at the television again.

The Dodgers were playing the Rockies.

"He should have retired years ago," Mac muttered as a close-up of the pitcher flashed on the screen.

"No way," Jericho argued. "You've got to think of things like leadership and experience. That team needs all of it they can get."

The pitcher walked the batter and he jogged to first base. Mac threw Jericho a smug look.

"They need wins more and they're not going to get them that way."

Shadow cleared her throat. "Good morning," she ventured.

"Shh," they said together.

She moved into the kitchenette without taking her eyes off Mac. He looked so...*relaxed*. At ease. Almost... lazy. He had taken that one day off in the canyon, she remembered, but there had been an intensity about that. This was different.

"Satellite dish working okay?" she asked conversationally.

"Fine."

"Great."

"I guess you two ate already."

There were wordless grunts.

"You know, we really should think about getting back to the canyon to pick up the trucks."

"Two more innings," Mac said.

"Ernie'll run us into Shiprock to get yours. He had to go home, but he'll be back in an hour," Jericho supplied. Then they both fell silent again.

Shadow made herself a sandwich and carried it back to sit on the floor beside the sofa. "You never said you liked baseball," she murmured to Mac.

There was so much she didn't know about him, she realized. He was almost unfolding before her eyes, layers peeling back, revealing a man inside who was inherently the one she knew, yet so much stronger somehow.

Not *quite* an emotional mess, she allowed. Had this man been there all along, waiting inside to come out? Or was he someone new, someone love had brought about?

He flashed a look at her and finally answered. "Only in September and October. The rest of the season is like watching grass grow. Now shut up and let us watch this."

There was the man she had first met. Shadow leaned back against the sofa to watch the game. But she couldn't keep her eyes on the television. She watched Mac as he muttered and argued with Jericho, and her mouth alternately gaped and smiled.

It was four o'clock before they made it back to the canyon. They dropped Jericho at his Land Rover, then sat with the engine idling after her brother turned his vehicle around to speed eastward again.

"Well," Shadow said finally.

Mac didn't answer. He was looking up at the mountain.

"How do you want to go about this?" she asked after another moment. His truck was on the western side of the range. They could drive around, or he could hike over. Either way, it would take several more hours to get to it.

She wondered if she would spend them with him or alone.

"Let's camp here one more night," he said suddenly.

Shadow's heart spasmed. *If only it could be that easy.* "I can't," she said softly. "I have to work tomorrow."

She had called the powers-that-be and had set the wheels in motion to try to get Diamond Eddie's job. It was what she had always wanted. So why did it suddenly feel like an intrusion?

She risked a glance at him. Mac only nodded.

He was stalling anyway. He knew it, and on some level he was pretty sure she did, too. Once, a lifetime ago, he would have kissed her soundly and said goodbye. Once, a lifetime ago, he *might* have suggested that she come back next weekend. But they had gone so very far beyond that point now, and he knew there was no way in hell he was going to be able to sleep without her again. Not tonight. Not tomorrow night. Not ever.

He didn't want to.

"I called the Smithsonian this morning. Before you got up," he said suddenly.

Shadow wasn't sure if he was changing the subject or not. "What about?"

"Diamond Eddie's treasure has thrown them into a hell of a tailspin. Nobody knows quite what to do with it. To their knowledge, a pot hunter has never stored his finds against a rainy day before. They tend to grab what they can in the dark of night and sell it immediately."

"So what do they want to do with the stuff?"

Mac shrugged. "I had their grant to work here. I found it—in a roundabout way of speaking. So they've technically got the rights to it. I guess they'll filter it all into their Anasazi collection."

Shadow nodded. "That makes sense."

"Some of the lesser pieces might be sold off through the New York auction houses," he went on. "It all needs to be sorted, cataloged. I told them I'd do it."

Her heart thumped. "How long will that take?"

"A month maybe, to get through the pots. I have no expertise with the rest—it's not really my area. When I get through the shards, I'll let them send a team to go through the other stuff."

"You hate working with a team."

He chewed his lip, still looking at the mountain. "I'll be out of here by then," he said finally.

"Will you try to put the life of She Who Waits back together?" She felt herself holding her breath as she waited for his answer.

"I've lost interest in that," he said carefully, "since I know she can't tell me where the Anasazi went."

"So what will you do then?"

"There are over a thousand other sites sprinkled across the Colorado Plateau."

A single hard shudder moved through her. Most of them were on the Res. "I've heard that."

"Maybe something in one of them can solve the mystery."

"Maybe."

"It'll take a lifetime to go through them all." Finally, suddenly, he looked at her. "You said that it didn't make any sense not to ever see me again. Can I take that to mean you'll visit my sites occasionally?"

His voice was so cautious, so wary. She wanted to reach out and touch him, to make it easier for him. But she couldn't heal him. Not completely. She had finally, really accepted that. Only he could heal himself.

Of course, she could keep prodding him in the right direction.

"I don't think I can do that without tearing my own heart out," she answered quietly.

His face changed, a million emotions flashing across it. Wariness almost settled there, but then there was only pain. It took her breath away, almost made her relent. Her hand seemed to move to him of its own accord, then she deliberately brought it back.

"What are you saying?" he asked neutrally.

"That walking away once almost killed me. I don't think I can do it over and over, Mac, leaving you, wondering if and when I'll ever find you again. I *know* I can't. Maybe it's wrong. Maybe I *am* rigid and bossy and there's something lacking in me, some . . . some spontaneity. But I need more than that. And if I can't have it, then I think I'm better off not having anything at all."

His expression seemed to settle. But his eyes closed down as he looked away. "Is that what you were coming to tell me in the Baja?"

She let out a shaky breath. "More or less. Before everything happened with Diamond Eddie, I thought I'd take a leave of absence from the museum. I have some money saved. I thought I could pretty much follow you around— if you'd let me—until it ran out. I wouldn't have to walk away from you. For a while." *I could postpone the inevitable.* But *was* it inevitable? She watched his eyes lose a little of their shuttered look and something in her heart dared to hope.

"You were going to give up your job?" he demanded. She would have given up her precious stability? Her family and home? That staggered him.

Shadow gave him a thin smile. "It wasn't much of a job. Three days a week, the same thing I'd been doing for seven or eight years."

"But now that you're going to have a better one, you're not willing to follow me?" he pushed.

She would, she realized. She would do it in a heartbeat. Instead she said, "That depends entirely on why you came back to the canyon."

He could have told her that it occurred to him that their thief had to be someone she knew. That he was concerned for her safety. That he had figured it out and was rushing

to protect her. He could have told her that a Mexican bartender with the wisdom of a sage had talked him into it.

And none of that would really be true. All his time for
excuses had run out now.

"Because I fell in love with you," he said roughly. "And
unless I found you, nothing was ever going to be right
again."

He looked up again to see that she was crying. *Crying?*
Shadow? "What the hell are you doing?" he asked, panicked.

"I love you, too."

His heart was moving hard. He reached out to clumsily
wipe her cheek. "Just like that?"

"It really doesn't have to be complicated." She managed a watery smile.

"It's the most complex thing that's ever happened to
me."

"That's because part of you still thinks I'm going to go."
She hesitated. "I won't, you know. I'm nothing if not per-
sistent."

He knew. Yet he still wanted to touch her, if only to re-
assure himself of it. He raked a hand through his hair instead. It seemed important that they get the talking out of
the way first. This was too...vital.

"So what do we do now?" he asked.

She shrugged. "You dig. I run the museum."

"Will they give you the job or hire from outside?"

She was on steady ground now. "I'll get the job," she
said confidently.

One corner of his mouth kicked up into a grin. "Yeah,
but do *they* know it yet?"

"They're about to." Suddenly her smile faded. "I can
come and go from your digs, if I know I'll always be able
to find you, that you'll be waiting for me to come back."

He didn't want to think of all the nights there would be
in between. Then he knew that it only made sense.

"One of the first things that drew me close to you was the sharing," he mused. "Doing things together. Balancing life. I'd hunt, you'd cook dinner. I'd look down the east rim for footprints, you'd take the west."

Shadow felt her heart surge. For the first time she truly started to believe it could work.

"The museum's closed every Monday," she interjected. "Eddie used to take weekends off, too. He'd leave me and the guides to run things."

He slanted her a look. "Eddie was a busy man."

"I could be a busy woman."

"I usually take a few weeks off between digs," he went on.

"And during those times we could be together all the time."

"Absence makes the heart grow fonder."

"Not to mention the rest of the body."

He laughed outright. "We'd have some wild reunions."

"Once a week. We'd only be apart four, maybe five days some weeks."

"And sometimes not at all."

"Yeah." Then, suddenly, he thought of something else. He looked at her sharply. "Seven *years?*"

Shadow frowned, not understanding what he was getting at.

"There was no way you could have known what you were going to tumble into in that canyon," he continued. "It's not like you were going to Acapulco or Palm Springs."

"I thought I'd find a big, bad pot hunter," she said cautiously. "I'd slay the beast and go home."

"So can I assume that you weren't protected—that you didn't . . . you know . . ."

Suddenly she understood. Her jaw dropped. "I never thought about that."

"And *I* sure as hell wasn't expecting you to fall at my feet. *I* wasn't prepared."

She put a hand to her tummy. Her touch trembled. "I never thought," she repeated, whispering. "I never...I didn't make a habit of..." She trailed off. "Oh, my God, Mac."

But she wasn't half as rocked as he was. She saw it in his face, dawning slowly, a look half of wonder and half of terror, and she could read his mind as easily as he always seemed to read hers. *Family.*

"Would it be so bad?" she asked softly. "Would it be terrible if I was pregnant?" Once again, she held her breath, waiting for his answer.

He swallowed slowly, deliberately. "I guess not, if Hopi doctrine holds any water."

"Hopi—oh." Her heart started beating hard. "You said it didn't."

"Not in my book. I want more."

Her pulse thundered. "I think you'll probably have more. Like two for the price of one." Somehow, impossibly, she was sure of it. It would have happened. They had been in the canyon, in an ancient place of legends, a place where the philandering Kokopelli had finally turned into his own mate's arms and had given her a child.

How many times had she thought she would be like She Who Waits? She gave a little, high-pitched laugh that was both overwhelmed and entirely happy.

"Oh, Mac," she breathed again. "I *want* this. I want it to be true so badly."

"How long before we know?"

"I...a couple of weeks, I guess."

"No sense waiting."

"Waiting?" she whispered. "For what?"

He finally let himself touch her hair again. It hadn't escaped him that she hadn't tied it up that morning. They had both changed, he realized, in subtle ways, in huge ways...together, sharing that, too. He tunneled his fingers all the way through its length, spreading the ends out in the palm of his hand.

He wanted to be able to do this forever. He wanted it to *endure*. He needed that as he had never needed anything before in his life. Maybe that was why his throat closed again, why suddenly he had to grope for words.

They came out hard, fast, without any of the finesse he'd spent days envying other men for. And she didn't seem to care.

"Marry me," he began.

"I already have." She put a hand to her belly again. "Where it counts."

But he shook his head. "I want it carved in granite. I need that. I need something I can touch, something that I can always look at and know it will last. That's something my father never had."

"You will," she reassured him. "I promise. Here, now, or in front of any shaman or justice of the peace you want."

He looked alarmed. "Uncle Ernie?"

"He takes some getting used to," she conceded, "but he's family."

Mac took the word gingerly to his heart. He held it there, testing it, and found it had weight and strength. Finally he reached out and gathered her all the way to him.

"If he's yours, I guess that makes him mine, too."

She nodded against his chest. "Until the end of time, Mac. You'll always have a home, a family, a haven, until all the sands run out."

* * * * *

COMING NEXT MONTH

Take 4 bestselling love stories FREE

Plus get a FREE surprise gift!

Special Limited-time Offer

Mail to Silhouette Reader Service™

P.O. Box 609
Fort Erie, Ontario
L2A 5X3

YES! Please send me 4 free Silhouette Intimate Moments® novels and my free surprise gift. Then send me 6 brand-new novels every month, which I will receive months before they appear in bookstores. Bill me at the low price of $3.21 each plus 25¢ delivery and GST*. That's the complete price and a savings of over 10% off the cover prices—quite a bargain! I understand that accepting the books and gift places me under no obligation ever to buy any books. I can always return a shipment and cancel at any time. Even if I never buy another book from Silhouette, the 4 free books and the surprise gift are mine to keep forever.

345 BPA AQS4

Name _____ (PLEASE PRINT)

Address _____ Apt. No. _____

City _____ Province _____ Postal Code _____

This offer is limited to one order per household and not valid to present Silhouette Intimate Moments® subscribers. *Terms and prices are subject to change without notice.
Canadian residents will be charged applicable provincial taxes and GST.

CMOM-295 ©1990 Harlequin Enterprises Limited

Because love is a risky business...

Merline Lovelace's "Code Name: Danger" miniseries gets an explosive start in May 1995 with

NIGHT OF THE JAGUAR, IM #637

Omega agent Jake MacKenzie had flirted with danger his entire career. But when unbelievably sexy Sarah Chandler became enmeshed in his latest mission, Jake knew that his days of courting trouble had taken a provocative twist....

Your mission: To read more about the Omega agency.

Your next target: THE COWBOY AND THE COSSACK, August 1995

Your only choice for nonstop excitement—

Kathleen Creighton's

RITA Award-winning author Kathleen Creighton
brings Midwest charm to the Intimate Moments
lineup in her ongoing miniseries, "Into the Heartland."
A WANTED MAN, IM #547, introduced Lucy Brown to
readers in February 1994. Now meet Lucy's brother,
Wood Brown, in ONE GOOD MAN, IM #639, coming
your way in May 1995.

Wood Brown had been to hell and back. And no
one knew his pain better than physical therapist
Christine Thurmond. But as she healed his battered
body and soul, she yearned for some loving all her
own. And only one good man would do....

The Browns—one sister, two brothers. Tragedy changed
their family forever, but never their spirit—or their love for
the heartland. Look for Rhett Brown's story in 1996 and
venture once again "Into the Heartland"—*because
sometimes there's no place like home*—only in

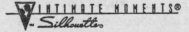

HEARTBREAKERS

Hot on the heels of **American Heroes** comes Silhouette Intimate Moments' latest and greatest lineup of men: **Heartbreakers.** They know who they are—and *who* they want. And they're out to steal your heart.

RITA award-winning author Emilie Richards kicks off the series in March 1995 with *Duncan's Lady,* IM #625. Duncan Sinclair believed in hard facts, cold reality and his daughter's love. Then sprightly Mara MacTavish challenged his beliefs—and hardened heart—with her magical allure.

In April *New York Times* bestseller Nora Roberts sends hell-raiser Rafe MacKade home in *The Return of Rafe MacKade,* IM #631. Rafe had always gotten what he wanted—until Regan Bishop came to town. She resisted his rugged charm and seething sensuality, but it was only a matter of time....

Don't miss these first two **Heartbreakers,** from two stellar authors, found only in—

INTIMATE MOMENTS®
Silhouette

HRTBRK1

Announcing
the New Pages & Privileges™ Program
from Harlequin® and Silhouette®

Get All This FREE
With Just One Proof-of-Purchase!

- **FREE Travel Service** with the guaranteed lowest available airfares plus 5% cash back on every ticket

- **FREE Hotel Discounts** of up to 60% off at leading hotels in the U.S., Canada and Europe

- **FREE Petite Parfumerie** collection (a $50 Retail value)

- **FREE $25 Travel Voucher** to use on any ticket on any airline booked through our Travel Service

- **FREE Insider Tips Letter** full of fascinating information and hot sneak previews of upcoming books

- **FREE Mystery Gift** (if you enroll before May 31/95)

And there are more great gifts and benefits to come!
Enroll today and become Privileged!

(see insert for details)

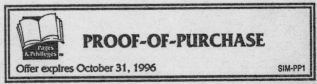